Acclaim for Stuart Kaminsky and Inspector Rostnikov

"Terrific . . . Exceptional."
—*Detroit Free Press*

"Deeply absorbing, full of character nuance and irony . . . Kaminsky's laconic tone and colorful prose bring [Moscow] and its denizens to life."
—*The Sunday Herald*

"Kaminsky excels each time he enters the harshness of post–Cold War Russia."
—*Publishers Weekly* (starred review)

"Kaminsky has staked a claim to a piece of the Russian turf. . . . His stories are laced with fascinating tidbits of Russian history. . . . He captures the Russian scene and character in rich detail."
—*The Washington Post Book World*

"As always, Kaminsky provides a colorful, tightly written mystery (he doesn't waste a word) filled with twists, counter twists, and a surprise ending that is plausible and clever."
—*Chicago Tribune*

"Stuart Kaminsky has created a sympathetic and engaging hero who solves mysteries in spite of the peculiar handicaps imposed by the police bureaucracy and exacerbated by KGB interference."
—*The Cincinnati Post*

TARNISHED ICONS

Stuart M. Kaminsky

IVY BOOKS • NEW YORK

Ivy Books
Published by Ballantine Books
Copyright © 1997 by Double Tiger Productions, Inc.

http://www.randomhouse.com

Library of Congress Catalog Card Number: 97-93208

ISBN 0-8041-1289-4

Printed in Canada

First Edition: July 1997

10 9 8 7 6 5 4 3 2

To Eleanor, Tim, and Catherine Mullin with thanks for thirty years of continued friendship, help, hospitality, and kindness. We think of you as an essential and supportive part of our family.

Happy families are all alike; every unhappy family is unhappy in its own way.

—Anna Karenina, Leo Tolstoy

ONE

Saint Petersburg, Russia, 1862

A WOMAN HAD BEEN BRUTALLY MURDERED. SHE WAS the baroness Anastasia Volodov-Kronof.

The baroness was a woman of great wealth and social power who threw an annual celebration with wine, wild fowl, and an assortment of cakes in the park near the new Hermitage. All were invited. The tradition had begun eight years ago when her husband died. The celebration on the anniversary of the baron's death was considered to be either a sign of respect for a loyal officer of the czar or a sign of relief that the widow was finally free of an abusive martinet. She had married the baron when she was a girl of fourteen and he an officer of thirty.

Her death did not sit well with the populace of Saint Petersburg in 1862. She was a benefactor, an emulator of the aristocracy of France that had repeatedly rejected her. Her husband was an official hero of his country. Though she lived like a grand dame of Western Europe, holding salons for young artists, she, in quite general but sincere terms, espoused the causes of justice, freedom for all, and an eventual abolition of some of the more unjust practices of the aristocracy.

It was said that Czar Alexander himself had invited the baroness to all palace parties and looked upon her with favor. In turn, she had prepared a will in which a very valuable gold wolf the size of a small dog, encrusted with jewels, would be given to the royal family upon her death for inclusion in the growing Hermitage collection. The wolf, a central figure of her former husband's crest, had been commissioned by the late baron and was completed according to the baron's instructions by a young French jeweler named Emile Toussaint.

Accused of the baroness's violent murder was a thin young man she had taken under her broad wing, into her ample bosom, and under the silk sheets of her French bed. In addition to her murder, the young man and three of his comrades were also accused of taking the gold wolf to sell to a wealthy foreign monarch to support a small group of anticzarist revolutionaries.

The young man was twenty-five, one of the new breed who wore long hair, mustaches, and black coats, and uttered proclamations about the rights of serfs. He was the grandson of a Decembrist, one of the officers who had staged a revolt against Czar Nicholas. His grandfather, Peotor Marlovov, had returned to Saint Petersburg from Siberia five years earlier, in 1857, under pardon from the czar. The old man had planted in his grandson the seed of revolution.

The thin young man and his three comrades, two of whom were army officers, were shackled together and flanked by a dozen armed soldiers as they marched through Senate Square by the Neva River. The strange-looking little man who was in charge of the armed escort marched next to Marlovov and his comrades. The two were a remarkable contrast. Marlovov, in spite of or because of his hard youth in Siberia, stood tall, thin, erect, and handsomely confident with his hair cut stylishly long in the French manner. If any look dominated his face, it was superiority. Though he had been named Vladimir, he called himself Louis.

The little man at his side was another matter altogether. He had great difficulty keeping up with the long-striding prisoner and the brightly uniformed guards.

His name was Colonel Dieter Fritch, a German in the service of the czar. Fritch, well dressed in a white uniform, was about forty, fat, and clean-shaven. His hair was short and he had a large round head that was unusually bulbous in the back. His soft, round, snub-nosed face was yellowish in color as if he had seldom ventured out into the daylight. He wore a perpetual knowing smile as if he kept a secret that he might some day share with you. There was something decidedly feminine about the little man except for his eyes below white lashes, moist eyes that were quite serious.

"If we were to walk a bit slower," said Fritch with a decidedly German accent, "I would not breathe so heavily and we could talk."

It was summer, and the trees were blocking a view of the admiralty facade.

Louis preened his mustache, shrugged slightly, and glanced down at the ridiculous little man. The other prisoners and the two armed guards slowed just a bit.

"Thank you," said Fritch, producing a large handkerchief and mopping his brow. "May we sit briefly?"

Louis sighed with annoyance and looked at his comrades and the guards, one of whom looked at the little German and nodded. The shackled friends strode to a concrete balustrade and sat. The German sat beside Louis. The soldiers stood.

The leader of the armed escort, a young lieutenant in the red uniform of the royal family's personal guard, said, "Ten minutes, Colonel. No more. We'll be in trouble if we don't deliver them for trial on time."

The wooden benches would be packed to see the men who had murdered the popular baroness Volodov-Kronof.

"You have not confessed to the murder," said Colonel Fritch, turning his large eyes on the handsome young poet. The other three accused looked straight ahead in marble silence. "You have refused to talk to a lawyer. You refuse to admit your guilt. You refuse to proclaim your innocence. You should be easy to convict and hang. Judge Volorov, at his own request, has been assigned to this case. He was a personal friend of the baroness's. He holds a long-standing grudge against the Decembrists and their survivors. He has no fondness for European dilettantes."

"Is that what you take me for?" asked the young man with a sigh.

"It is what the judge and jury will take you for," said Fritch. "And, I must confess, it is what you appear to be."

"You have read my poetry?" asked the young man, crossing his legs.

"Some. The thin book published by the baroness."

"And?" asked the young man.

"You are more interested in the review of your work by a foreign member of the czar's staff than in possibly saving your life?"

"Your assessment of my work?" the young man repeated.

"Self-indulgent. Mediocre. Unoriginal. Insincere," said Fritch. "But what do I know? I'm a soldier, not a critic of poetry."

"Went to the theater," the young man said, looking toward the river. "The play was about the Russian fool Filatka. Laughed a lot. They had a vaudeville show as well, full of amusing verse lampooning lawyers, so outspoken that I wondered how it got past the censor. Civil servants are such swine. . . . You won't catch clods like them going to the theater, not even if they're given free tickets."

"Gogol, 'Diary of a Madman,' " said Fritch, recognizing the quotation, "but you left out merchants and newspapermen who criticize everything."

The young man looked at the colonel with a new respect.

"You do read."

"With slowly growing skill," said Fritch. "And I send people to prison, into exile, or before a firing squad. Occasionally I help them if they are innocent. Are you innocent of this murder, Vladimir Marlovov?"

"I am guilty of the murder," the young man said with

little interest. "These three others are completely innocent. And I prefer to be called Louis."

"More French," said Colonel Fritch.

"Five more minutes," said the lieutenant.

A warm wind blew down the corridor of buildings.

One of the two soldiers under arrest, a young man with wild hair and in need of a shave, muttered, "We are all equally responsible for what took place."

"They mean to kill us," said Marlovov with a shrug. "There is little we can do."

The little man stood and began to pace slowly in front of the four young men.

"The murder happened only two days ago," he said, "and you have refused to speak to a policeman or a lawyer."

"And soon we will face a jury and judge," said Marlovov, "who will convict us in rather short order."

Fritch wished they were in his curtained office with the big desk. A little intimidation, with time to break down the suspects would work better than hurried talks in the square with a third-rate poet who was decidedly unlikable. Work on them individually. Find a weak one. But the czar had personally given Fritch his instructions, and there was to be no delay.

"Facts," said the little German. "On the morning of July the third, there was a scream in the apartment of the baroness. It was heard by a maid, who came running into the lady's chamber, where you stood nude over her equally naked body on the bed. In your hand was a knife covered in blood."

"Rather damning evidence," admitted Marlovov.

"And your three friends, all members of the new Decembrist movement, were described by witnesses as leaving the apartments of the baroness carrying something in a blanket. The famed golden wolf had been removed from its place on the marble pedestal in the bedroom."

Marlovov sighed. "I was in the washroom undressing

and bathing. I had to pay frequent sexual dues to the baroness in return for her patronage. The baroness, as you know, was well past sixty. She wore too much makeup. When I came out of the washroom, I saw her on the bed, a knife by her side. I realized she must have been murdered when I was bathing. I picked up the knife to protect myself from the killer. Then the maid came in."

"Your story is ludicrous. If she was dead," said Fritch, "how could she have let out the scream that brought the maid rushing in?"

The sigh this time was enormous.

"It was not she who screamed," said Marlovov. "I screamed when I saw the body. Now you may add cowardice to the other traits of which you will accuse me and my friends. Besides, I've confessed to the crime."

"How long were you in the washroom?" asked Fritch.

"Ten minutes, perhaps more, as long as I could prolong it and put off my duty to my patroness," said Marlovov.

"Is there any other way in or out of the bedroom besides through the door the maid entered when she heard the scream?"

"A door to the balcony," said the young man. "Three flights up. Another door to the corridor leading to the rear of the apartment, the kitchen."

"How many servants were present in the apartment when the murder occurred?" asked Fritch.

"Surely, you must know that."

"Humor me."

"Just the maid," he said.

"Could she have killed the baroness, gone out to the parlor, and rushed back in when she heard your scream?"

Marlovov began to laugh.

"I can see her now," he said, "before the judge and jury, a frightened, skinny little dolt, half the size of the cow I bedded. The idea is ridiculous."

"Do you know who else has apartments in the building where your . . . patroness was murdered?"

Again Marlovov shrugged.

"Five others. Each floor was a complete suite. I knew none of the other tenants except to exchange nods. I didn't wish to. Anastasia did not wish me to."

"Odd," said Fritch, rubbing his forehead. "I would have thought that since she had paid for you she would want to show you off to everyone."

"We had readings in her parlor. Her friends attended."

"But none of her neighbors?"

Louis shrugged again.

"Who knows? They were all much the same. Eating what they could get, drinking what they could reach."

"So," said Fritch, "who murdered the baroness and who took the golden wolf?"

"Who knows?" said Louis. "We are all to be shot for it. I repeat, you have my confession."

"You can save the lives of your friends," said Fritch. "I am empowered to grant them immediate exile to Siberia if you turn over the wolf. Only you will be tried."

"And shot," said Marlovov.

Fritch looked at all four of the young men. The four men looked at one another, and in their look was an agreement. They would die together.

Fritch understood. These young men would die for a losing cause. The German was equally willing to die. He had sold his loyalty to the Russian monarch and the sale was final and he would honor it. The only difference between himself and the quartet of revolutionaries was the object of their loyalty.

Marlovov now stood. He towered over the little man. The guards flanked the young men and began to lead them off in the direction of the court. Fritch did not join them. He did not move till they were out of sight, though he could still hear the distant rattling of their chains.

He patted real and imaginary wrinkles in his uniform, adjusted his cap, and made his way to the chambers of General Androyanov. A tall young officer disappeared through a door and returned within a minute to usher

Fritch into the large office. The tall man departed, closing the door behind him. The general's chamber was a large office, much larger than Fritch's office across the river.

The general was a tall, robust, imposing man in his sixties. He had pure white flowing hair. He stood at a mirror in the massive office adjusting his uniform. Androyanov was known to be a personal friend of the czar himself.

Satisfied with his appearance, the general turned to face the perspiring German. Fritch stood at rigid attention.

"I can see from your face that you have failed," said the general in French.

"They are true believers," answered Fritch in French.

"Torture?"

"We would take their dignity but would not obtain the wolf," said Fritch.

The general nodded. He had come to accept the perceptions and talents of the German. He turned in his chair and looked out of his windows at the three-story yellow Menshikov Palace directly across the river from the Senate. The modest palace had been built by Aleksandr Menshikov, who rose from being a stable boy to become the best friend of Peter the Great and eventually the second most powerful man in all of Russia. The building was constructed in 1710, the first stone palace in a city of cathedrals and palaces.

"Do you know why I like this view?" the general said, actually pointing to the window.

"It is a historic and beautiful landmark," said Fritch.

"I was a stable boy like Menshikov," said the general. "Did you know that?"

"Yes, I know that. Your service to the czar, your many accomplishments are well known."

The general adjusted his collar. Folding his large hands on his massive desk, he looked up at Fritch.

"The wolf is lost," he said.

Fritch nodded.

"I shall tell the czar," the general said, still in French,

"and assure him that we will not rest till it is recovered and any others involved in this revolutionary pimple of a movement are squeezed until blood flows. Time will pass. We will fail. There are many in court who will be pleased at our failure, Colonel, because I am the only general in the czar's army who is not of noble birth. But I shall not fall. You understand?"

"Fully," said Fritch.

"A baroness is dead. Four men will be shot. Others will probably follow. You and I will battle to retain our positions, influence, and dignity, and the czar shall suffer yet another disappointment. Colonel, have you ever seen the golden wolf?"

"Never," said Fritch, knowing the white collar of his uniform was turning dark from perspiration.

"Pity," he said. "It is truly magnificent."

In the distance, outside the window a volley of shots crackled. Neither man moved.

"Brief trial and swift justice," said the general. He stood with a sigh. In Russian he said, "Let's bring the bad news to the czar."

TWO

Moscow, Russia, 1996

KATRINA IVANOVA HURRIED ALONG THE SNOW-covered Taras Shevchenko Embankment by the Moscow River. When she had finished her shift as an elevator operator in the Ukrainia Hotel, it had been just before midnight, which gave her half an hour to rush down the embankment, go under the Bordino Bridge, hurry through the garden in front of the Kiev railway station, and get to the Kievskaya metro station.

If she missed the last metro, she would either have to take a cab, which she could not afford, or go back to the hotel and ask Molka Lev to help her sneak into an empty room for the night. Katrina did not want to ask Molka Lev's help. She did not want to ask anyone's help. She had, in her thirty-two years, been less than pleased with the help offered to her by almost all men and most women. There was always a price to pay.

It was December and a light snow was falling on two days of old snow blown about by a bitter wind off the river. Katrina did not mind the cold or the snow. The colder it was, the less likely she was to be bothered by a drunk or a mugger or one of the new gangs of children who robbed, raped, and murdered. At this hour and in this weather she was unlikely to be disturbed.

A voice, an almost animal wail, rose in the wind in front of her. Katrina's left boot struck a patch of ice under a thin spot of snow. She almost slipped but held her balance and managed to keep from falling.

Katrina was bundled tight in a lined cloth coat over a wool sweater with a high neck. A wool hat was pulled and tied to cover her ears and pink cheeks. Katrina Ivanova knew she was no beauty, but she was certainly not ugly. Her body was straight and solid if a bit heavy, and her skin was pink and clear. Her hair was as blond as it had been on her third birthday.

There was another sound ahead of her in the near darkness. This too was a voice, a deeper voice, wailing in the wind. Someone was ahead of her along the embankment, out of sight to her left. She would not be able to avoid it.

Maybe it was just the rustling of wind and snow in the trees, or a stray dog, or even two men arguing on the bridge still far ahead, their voices carrying far in the night.

The incidence of attacks on women had, since the end of the Soviet Union, risen so dramatically that the statistics published in the newspapers and given on television were no longer reliable. Rapes and murders were up two or three hundred percent. Gangs slaughtered one another on the street. Criminals, with guns visible under their jackets, were welcomed into the best hotels, including the Ukrainia.

Katrina was good at statistics. She loved statistics. There was certainty in them. Before her, through the haze of white, she could see the lights of Bolshaya Dorogomilovskaya Street, where the bridge crossed into the heart of the city.

She stood silently for an instant. No more voices in the wind ahead of her. Another fifty yards to go. No one in sight. The street lamps along the embankment were on, though they were dimmed by the swirl of snow. She could hurry and risk falling or she could go a bit slower. Katrina chose to hurry.

Suddenly in front of her through the whoosh of a gust of wind she heard four sharp, loud cracks like a steel cable striking a metal beam. Now she was sure. There was a moan and then three, four more loud cracks just ahead.

Katrina was frightened. There was no doubting that now, no lying to herself. About twenty-five yards ahead of her a hunched creature suddenly came up from the riverside. It looked like a bear. The creature looked around and saw Katrina.

Katrina, seeing something glitter in the creature's hand, reached into her heavy red plastic purse and pulled out a Tokareve .762mm automatic. She had purchased it from a waiter in the hotel kitchen almost a year before when she had realized that the new Russia was a place of madness where statistics might be meaningless.

The bearlike figure began to raise its right arm, and Katrina could see that there was something in its hand. She dropped her purse gently in the snow, gripped the pistol in her wool-gloved hands, and leveled the weapon at the hulk pointing at her.

She fired first and the creature stood straight up. It was a man in a long coat and fur cap, and he definitely had a weapon in his hand. He staggered back. Surprised at the shot? Hit by a bullet? Then he fired. Katrina felt a sudden squeezing of her left arm, as if some great gorilla had grasped her in anger. Before she could fire again, the man ran in the direction of the bridge. Actually, it was more like an animal lope than a run, a strange lope that even at this moment seemed odd. Then he was gone into the darkness. She could hear him moving farther and farther away. Her arm hurt and she was frightened. She picked up her red purse and hurried toward the bridge, screaming for help. She hoped someone would hear her and come to help her, though she knew that few would be brave enough to respond to the midnight cries of a woman so far from the busy, lighted streets.

Katrina felt dizzy. Weapon still in her hand, she moved forward. She tried not to look down as she shuffled, but she could not resist and she knew she was bleeding. She could see the dark drops falling onto the snow in front of her, and she looked back to see their dim trail behind her. Katrina was lost in weeping panic as she hurried forward.

The footsteps in the snow where the man who shot her had come up from the embankment lured her toward the edge of the drop to the river. Lights from the other side of the river reflected off the water—bobbing jigsaw pieces—and she saw them. About ten feet down. There were four figures laid out in a line almost perfectly straight, as if they had arranged themselves and were about to make identical snow angels. But these figures did not move.

The light wasn't good enough to see clearly, but Katrina knew. In her heart she knew that the four were dead, murdered by the creature who had shot her.

She trudged forward, too weak and frightened now to scream. He would leap out. She knew it. From behind a clump of snow-covered bushes or a stone block that marked the drop to the river. Something moved ahead. She fired again, not trying to hit anything but trying to keep the creature at bay.

A dog scuttled out from behind a stand of birch trees and fled in fear into the narrow parkway away from the river.

Katrina reached the street. She saw the frightened faces of three bundled old men. She passed out.

When she opened her eyes, a broad flat face appeared before her. She tried to bring it into focus. For an instant she thought it might be the man from the river, but something about the concern in his eyes and the warm feeling of a white room calmed her.

"We're in a hospital," the man said gently. "You have lost some blood but you will recover. Agda is being brought here in a police car. We found her name in your purse."

Katrina nodded, her mouth painfully dry.

"Water," she whispered.

The burly man poured a glass of water from a pitcher next to her bed.

"Just a sip or two," said the man.

She nodded and did as she was told.

The man appeared to be in his fifties. He had dark hair just beginning to turn gray and the body of a small delivery truck. Under his coat he wore a yellow turtle-neck sweater that gave him the appearance of having no neck at all.

"My name is Chief Inspector Porfiry Petrovich Rostnikov," the man said. "My colleague is Inspector Timofeyeva."

Katrina turned her eyes but not her head to a second figure in the room, a young, pretty, blond woman defi-nitely on the solid side. The young woman was wearing an open dark coat and a long red scarf. She could have been mistaken for Katrina's younger sister.

"We are with the Office of Special Investigation, Petrovka," the man said. "Can you talk?"

"Yes," she said dryly. She took another small sip of water. "Will I be able to use my arm again?"

"Yes," said the young woman. She stepped to the edge of the bed and touched Katrina's right arm gently. "The wound is not bad. What happened?"

Katrina told her story. The young woman took notes and the man stood, hands in his pockets, listening. When Katrina finished, the man said, "You did not recognize the man you shot?"

"Did I shoot him?" Katrina asked.

"There were two sets of blood drops," he said. "Yours and someone else's. Yours went straight to the street. The other person's went into the park. He apparently got into a car he had there."

"Are you sure it was a man?" the young woman asked.

Katrina nodded yes and said, "At first I thought it was a big animal."

"I mean," said the young woman, "could it have been a woman?"

"No," said Katrina.

"Could you identify him?" the young woman asked.

"No," said Katrina. "But you said I shot him?"

"It appears so," said the man.

"I'm going to show you photographs of the four dead men," Elena Timofeyeva said. "Can you look at them?"

Katrina closed her eyes and nodded another yes. Elena held up Polaroid head shots of the dead men on the river-bank. Each face was eerily illuminated by the white flash of necessary light. Katrina looked at the four faces. Two of them had their eyes closed. Two had open eyes. One of the two with open eyes looked frightened. The other with open eyes looked angry. All four had dark holes in their foreheads and faces. Three of the men were young, possibly even in their teens or twenties. The defiant man was older, but she couldn't tell how much older.

"No," Katrina said. "I've never seen them."

Elena put the photographs away.

"Anything you can tell us about the man who did this?"

Katrina thought and remembered the man coming up from the riverbank, aiming at her and then . . .

"He walked funny," she said. "Like an animal."

"You say he moved quickly," said Rostnikov.

"Yes, I think so, very quickly. Not like a cripple."

Elena Timofeyeva glanced at Rostnikov, who continued to look down at the woman lying in the bed. Only six months earlier, Rostnikov, at the urging of his wife and son and his wife's cousin Leon, who was a doctor, had agreed to allow the removal of his left leg just below the knee. It no longer made medical sense to preserve a gradually decaying leg, subject to infection and providing no support.

It had taken Rostnikov weeks to come to terms with this truth. He had earned the withered leg as a boy soldier fighting the Nazis. He had destroyed a tank. The tank had almost crushed his leg. For almost half a century

Rostnikov had lived with the pain from the leg. Because he was a war hero, he had been allowed to become a policeman after the war. He was powerful. He was calm. He possessed the one attribute that made him an ideal member of the police in the cold war period—he had no ambition other than to live with his wife and his son and do his job.

He had moved up the ranks as a street officer and then as a detective in the office of the procurator general of Moscow. When he ran afoul of some of the powerful and displayed a determination that could not be blunted even by political expediency, he was eventually transferred to the supposedly dead-end job of investigator in the Office of Special Investigation, a dumping ground for cases no one wanted.

With an irony that was not lost on some of the more intelligent of the members of the National Police and the KGB, the Office of Special Investigation not only took on dead-end cases but also managed to solve most of them. Rostnikov had gradually brought other investigators from the procurator general's office. Their moment of initial glory came when Rostnikov's people thwarted an attempt on the life of Mikhail Gorbachev. They had since managed to walk the line that allowed them to survive the political breakup of the Soviet Union and the Communist Party.

Through all this, Porfiry Petrovich Rostnikov had been accompanied by his withered left leg. It was not an easy decision to let it go.

Rostnikov's surgery had been performed in Moscow by an American surgeon obtained through a friend in the FBI who had been assigned to counsel the Russian police on dealing with organized crime. Within days after the surgery Rostnikov had begun learning to walk with a prosthetic leg. Gradually the pain went away. In its place was an occasional soreness where what remained of his leg had to be fitted into the device he now had to endure. He walked with only the slightest of limps, and though

he told no one, there were many times when he missed
the leg that had given him half a century of torture. He
even wondered what had happened to the leg, but he had
decided never to ask.

Rostnikov said to Katrina, "The ground was trampled
by the first police who arrived, but basically, the prints in
the snow were clear."

A tall, thin woman in white, who Rostnikov guessed
was probably from Uzbekistan, came into the room and
whispered to Rostnikov. He nodded and looked down at
Katrina with a smile.

"Inspector Timofeyeva has a few more questions.
Your friend Agda is here."

As Rostnikov left the hospital room with the nurse, a
woman came quickly in. She was a short older woman in
a heavy coat. Her dark hair was a wild mess, and she was
pink-cheeked from the cold. Rostnikov was already out
of the room when the tearful Agda bent over to kiss her
friend on the mouth and whisper to her.

Elena stood back waiting. In spite of the difficulty of
getting information through the outdated computer network, Rostnikov and Elena had known a number of
things about Katrina Ivanova before they talked to her at
the hospital. They knew her age, that she had come from
Georgia as a child, that she had never used her gun
before, that she was a reliable employee of the Ukrainia
Hotel, and that she had a long-term relationship with
Agda, who played the violin with a band at the Metropole Hotel. Elena stepped farther back to give them some
privacy.

Before he had taken five steps into the hospital corridor, Rostnikov found himself facing a man of about
forty, slightly shorter than himself and considerably
lighter. Through the man's open jacket it was clear that
he was remarkably muscular.

Though it was warm in the hospital, an unusual phe-
nomenon for any Russian building in the winter, the man
did not remove his small fur cap. He was clean-shaven

and light-skinned, with light brown hair and cheekbones tightened in determined anger.

"What happened?" the man demanded. Rostnikov could not quite place his accent.

"Who are you?" Rostnikov asked.

"I asked a question," the man said, standing very close to Rostnikov. People passing in the hall tried to ignore the two men, who looked as if they might be about to engage in a monumental brawl.

"As did I," said Rostnikov. "My name is Porfiry Petrovich Rostnikov. And you are?"

"Belinsky, Rabbi Avrum Belinsky."

"Ah, yes. I wanted to talk to you. Your name was on cards in the wallets of four men murdered tonight. You knew the victims?" Rostnikov handed the rabbi the Polaroid pictures.

"My question first," said Belinsky. "I've seen the bodies. Identified them. I have no need of photographs to remember them."

The man seemed nothing like what Rostnikov expected in a rabbi.

"Four men were murdered on the Taras Shevchenko Embankment slightly after midnight," said Rostnikov. "Judging from the names we retrieved from the bodies, the four men were Jewish."

"With the two last month, that makes six," Belinsky said. "All from our congregation. We can't and won't lose more Jews. What are you doing to find the murderers?"

"What can you do to help us?" asked Rostnikov, thinking he felt a twinge in his no longer extant left leg.

"More questions for answers," said Belinsky impatiently. "I have some information that might be relevant. But how do I know you and the rest of the police will bother with the murders of Jews?"

"My wife is Jewish," said Rostnikov. "And my son, therefore, is half Jewish. In the old Soviet Union and the days of the czars, that would have made him entirely

Jewish. As he discovered when he was in the army, under our new system too, he is considered Jewish."

"And you don't want that," Belinsky said sarcastically, now taking off his jacket and draping it over his arm.

"I needn't tell you it is difficult to be Jewish in Russia, now and always, Avrum Belinsky," said Rostnikov. "You are not Russian, are you?"

"I'm Israeli," said Belinsky. "I came here to help re-build the Jewish community. We are not to be stopped. A Jewish community center just opened in Saint Petersburg where they estimate there are one hundred thousand Jews. There were only some sixty synagogues in all of the Soviet Union, half of them in Georgia. Now we are trying to reignite Judaism in Russia, to give dignity and faith to those who have too long been without it."

"Is that a sermon?" asked Rostnikov.

"It comes from one of my sermons," Belinsky admitted. "When you check on my file, you will find that I was an officer in the Israeli army, that I have been twice wounded. I volunteered for this job when a group of Jews in Moscow requested assistance. I was, you will also discover, a member of the Olympic team in Germany when the mas-sacre took place. I knew the men who died there as I knew the men who have died here."

"You were a wrestler?"

"Greco-Roman," Belinsky said.

"You lift weights?" asked Rostnikov.

Belinsky looked irritated.

"Yes," he said.

"There will be a meeting in a few hours of the Office of Special Investigation, in which I work," said Rost-nikov. "I will ask that I be assigned exclusively to this case with adequate support."

Belinsky nodded, still wary.

"Don't do anything on your own, rabbi," Rostni-kov said.

Belinsky didn't answer.

"Now," said Rostnikov, "let's go to the canteen for some tea and talk."

Belinsky hesitated and then nodded in agreement.

Sasha Tkach was running late. It seemed as if there were a few truths by which he could live with some certainty. First, he would never get enough sleep. Second, he would always be running late. Third, he would never escape from his nearly seventy-year-old mother, Lydia, who, though she now had a tiny apartment of her own, spent almost every evening and many nights in the already cramped apartment of her son, his wife, and their two children. Sasha had found her the small but neat room in a concrete one-story apartment building. Elena Timofeyeva, the only woman in the Office of Special Investigation, had arranged it.

Actually, Elena, who lived in one of the two-room apartments in the building, had enlisted the aid of her aunt, with whom she lived. Anna Timofeyeva, who still had friends who owed her favors from her days as first deputy director of the Moscow procurator's office, had gotten Lydia into the building. Anna had laid down a series of rules by which Lydia Tkach could live there. The rules were in writing. First, Lydia could visit Anna and Elena only when invited or in the case of a real emergency. The determination of whether the situation was an emergency would depend on Anna's assessment of information given in no more than two sentences. Second, Lydia must wear her hearing aid when visiting. If it was broken, she could not visit. Third, discussions of her son's job or complaints about her daughter-in-law were not to be tolerated. Although it wasn't a rule, Anna made it clear that she did not particularly want to hear about Lydia's grandchildren unless it was Anna who brought up the subject. Lydia had agreed to abide by the rules. She still spent as much time at her son's apartment as her daughter-in-law Maya's tolerance would permit. As much as Maya disliked the frequency of her mother-in-law's visits, she had to admit that Lydia's willingness to take care of the children while Maya worked was extremely helpful.

Sasha was an investigator in the Office of Special Investigation. He and Emil Karpo had been transferred to the office with Rostnikov when Rostnikov had lost favor within the procurator general's office. The Office of Special Investigation had been a strictly ceremonial dead end until the often confused regime of Yeltsin and the reformers, when it took on more important cases, often politically sensitive ones, that the other investigative branches—State Security (formerly the KGB), the Ministry of the Interior (including the mafia task force), the National Police (formerly the MVD), the procurator's office, the tax police—did not want. It was not uncommon for disputes to rage at a crime scene as to which of the investigative branches had jurisdiction. Often, two police districts would engage in heated argument in front of the public about who was in charge. The criminal investigation system of Russia was not quite in a shambles, but everyone seemed to be lying back and waiting to see if the reformers would hold on to power or the new Communists and Zhirinovsky Nationalists would combine and seize control. No one wished to fail. It was easier to shift the difficult cases to the Office of Special Investigation.

Sasha, who was over thirty but looked no more than a few years past twenty, dressed quickly to the morning din of his apartment. Lydia has slept over, and now, refusing to wear her hearing aid, she was shouting about having slept badly. Pulcharia, who was nearing four years old, was telling Maya, her mother, that she did not want to stay with Grandma Lydia. Illya was gurgling calmly in his makeshift crib.

Sasha examined himself in the mirror of the tiny bathroom. The bulge of the gun in the holster under his jacket did not show. The suit he wore was baggy and a bit frayed. A new suit was out of the question. His salary and

Maya's combined were barely enough to keep the family fed, dressed, and in a reasonable two-room apartment. He adjusted his shirt, slightly yellow from too many washings, and decided this was the best he could do. Besides, he would be out on the streets in his coat and scarf most of the day.

He was alone in the bedroom with the baby. When Lydia slept over, which was often, she slept in this room on the bed with Pulcharia. The baby slept in the other room. Even with the door to the bedroom closed, Lydia's snoring could be heard just below the decibel range of a metro. Pulcharia had always been completely oblivious of her grandmother's snoring.

Sasha stepped out into the combination living room/ dining room/kitchen where he and Maya slept on the floor. The futon had been rolled up and stored, and the room was reasonably neat, but the look from Maya as their eyes met let him know with sympathy that neither of them would escape the apartment this morning without conflict. Maya, dark, pretty, showing no sign of having had two babies, shrugged slightly and shook her head, her short, straight dark hair moving in near slow motion.

Maya was dressed for work, dark skirt, green blouse, shoes with a low heel. She looked beautiful. He wondered how many men made passes at his wife in the course of her day at the Council for International Business Advancement. Sasha tried to ignore his mother and moved to give his wife a kiss. She was already made up, so the kiss was nearly chaste.

"Me," said Pulcharia, knee-high to his baggy trousers, holding out her arms.

Sasha picked her up, kissed both her eyes and nose and hugged her, thinking that in spite of Lydia's insistence that the child looked like Sasha's grandmother, Pulcharia was clearly Maya's child. This was how Maya had looked as a child. They had photographs. Lydia denied the striking resemblance and insisted that her grand-daughter was a replica of Lydia's own mother.

Sasha put his daughter down and accepted a cup of coffee and a slice of bread from Maya. Only then did he turn to his mother, a small, wiry woman with a deter-mined face that would have been considered handsome were it not for her nearly constant scowl. There was more than a bit of gray in her short, wavy hair. She wore a sag-ging, heavy blue robe and regarded her son with a look of determination.

"Dobraye utra," Sasha said, continuing to eat. "Good morning, Mother."

"Two things," Lydia shouted as Pulcharia sat herself down at the table near the window and ate last night's bean soup and a large piece of bread. The child had the enviable ability to tune out her grandmother.

"Yes, Mother," Sasha said, sitting in front of a bowl of soup and joining his daughter. He was sure that Maya had finished eating sometime before.

"First," said Lydia, "the child kicks in her sleep. She moves all around. I can't sleep."

Lydia's unceasing snoring was evidence to the contrary, but Sasha looked up as his mother moved toward him.

"I'm afraid you'll just have to sleep in your apartment more," he said.

Hovering over him, she ignored his comment. Maya looked at her watch, gulped down the remainder of her coffee, kissed Pulcharia, gave Sasha a look of sympathy, and moved to give the baby a good-bye kiss. "Second, this apartment is too cold," Lydia said.

"Everyone's apartment is too cold or too hot," said Sasha. "It is a fact of winter life in Moscow."

"I intend to complain," Lydia went on.

"To whom?" he asked, dipping his bread into the soup.

"Third," Lydia said. Maya was putting on her coat.

"I thought you said there were only two things," Sasha said before he could stop himself.

"Grandma did," Pulcharia confirmed.

"You have still made no effort to be assigned to an office job," Lydia said.

"I don't want an office job," Sasha said with what he thought was remarkable composure considering that he had gone through this conversation with his mother perhaps a hundred times before.

"You have a family," she said.

Maya closed the door quietly and escaped.

"Yes," he said.

"People try to kill you. You do dangerous things."

"Sometimes," he said.

"You're like your father," Lydia said. "You have a temper. You're easily angered and your emotions get you into trouble."

Sasha checked his watch. On this point, he knew, his mother was right. Sasha's father, whom Sasha did not even remember, had been an army officer. He had died on duty in Estonia when Sasha was two. The official cause of death was pneumonia, but Lydia was convinced that he had died of debauchery.

"Your father was always volunteering to go to distant places, even Siberia," she said, "because of his hot blood."

And, Sasha was certain, to escape from his wife, who had been a beauty but who almost certainly had the same personality then as she was displaying now.

"Today you ask for a transfer to a ministry office position," she insisted. "I will go back and see some of my old friends. They have already said they would help."

Sasha took his and Pulcharia's bowls and put them and the spoons in the small sink behind him.

"No, Mother," he said.

"Then I will talk to Porfiry Petrovich again," she shouted.

To this the baby reacted with a scream followed by crying. Lydia didn't seem to hear him. Pulcharia ran to the crib, where she had some success in quieting little Illya.

"Porfiry Petrovich has no power to transfer me," Sasha said. "Besides, he would not do so without my consent, even if he could."

"Colonel Snitkonoy," she said. "I'll go directly to him."

"He will pat your hand, tell you he understands, promise to see what he can do, and then forget you came except to tell me that it would be best if I did what I could to keep you away from him."

"Stubborn," she said. "Like your father."

Sasha nodded.

"He needs a new diaper," Pulcharia called. "He stinks."

"The baby needs a new diaper," Sasha shouted, walking across the room to take his own coat and wool cap from the rack near the door. "And I am very late."

"This conversation is not over," Lydia said.

"Of that I am certain, Mother," he said, buttoning up.

"Gloves," Lydia said.

He pulled his gloves from his pocket and displayed them.

"He stinks," Pulcharia repeated, leaning over the railing of the crib to get the odor more directly.

Sasha hurried back across the room, kissed his mother's cheek, and marched quickly toward the door.

"I don't want to stay home with Grandma," Pulcharia said as he opened the door. There were tears in her eyes.

"She loves you," Sasha whispered so that his mother could not hear. "You must stay with her."

"Yah n'e khachooo," said Pulcharia. "I don't want to."

"I'll bring you something special," Sasha said, taking his daughter in his arms and kissing her again. "Now I'm late."

"We'll go for a walk," said Lydia, moving to the crib. "We'll go to the park."

"Okay," said Pulcharia.

When Lydia had worked in the offices of the Ministry

of Public Affairs, she had frequently lived with Maya and Sasha and it had been almost tolerable. Now Lydia was retired, on an insignificant and often unpaid pension, and had plenty of time. In spite of the pitiful pension, Lydia was not poor. During her more than forty years in the ministry, Lydia had quietly managed to put away money. What little she saved, she converted from rubles into jewelry, jewelry she bought from people who needed cash for bread. Gradually Lydia learned enough about jewelry to know what she was buying and to make sometimes remarkable purchases. She kept everything in a box she hid carefully wherever she was living. Then, after she had officially retired, with the Soviet Union in the process of falling, Lydia sold her jewelry, piece by piece, at a profit, to the sudden influx of entrepreneurs, carpetbaggers, and outsiders in Moscow.

While Yeltsin stood on the top of a tank proclaiming the end of Communism, Lydia was going to the proper ministry offices and arranging to buy government Bread Shop 61 half a block from where she was living near Solkonicki Park. When Gorbachev had started using words like *perestroika*—the restructuring of the Soviet communist system—and *glasnost*—openness to express one's opinions—Lydia had called a cousin who was a farmer on a collective outside of Kursk and made a deal with him. It was simple. If the government ever did fall and the farmers became free to own and deal, she would be willing to purchase all the wheat he could produce on his land and that of some of his neighbors. It was not an enormous amount, but it would be enough to supply flour for the bread she planned to sell. Lydia's cousin even knew someone in Kursk who could convert the wheat to flour at a reasonable rate, with her cousin, of course, getting a small commission for that service. Lydia and her cousin would annually reset the price, and she would make it a fair one. Living in fear of having no government to which to sell his crop, her cousin and his friends had readily agreed. Then she had made the necessary

vzyatka—the unofficial bribes needed to get services—
obtained the necessary purchases, and became the owner
of a bread store. The bureaucrats who had sold her the
government store that they now deemed worthless were
happy to take her money even though its value was dropping crazily. She had bought the store and had full papers
and rights to it. It had even left her with significant
savings.

While the people of the right and left and middle were
marching and buildings were in flames, Lydia offered
each of the state employees who worked in the store the
opportunity to stay and work for her with the incentive of
bonuses if business went well. Some stayed. Some left.
They all thought she was a bit mad. Gradually the bread
shop workers learned that it was to their advantage to
produce and to be reasonably respectful to customers.

Now, more than three years later, Tkach's Bread Shop,
which sold only one size of loaf at a price lower than
competing shops, was a thriving business with long lines.
It was an assembly line of bread, and prices were listed in
rubles and dollars.

Once, a little more than a year before, a gang of young
men, too few to be called a mafia, too many to be
ignored, and too violent to be reasoned with, had come to
the shop and demanded a regular weekly protection payment. The bread shop manager had called Lydia, and she
had agreed to meet the gang the next Tuesday morning.
When the gang of tattooed young men in leather jackets
arrived, they were greeting by the old lady and three men
who displayed both their weapons and their police identification. One of the policemen looked like a boy but had
a glint of near madness in his eyes. A second policeman
was bulky and looked a bit dull-witted. The third was tall
and dressed in black, with a paste-white face and sparse
combed-back hair. Ultimately the gang decided the
money they might collect from the bread shop was not
worth a confrontation with these three. Six months later a
larger, older gang of Georgians also backed down when

Sasha and his fellow policemen showed up. The few rubles they would collect from Lydia were simply not worth dying or going to jail for.

Now, with no protection to pay, Lydia was even further ahead of her competition, and the bread shop thrived. When Lydia died there would be a significant business to be left to her son and grandchildren. She had arranged the proper papers and paid the right people so that this could come to pass.

Somehow, though she didn't tell him, Lydia expected Sasha to know all this and be grateful. Normally, however, he had other things on his mind, dangerous things that worried Lydia.

Sasha put his daughter down and went through the door, closing it quickly behind him. As he ran down the stairs, he brushed back the strand of hair that had regularly fallen across his eyes since he was a boy. There was more than a bit of truth in what his mother had said. There was danger, now more than ever before, and there were always bribes and women. He did have a temper. There was, however, a great deal to be angry about.

One of those things was a violent rapist who had survived long enough to earn a nickname, the Shy One. He had managed to commit at least twenty reported rapes without once being seen by his victims, who ranged in age from sixteen to sixty-seven. He had come upon them from behind and dragged them to a dark street or park or train yard. He warned them not to scream, and then he raped them from behind.

The first reported rape had been over two years ago. The rapist had worn a condom and left no semen traces to analyze. After each sexual attack he had beaten the victim, hitting each woman in the head when he was finished. With each attack the beatings had grown worse. All of the victims had received hospital treatment. Seven had required surgery. Two had lost sight in one eye. And the Shy One left no clue at all, which was why the National Police were happy to turn the case over to the

Office of Special Investigation and why the Wolfhound had turned it over to Sasha and Elena Timofeyeva with the vague suggestion that Elena might be used as a decoy and Sasha, with his youthful appearance, might watch over her with little suspicion falling on them. The Wolfhound's ideas were always vague, intentionally so. If his investigators succeeded, he could take credit for their success. If they failed, he would view their failure with paternal sympathy and clear disappointment.

The Shy One had no time pattern, no particular night of the week, no pattern of months, and only the vaguest broad sector of operation. Some of the victims said they heard a car door close immediately after they were attacked, but none could identify any car.

Sasha tried to come up with an idea as he jogged to the bus, but all he could think of was that his mother would be there when he got home and he would have no peace.

Emil Karpo had awakened at five in the morning, just as he had done for more than twenty years. He had awakened in total darkness without an alarm clock. He turned on the small table lamp next to his narrow bed and rose slowly. For weeks after Mathilde Verson's death, he had slept with the small light on as he had as a young boy. Then, one night, he had turned it off. He slept without clothes despite the weather. Though the past night had been cold, it was no colder than a typical Moscow winter night. On warm nights in the summer, he slept on top of the thin sheet and thick blanket. On cold nights like last night, he had slept under the thick blanket that had been a gift from Mathilde. Mathilde, who had been torn to pieces in daylight on a busy street. She had been caught in the crossfire between two rival mafias. Mathilde had been a full-time telephone operator and a part-time prostitute with a sense of humor Karpo did not understand. They had, over the years, moved from a regular Thursday rendezvous to a teasing friendship to a serious relationship. Karpo wondered what there was in him that had made the bright, pretty woman want to be with him.

Emil Karpo had no illusions about himself. He was tall and incredibly gaunt, though he worked out in his room each morning. He was very pale and wore his straight and thinning hair brushed straight back. Until Mathilde, he had never worn anything but black. She had gradually changed that, but now he was back to his black attire. With Mathilde he had smiled a few times, very small smiles that only someone watching closely would have noticed. People did not tend to watch Emil Karpo closely. He was well aware that both the criminals and police referred to him as the Tartar or the Vampire. Neither name displeased him. It did not hurt to have a reputation. But Mathilde had seen past his white, cold image. *Zeema*, the winter, suited him and now it was *Dikabr'*, December, which suited him best of all months.

He looked around the room. Against one wall was a bookcase filled with black notebooks covering the details of every case on which he had ever worked. He had a special marking on those books containing cases that had not been solved. On the desk before the bookcase stood an old table. Two months ago, Karpo had purchased a computer, which rested on the table. It was crude, an old Macintosh II, but it had been expensive. That didn't matter to Karpo. He had saved most of his salary. He could have lived better, perhaps eaten better, certainly dressed better, but he had simply put his money—cash— in a well-hidden place outside of his room.

Karpo was slowly transferring all of the data from his black books to the computer. He had been reading books on computers and had become convinced from using the one belonging to the Office of Special Investigation that a careful recording of the data in his notebooks might enable him to cross-check information from thousands of crimes and perhaps find information that would tie some things together.

On the wall near the door to the hall sat a chest of

drawers, so old it was almost an antique. There was a painting on the wall. Mathilde had painted it. Craig Hamilton, the black FBI man who had been one of the agents assigned to help in the Russian fight against organized crime, lived in Washington and was a lover of art who frequently visited the National Gallery with his family. He had declared Mathilde a talented artist. Mathilde had given the painting to the Rostnikovs. Karpo had come to his room shortly after her death to find the painting on the wall. Each morning he paused, as he did now, before he began his workout to gaze in the semidarkness at the reclining figure of a woman looking up a grassy hill, her face away from the viewer, her red hair, like a young Mathilde's, billowing in a gentle wind. At the top of the grassy hill stood a small house. On the wall behind Karpo's bed was the door to the closet where his dark clothes hung neatly in front and the clothes that Mathilde had bought, made, or convinced him to purchase were in boxes on the shelf. The fourth wall was to the right of Karpo's bed. It had the single window that Emil Karpo opened only in the morning to determine the weather.

It was little more than the cell of a monk. Karpo, in fact, had set up the room to resemble that of Lenin's original Moscow room. Emil Karpo had zealously believed that Marxism would eventually weed out the corruption of individuals and that Communism would unite the world. He had been certain of his convictions from the first meeting he went to as a small boy holding his father's hand, when he saw the red banner with the hammer and sickle covering the large wall behind the speakers who stood on the low platform and shouted with passion of the transformations that Soviet Communism would bring to the world. On that night, at that meeting, the workers, except for his father and a few others, had shouted till it hurt the boy's ears. His father, whom he now resembled, had simply squeezed the boy's hand.

Karpo had become a policeman in order to help stop

those who broke the laws of the state and impeded the progress of the Communist dream. The Party, flawed as it might have become, had been his religion. Now the Soviet Union was gone and a group of opportunists calling themselves Communists were threatening to take over the government in free elections. But Karpo knew theirs was not the Communism in which he had believed. That was dead. These new Communists said they would rid Russia of the mafias and reunite the Soviet Union. Karpo, who was on the cold concrete floor doing push-ups, knew that it was too late. The people had exchanged the corruption of Communism and its promise for the corruption of capitalism and its inflation, lack of direction, and the growth of a wealthy criminal element. The bribes were still necessary. The food was more scarce. The political promises now were more hollow.

It was not Communism that had failed. It was humanity. The animalism of humanity, the weakness of people, the ease of corruption, the lack of real commitment from top to bottom, had destroyed the dream that could have been a reality. It had all relied ultimately on faith, not on God and not on the system, but in people, the Russian people, the Soviet people, to commit themselves to Communism and its ultimate promise. Karpo now had little faith that the people had the ability to escape centuries of corrupt survival under any system. Capitalism was not the savior. It was only another facade behind which the weak and uncommitted—almost everyone—could hide.

Only Mathilde had helped him through, and the example of Porfiry Petrovich Rostnikov, who behaved as if nothing surprised him, as if society was mad regardless of who controlled it, as if only individual people— women, children, the innocent and relatively innocent— counted. Rostnikov's attitude had frequently gotten him into trouble with the MVD, the KGB, and military intelligence, but he had managed to survive. Karpo had decided early in his career that he would stay with and respect this limping eccentric man who frequently smiled at the folly of the world.

Karpo finished his one hundredth push-up, rolled onto his back, put his legs up on his bed, and began to do his several hundred abdominal crunches. He had no need to count. His body told him how many he had done. Next he propped himself on his arms so that his long legs could reach into the air. He began pumping his legs, bicycling, slowly for a minute or two, then faster and faster. He continued for fifteen minutes and was barely breathing hard when he stopped and rose. He had worked up a very slight sweat, and in spite of the coldness of the room, he was warm. He got a towel from his bottom drawer, one of the three towels he owned, took the blue plastic box with the bar of soap inside, wrapped the towel around himself, and went into the hall. It was not yet six. The narrow hallway with the dull gray walls was empty. Even those who had to be at work early waited for the policeman to take his morning shower and get back to his room before lining up to douse themselves in the trickle of quick cold water. No one wanted to run into the Vampire. It was an unwritten rule of the building off Vernadskogo Prospekt. Many wondered why a policeman, a detective, chose to live in a place like this when he could certainly do much better, but he had been there as long as any of them could remember.

Back in his room, Karpo, fully dry, hung his towel on a bar next to the window and slowly dressed. His watch told him that he had two hours to work on his computer. Already he had uncovered some interesting data that he wanted to discuss with Porfiry Petrovich. Karpo had a possible lead in the case of the person who had been sending letter and box bombs to seemingly unrelated Moscovites. One of the victims had died. Eight had been seriously injured.

He focused on this as he worked on his computer. All else was blocked out, even the call the night before from Pankov, the small, quivering assistant to the director of the Office of Special Investigation, Colonel Snitkonoy, the Gray Wolfhound. Pankov had simply said that the director ordered the appearance of all members of the office for a meeting the next morning at nine. The morning briefing was always scheduled, and Karpo thought briefly that there must be something of great importance at issue if a call had to be made. He knew better than to ask Pankov what the issue might be.

He would know soon enough.

THREE

ELENA TIMOFEYEVA SAT AT THE TABLE IN COLONEL Snitkonoy's office between Porfiry Petrovich and Emil Karpo. To the right of Karpo sat Sasha Tkach, who looked decidedly tired. To Rostnikov's left sat Akardy Zelach, who looked more than uncomfortable. The hulking, stoop-shouldered creature who was known for his loyalty but not his intellect, looked decidedly concerned. To Zelach's left was an empty chair, and this struck Elena as most unusual. That was the place of Major Gregorovich, the second in rank in the office, the man who everyone knew disliked Rostnikov, thought the Wolfhound a fool, and leaked information to other investigative offices. Gregorovich had been responsible for particularly sensitive cases involving the military or other investigative agencies. Officially he was assigned to the office only temporarily, but the assumption was that he was there to watch the Wolfhound and, at some point in the future, as a reward for his reliable revelation of the investigations of the Office of Special Investigation to other agencies, to take over when the Wolfhound moved on or retired.

But the major was now missing from the table. Elena assumed the man must be ill, on a secret assignment, or dead. The latter possibility did not cause her distress. To the left of the empty seat sat Pankov, almost a dwarf, notebook open before him, stack of reports rising like a small fortification before him to ward off the director's wrath. Pankov fidgeted, as always, and tugged at the too-tight collar of his familiar gray suit.

It had also not escaped Elena's attention that a new member of the office had joined them. There was not enough room behind the table except for Major Greg-orovich's empty seat, so a chair had been placed at one end of the table next to Sasha. In the chair sat Iosef Rost-nikov, Porfiry Petrovich's son. He smiled at Elena, who resisted smoothing her hair and looking at him. Iosef, tall, broad like his father, and with a handsome face and curly dark hair, had begun to smile more like his father. For more than a year after being released from the army and serving in the purgatory of Siberia or the battle-ground of Afghanistan, Iosef had devoted himself to drama, antigovernment plays in little theaters, plays that Iosef often wrote and acted in. At some point, a change had come to Iosef Rostnikov. He had given up the theater and applied for the National Police which was a bit reluc-tant to take on the son of Porfiry Petrovich Rostnikov, who might pass information on to his father. However, they were offered little choice. He was qualified and a directive came down from the Ministry of the Interior that he should be hired. Iosef had been on patrol with a taciturn young partner calming drunks and feuding fami-lies, rousting teenagers, taking notes on beatings and rob-beries, and learning what he could. The National Police had been only too happy to let the younger Rostnikov join his father in the Office of Special Investigation when the request had come through.

But something else had happened to change Iosef. He had declared one night at a party in his parents' apart-ment, a party where he had been accompanied by one of the most beautiful girls Elena had ever seen, that he intended to marry Elena Timofeyeva. At first, Elena had considered it a drunken joke. But he had continued to pursue her. In the mirror each morning Elena saw a smooth-skinned, pink, and good-looking if a bit pudgy face with straight blond hair. Elena fought an endless battle to keep her weight down. She had before her the image of her aunt and her mother and was convinced that she was doomed to become a compact tank. She had, the year before, had a brief affair with a Cuban policeman while on duty with Porfiry Petrovich for an investigation in Havana. The policeman was married, and she was never quite sure whether he had been truly attracted to her or had seduced her to keep track of Rostnikov's investigation. She had decided it was probably both.

Elena looked at the clock on the wall. It was about thirty seconds to nine. She glanced at Rostnikov, who was drawing pictures of birds in his open notebook with the word 'colors?' neatly printed at the bottom of the sheet.

At precisely nine the door to the office opened, and a man in a blue suit and matching striped tie stepped in. His hair was dark and cut short. His body was lean. He stood before them, hands folded in front of him. He looked at each of them. His face was rugged and clean-shaven, his most notable feature being his bushy eyebrows, which made him look just a bit like a younger, trimmer version of Leonid Brezhnev. Elena guessed his age at a little over fifty. Rostnikov looked up from his notebook, and his eyes met those of the man who had entered and now spoke.

"My name," he said in a confident tenor, "is Igor Yakovlev. Colonel Snitkonoy has been promoted and made general. His presence was required in Saint Petersburg, where he will be head of security for the Hermitage. This is a permanent appointment. Major Gregorovich has been transferred and will be providing security for a prominent member of the congress, Citizen Zhirinovsky."

The transfer, Elena knew, was a nightmare any sane person would dread, to be responsible for the protection of the probably mad regressive Nationalist who cried out for assassination from those he offended on a daily basis and who blamed the Jews for a long list of the ills of Russian history. The crazy Zhirinovsky was reportedly half Jewish himself.

Yakovlev looked directly at each of those around the table. Pankov clearly knew what was happening. Karpo showed no particular sign of interest. Rostnikov studied the face of the man before him. Sasha was alert and wary. Iosef had an open look of curiosity. Zelach seemed confused and looked around the table for reassurance. None came.

"I," said Yakovlev, "am the new director of the Office of Special Investigation. I expect you to function with the efficiency you have displayed since the establishment of this office. While we give great credit for this success to Colonel Snitkonoy, I intend to function at an even higher level. I know about each of you, your strengths and weaknesses, your loyalties."

With this he looked directly at Rostnikov.

"My background, as Inspector Rostnikov knows, was in the former KGB," Yakovlev said. "I no longer hold any rank within State Security. I renounced such rank to accept this position when it was offered by a member of the government through the Ministry of the Interior. I see it as an opportunity. That is all you will ever hear from me regarding my background or professional life. I have no doubt that Porfiry Petrovich will give you further information about me if he so chooses or I do not order him to give no further information. I will not so order him. Questions?"

No one spoke or moved.

"You will all, including Citizen Pankov, receive a raise of ten percent effective immediately," he said. "I expect a fifty percent greater effort from you in return. Next, these morning meetings will end. They are a waste of time you could be spending at work. We will meet infrequently as needed. Meanwhile, I am officially naming Inspector Rostnikov assistant director of this office. He will move into the office formerly occupied by Major Gregorovich. You will report to him, all of you except Pankov, who will report to me only. Chief Inspector Rostnikov will meet with me on a regular basis to report on your

progress and to receive new cases that come to my desk.
You will come to me directly only if I send for you. You
all understand?"

A few said *da* while others, including Elena, nodded
their heads.

"Good," he said. "You all have work. You are all dismissed with the exception of Chief Inspector Rostnikov.
Pankov has already prepared all the necessary papers for
your salary increases and I have signed them. The money
for these raises will come out of the office's annual
budget. The salary of the director will be reduced to
cover this fiscal charge."

Slowly, one by one, a bit dazed, they all stood up,
Karpo first, followed by Sasha and Elena. Iosef looked at
his father and then at Yakovlev, who hovered over Porfiry Petrovich. The new director's hands were now
folded behind his back. He continued to stand tall.

Iosef got up and a confused Zelach followed him.
Pankov took up the rear and closed the door behind them.
When they were gone, Yakovlev said, "Well, Washtub?"

"Well, Yak?"

Yakovlev smiled, his bushy eyebrows rising. He
reached into his pocket and pulled out a pair of glasses,
which he carefully placed over nose and ears.

"I need you," said Yakovlev.

Rostnikov shrugged.

"I need a one-legged troublemaker whose sarcasm
matches Gogol's," the Yak said. "I need an honest man. I
need the loyalty you get from those who will now be
working for you. I am not simply flattering you. I need
you, Porfiry Petrovich."

"I know," said Rostnikov. "But you are giving me
more credit than I deserve."

"I reserve the right as your superior to maintain a small
pocket of doubt on all these counts."

"It would be foolish to do otherwise," said Rostnikov.
"And you are no fool."

"We have been on opposite sides on more than one

occasion," said Yakovlev, moving to the end of the table and taking the seat Iosef had vacated.

Rostnikov nodded. He turned his head to face the director at eye level. The turn was awkward with his artificial leg, but it was not painful. Rostnikov knew the man before him as a ruthless member of the KGB. He had served under a general who committed suicide when the coup against Gorbachev failed. The suicide had been announced officially as a heart attack. Yakovlev had not been promoted. Nor had he been dismissed or demoted. He still had his protectors. Since the fall of the Soviet Union Yakovlev had moved into the shadows till this moment. He was smart, but more important, he was *khitry*, cunning. Rostnikov knew he had killed on more than one occasion at the order of the now deceased general and probably others as well. There were stories of interrogation sessions conducted by the Yak in Lubyanka, sessions that the subject did not survive.

"Everyone who was at this table, with the possible exception of Pankov and Zelach," said the Yak, "knows that the Wolfhound is a fool. He is, however, a threat to no one, and he looks good in uniform. I expect he will be a great success in Saint Petersburg and consider himself fortunate to have gotten what he considers to be a promotion."

"You may underestimate him," said Rostnikov.

"You contradict me?" said Yakovlev, suddenly standing. "That is precisely what I need from you. Honesty, intelligent assessments of people and situations, and loyalty. Do I have them?"

"May I expect the same from you?" said Rostnikov, putting an *X* through two of his birds in flight.

"Would you believe me if I simply said yes?"

"Yes," said Rostnikov. "With the knowledge that a situation might well arise in the future. If that were to happen, I would hope that you would give me some advance indication that I could no longer rely on your loyalty."

"The answer to your question," said Yakovlev, "is yes."

"And my answer, too, is yes," said Rostnikov.

"And now we can get to work," said the Yak. "I want a briefing on the murder of the four Jews last night."

Yakovlev moved behind the desk that had a day or two ago belonged to Colonel Snitkonoy. He folded his hands before him and waited. From behind the table where he sat, Rostnikov opened the file he had brought with him.

He had been honest with Yakovlev, though he had not revealed that he had learned of his appointment four days earlier from Anna Timofeyeva, who had gotten the information from an old friend in the procurator general's office. Anna had told no one else, not even her niece. In part her motivation was to suggest to him that he protect Elena, but she knew he would do so to the best of his ability in any case. In part it was to prepare him for a man who could not readily be trusted. It was, in fact, likely that Rostnikov was aware of the change before Colonel Snitkonoy himself.

Yakovlev, Rostnikov decided, had been reasonably honest with him. However, Anna had also suggested to Porfiry Petrovich that it had been Yak's idea to leak the news of his appointment through the unwitting dupe in the procurator general's office. Yakovlev would have wanted nothing unexpected from his new second in command at this meeting. He would have wanted Rostnikov to have some time to come to a conclusion about the abrupt change.

Rostnikov looked at the open file, closed it, and did what he knew Yakovlev wanted. He told him what had happened in simple terms and gave some of his ideas on how he planned to follow up.

Outside the office on the top floor of Petrovka, there came the sudden barking of dozens of dogs, the National Police dogs. With the rise in gang activity and street crime, there should have been more police, but police were expensive compared to dogs, so there were now more dogs, and they were louder when something upset them or it was time to eat. Occasionally a dog would disappear, and the rumor ran through the building that some patrol officers were taking the dogs home for food.

Rostnikov finished his presentation over the sounds of the yowling animals.

"It is my understanding that the foreign press already knows about the murder of the four Jews and the two others," said Yakovlev. "The *New York Times* and CNN will have the story. It was given to their correspondents by a very angry rabbi whose phone was wired, a rabbi who is probably also an Israeli informant."

"I have met the man," said Rostnikov.

"I can keep some of the circumstances under cover," said the Yak. "For a while. But an outburst of overt and violent anti-Semitism at this point in the history of our country could be a political bombshell."

"I understand," said Rostnikov.

"Good," said Yakovlev. "Find me this killer or killers. Find them quickly. Do not arrest them. Find them and report to me with a concise single-page report. Find them before they kill another Jew."

Rostnikov nodded.

There were three men in Moscow whose lives were very much involved in the report Rostnikov gave to his new director. At the moment Porfiry Petrovich began his report, the first man, who lived in one of the concrete-and-granite apartment towers built under Stalin in the 1950s, was just arriving at work. The building where the man lived was beyond the Outer Ring Circle. It took him nearly forty minutes from the Rechnoi Vokzal metro station each morning to get to Moscow and forty minutes when he left his work to go home. The man lived with his wife and seven-year-old daughter, who excelled at mathematics to the point where she was frequently singled out in her school for special honors, and the man and his wife were told that the girl had a very bright future.

He knew his assignment for the day. It seldom varied since his promotion, and he seldom had to think about what he was doing. Intelligence was not called for. Through much of that day as he worked, this man with a wife and brilliant daughter went over his plan: where he would find his next victim, when he would do it, where he would take her. From time to time, he would ask himself why he was doing this. Why had this obsession gradually come over him? He knew he couldn't and wouldn't stop. He knew that the pitiful whimpering of the women or their stunned silence tormented him. And he feared that with each attack he grew more violent, out of control, feeling a monstrous anger. But he could not stop. He had, he knew, been given a nickname, the Shy One, but that might well turn into a more tainted name in the future.

But now he simply planned and hoped that the thing that had taken him would pass as it had come and he would learn to live with or even forget what he had done in the past and what he planned to do this very night.

The second man was named Yevgeny Tutsolov. He lived with another young man named Leonid Sharvotz. Both men were in their late twenties. Late the night before, a third man, Georgi Radzo, who was almost fifty, had sat on a chair in the small room looking at Yevgeny silently. The older man was extremely powerful from more than twenty years of loading heavy crates onto trucks. Each day he loaded for nine hours with an hour to eat lunch. He was still loading trucks, but that should soon end. Yevgeny had sat soberly, calmly as the older man had bandaged his shoulder.

"The bullet went through," the older man had said. "I think you will be all right. It didn't strike anything vital and slid over the bone and out."

Yevgeny Tutsolov had wanted to curse, but instead he shook his head and said, "The unexpected. Always the unexpected. I kill the Jews, lay them out. It all goes well and then there is this madwoman pointing a gun at me."

"It didn't go well," the other young man, Leonid, said, seated forlornly on his bed. "Igor . . . you killed Igor."

"It was necessary," Georgi said. "Yevgeny had no choice."

"The one who shot you, she didn't get a good look at you, did she?" asked Leonid as the older man sat back to inspect the bandage he had put in place. He had seen far worse injuries on the loading dock. He nodded, satisfied with his first aid, and the wounded Yevgeny put on a clean shirt that buttoned in front. Putting it on was not particularly painful. He was sure he could work his shift the next day.

"It was dark. She was too far away. Even if she saw my face in the light from a streetlight, I'm sure she was too frightened to see clearly. If she had been closer, I might well be dead now or wounded and in the hands of the police. I don't like counting on luck."

Yevgeny's luck had indeed been bad. Herding the four men down the embankment, he had cracked his knee on an unseen rock covered by snow. He had been forced to limp through the execution.

It had taken a good part of the savings of all three men to purchase the AT-9, the American 9mm semiautomatic carbine, that Yevgeny had used. The carbine had the advantage of being relatively light and small. It had also been expensive, even in today's Moscow gun market. He had killed the first two Jews with it a week earlier, and it had handled perfectly. And he had killed the other three Jews and Igor with barely a second of panic when the weapon seemed to jam, only to come alive when Yevgeny hit the bullet cartridge firmly into place with his gloved palm.

That had been the night before. Now, in the morning, the powerful older man was at the loading dock where he worked, and the two young men were alone. The wound had throbbed slightly, and his knee had been sore enough

to wake him once or twice, but the slayer of the four
young men on the riverbank had managed to sleep. He
dressed and prepared for his day, confident that he could
hide the wound on his arm and that he would not limp.

"Will this be enough?" asked Leonid, who was tall and
thin with a decidedly boyish face that had been passed
down for generations in his family.

"Enough?" asked Yevgeny.

"Will the Jews go now?" the young man asked.

Yevgeny Tutsolov shrugged. He could feel the shrug
in his wounded shoulder.

"Perhaps, perhaps not," he said. "They are stubborn.
Jews are smart and they have learned to survive. I think it
will take more. I think it will require the particularly
gruesome death of the Israeli rabbi."

"Belinsky," said Leonid, who wanted to ask why it had
been necessary to kill Igor. He wanted to ask but he was
afraid. Yevgeny and Georgi had felt it necessary to kill
the man who had been their partner, who had helped plan
the murders, whom they had known for many years.
Leonid was aware of the reasons. The reasons were good,
but were they good enough?

"Belinsky," Yevgeny confirmed. "Before we kill him,
we will try a good beating. A good beating may make
him less enchanted with organizing the Jews of Moscow.
Killing him might make him a martyr, but I think, ultimately, we will have to kill him."

Within two miles of where Rostnikov was giving his
report to his new superior, in an upscale apartment
building on Chekhov Prospekt half a block from the
Rossia Cinema, another man stood before a worktable in
the tiny room off his bedroom, a room he kept locked and
for which he alone had a key.

Alexi Monochov lived with his mother and sister. The
sister had Down's syndrome, which was still popularly
known as mongolism in Russia. Nonetheless she was

able to hold down a simple job not far from the apartment, though they did not need the money.

Alexi's father, whose name was Ivan, had secured for the family a large apartment and a steady and more than adequate income before he died. The father had worked in the Bureau of Energy. When he was told that he was dying of prostate cancer as his father had before him, Ivan had begun taking home documents that were buried in the files. He copied them. He hid the originals. Then he systematically took the copies to fourteen well-to-do government employees and businesspeople and threatened to release the documents, which would certainly send the men to prison or maybe to their deaths. Ivan had been sensible enough to demand a not unreasonable monthly amount from each of the men to be paid to his widow. The documents would be sent to the proper authorities if anything were to happen to any member of his family or if the money should stop. None of the men had any idea that any others were also being blackmailed.

In the old Soviet Union there might have been questions about the sudden solvency of Ivan's family, but one of the men on Ivan's list had seen to it that such questions were not asked, and in the new Russia nobody cared about where people got their money. Illegality was simply assumed.

Now, with his sister and mother out of the house shopping and his bedroom door locked, the son of Ivan selected the proper tool, a tiny eyebrow tweezer.

He worked slowly, carefully, with a certain pride in his skills and secure in the knowledge that what he was doing was right. He completed his task and left his workroom, locking the door behind him. His mother and sister had not returned. That was good. He dressed warmly, put on his boots, and left the apartment.

The nearest mail drop was two blocks away. He walked six blocks down Gorky Prospekt to Mayakovsky Square. It was there, at the Belorus railway station, that he mailed his latest letter bomb.

* * *

It took Rostnikov, with the help of his son and Elena Timofeyeva, no more than twenty minutes to move into the office that had belonged to Major Gregorovich. It was Yakovlev who had insisted on the immediate move. Rostnikov understood. Take command, make changes. Show who is in charge and how things will work.

Porfiry Petrovich's office was directly across the hall from the room that had been divided into cubicles where the investigators of the Office of Special Investigation worked and where Rostnikov, until this morning, had himself worked.

For Rostnikov, the primary virtue of the office was the view from the window into Petrovka Street, where one could see the trees, buses, vendors, police vehicles, and pedestrians.

On the desk was a telephone, a large plastic container of plastic paper clips, a pad of paper, and a black cup filled with sharpened pencils.

The wooden desk chair was swivel mounted. Rostnikov resolved to give it a try, but he felt certain that he would eventually go back to the solid, heavy wooden chair that would play no tricks on him. On the other side of the desk were three chairs facing where he now sat.

In the corner of the room was a steel three-drawer filing cabinet that had no locks. It contained about fifty new, quite empty files and those that Rostnikov had brought with him from across the hall.

Alone in his office, Rostnikov considered removing his prosthetic leg, giving the stump a rest and a massage. But that would require pulling off his pants.

While he was considering this, the phone before him rang. He picked it up and simply said, "Rostnikov."

"You've been promoted?" said the voice. "I called your old office and talked to someone named Zelach who told me. Congratulations."

"Thank you," said Rostnikov.

In the past, during the more than a dozen calls he had

received from the voice, Rostnikov had tried without success to trace the caller. The caller had used his considerable expertise to thwart such efforts, keeping his conversations brief. And Rostnikov had listened calmly, making notes, putting together scraps of information, peculiarities. He didn't have much, but it was building.

"I've sent another one," the man said.

"To whom?" asked Rostnikov.

The man laughed and said, "You have a sense of humor. That is something I like in you."

"It pleases me that I amuse you," said Rostnikov.

Someone knocked at the door. Rostnikov put his hand over the receiver and said, "Come in," without raising his voice. Karpo, Sasha, and Elena entered. Karpo closed the door behind them as Rostnikov motioned for them to sit across from him.

"Are you listening?" the caller said.

"Attentively," said Rostnikov, then he mouthed "the bomber" to the three inspectors across from him.

The calls from the bomber had begun more than four months ago. He had simply called Petrovka and asked to speak to whomever was in charge of the investigation of the punishments being mailed. Rostnikov had reported all of this to Director Yakovlev just an hour earlier. Yakovlev had shaken his head slightly, saying, "If only the members of this office know this, impress upon them the need to tell no one."

Rostnikov had agreed. In fact, he had already done so. Now, in the coming together of black and bird in the drawing in Porfiry Petrovich's notebook, the bomber was calling again.

"Your family is well?" asked the bomber.

"Very well," Rostnikov said.

"And the new leg?"

"I am adjusting to it," said Porfiry Petrovich.

In the past three years, the bomber had sent letter bombs to nine people. Since the victims, one of whom died, included some prominent scientists and even an assistant deputy minister for energy, the Ministry of the Interior had sought a quick end to the bomber, but he had proved quite difficult to catch, and word had leaked to the media that there was someone sending letter bombs in Moscow.

From their conversations, Rostnikov had concluded that the man was a great admirer of the American Unabomber and that their causes were similar. Therefore Rostnikov had enlisted the aid of the FBI agent Craig Hamilton, who was assigned, with a varying number of other Americans, to act as a consultant to combat rampant organized crime in Russia. Hamilton had supplied all the information he could obtain about the Unabomber and what had been done to apprehend him.

"I've decided to stop soon," the bomber said.

"Good," said Rostnikov, looking over at the three people across from him who listened silently.

"On one condition," the bomber went on.

"That does not surprise me."

"I have prepared a document citing why I have sent these bombs. The document has been sent to you personally. Don't worry. It doesn't contain a bomb. The document is to be read on Moscow Television News every day for a week. It can be read in five minutes."

"I can't guarantee the cooperation of the media," said Rostnikov.

"Then, unfortunately, there will be more bombs."

"Well," said Rostnikov, "let's talk after I receive the document. Give me a number where I can reach you."

The bomber laughed again.

"I like you, Washtub," he said.

Rostnikov made a note on his pad. Other officers and many habitual criminals called him the Washtub. It might mean something. It might not. The bomber was no fool. However, Rostnikov knew a great deal about the man, enough so that the bomber would have great reason to be concerned if he knew the extent of the information.

"Give my regards to your wife and the two little girls," the bomber said.

"And give mine to your mother and sister," said Rostnikov.

It was a risk. Rostnikov had come to the conclusion but not the certainty that the bomber had a mother and sister, that his father was dead.

The bomber hung up. Rostnikov also hung up and sat back, forgetting the swivel of the chair he was in, and almost fell backward. Sasha started to rise from his chair to help, but Rostnikov smiled and sat erect. Now he was certain about the bomber's family. He was also certain, and had been for months, that there was a connection among all the bombing victims. They all worked in jobs or held positions involved in providing public and private energy. The victims ranged from low-level electricians to scientists to the government's deputy director of energy.

Only once had the bomber said anything related to his choice of victims: "The madness must be stopped. Those who produce it must be stopped." Rostnikov certainly agreed that the madness had to be stopped, but it was the bomber's madness.

"The list," he said, looking at Karpo.

Karpo nodded. A long list had been compiled of people related to the production of energy or research on energy who lived in and around Moscow. Every one of the more than seven hundred had been contacted and told to be very wary of suspicious mail. They had also been given a code that was to alert them if the police believed a bomb had been sent. Each person on the list would be called, and the only thing said would be "penguin." The National Police had agreed to give total cooperation, and within the hour twenty secretaries, officers, and mainte-nance workers would be making calls and saying the single word. None of the callers would have the slightest idea why they were making these calls or what they might mean. It was the responsibility of each caller to reach the people on his or her list, either at work or at home, as soon as possible.

"Alert the mail room," Rostnikov went on. "I should be receiving a letter or package from the bomber. I doubt if it is a bomb, but . . ."

Karpo nodded. He would tell the mail room to put any letters or packages to Inspector Rostnikov on a separate table. They would also be told to touch the items as little as possible.

Karpo and Elena looked at Sasha Tkach.

"Yes?" asked Rostnikov.

"Emil has an idea about the Shy One," said Sasha, who looked decidedly tired.

"The rapist began five years ago," Karpo said. "Four years before that, a woman of sixty was attacked in the hallway of her apartment building. She was large and singularly determined. She fought off the attacker, and he fled when the door to another apartment opened. The woman called the police and reported the attack as an attempted robbery. However, the method was identical to that of the rapist."

"Four years earlier," said Rostnikov.

"Correct," said Karpo.

"Conjecture?" said Rostnikov.

Conjecture was not Karpo's strength.

"It was his first try," said Sasha. "He failed miserably and didn't get up the courage to try again for four years."

"Perhaps," said Rostnikov. "How did you find this case?"

"Computer," said Karpo. "Cross-check of my open and closed files and the central Petrovka files. I searched for attacks on women from behind, the presence of a knife, the warning. It turned up this case."

"How does it help us?" asked Rostnikov.

"The intended victim saw the attacker's face," said Elena. "At the time of the crime, she said she would never forget him."

Rostnikov nodded. There was no need to tell them what to do, only who should do it.

"Sasha, Elena, you keep this. Emil, I need you on the bomber. You get Iosef. I'll keep the murder of the young Jews. Zelach can help."

The three investigators got up. Elena and Sasha wanted to discuss what had happened only this morning, what it meant. Who was Yakovlev? Why had they gotten raises? Karpo had no such questions.

"When I was a child," said Rostnikov, leaning forward to draw a bird on a branch over the word *washtub*, "my favorite color was blue. Now it is red. What is your favorite color, Elena Timofeyeva?"

She was the least accustomed to such displays of curiosity by Rostnikov, who always seemed genuinely interested in the answers to questions that appeared to be of no great consequence.

"Purple," she said.

Rostnikov looked at Sasha.

"Green," he said.

It was Karpo's turn.

"Black," he said.

Rostnikov had not really expected an answer from Emil Karpo. He looked up and saw something in the man's eyes that caused him concern.

"Thank you," said Rostnikov. "Send in Zelach, please."

The trio of inspectors left.

Moments later a nervous Zelach knocked at the door, waited to be told to enter, and then slouched in to stand before the desk.

"Sit," said Rostnikov.

Zelach sat.

"How is your mother?" asked Rostnikov.

"Well," said Zelach, "she'll be happy to hear about the raise. It is true?"

"True," said Rostnikov. "Director Yakovlev is a man of his word."

He did not add that his word was often something others did not like to hear.

Zelach was forty-one, unmarried, lived with his mother, and was both loyal and far from bright. When he was told to do something, he would do it, even if it might cost him life or limb. Zelach had lost part of his eyesight in an attack by a criminal two years earlier. His recovery from that and other injuries in the attack had resulted in a long convalescence.

Zelach was dressed in worn but neat slacks, shirt, and jacket, all selected by his mother.

"Two questions, Zelach," said Rostnikov, "and then we go to work. First, what is your favorite color?"

Zelach looked decidedly confused.

"Orange," he said. "My mother's is white."

"So is my wife's. Second question," said Rostnikov. "How did your father die?"

Zelach looked even more puzzled.

"You know. He was shot."

Zelach's father was a uniformed officer. He had been shot while trying to stop a black market deal in a garage. There should have been no shooting. It was a minor crime, and the black marketeers would probably have been able to bribe their way out of any serious punishment. Still, one had panicked and a single 9mm bullet had taken the life of Zelach's father.

"How did you feel about it?" asked Rostnikov, thinking about the bomber to whom he had just spoken.

"Feel? Sad, angry. I wanted revenge."

"Revenge," said Rostnikov, putting the finishing touches on his bird. "Did you ever get your revenge?"

"No," said Zelach.

"And plainly it has not driven you mad," said Rostnikov.

"No," said the even more confused Zelach.

"Do you still think of revenge?"

"No," said Zelach.

"Come," said Rostnikov, rising with difficulty. "Later we'll have birds to draw, colors to see. Now we catch a murderer."

FOUR

LUDMILLA HENSHAKAYOVA WAS STARTLED BY THE knock at her door. She had been sitting at her window looking out at the snow starting to fall again. In the corner a man on the television screen began to laugh. Ludmilla didn't know why he was laughing and she really didn't care. He and the electric picture box were there for mindless company. Ludmilla did not like to be alone.

Another knock.

Ludmilla did not live in the best of neighborhoods. Her apartment building was in fatal disrepair, and from her window not far from where the trolleys turned she could see only the ancient cemetery and its occasional visitors. Mostly, from the window, she watched the ugly huge crows perch on the tombstones, leaving their claw prints in the snow. Ludmilla was nearly seventy and barely able to survive on her pension plus the money she made selling flowers in front of the Bolshoi when the opera, ballet, or other event was going on. Such events were frequent, and Ludmilla needed the money badly, but recently the cold had gotten to her, and Kretchman, the flower supplier, had suggested that she stop until the weather grew warmer. But how could she?

A third knock.

Ludmilla sighed and over the sound of the laughing man on the television shouted, "Who?"

"Police," came a woman's voice.

"I don't believe you," said Ludmilla, looking at the dead bolt and four locks on her door.

"I'm here with another officer," the woman who claimed to be a police officer said. "We'll slip our identification cards under the door."

Ludmilla still sat. The man on the television had stopped laughing. Perhaps the snow would stop soon. There was a Mozart opera at the Bolshoi. She couldn't remember which one, but there would be Americans, French, Canadians. They and the newly rich young Russians were her customers.

The cards came under the door.

"They could be forged," Ludmilla said. "Anything can be forged if you have the money."

"We are here to talk to you and about the man who attacked you," came a young man's voice.

"That was ten years ago," said Ludmilla.

"Almost," said the woman outside.

"I don't want to talk about it," Ludmilla said firmly.

"We think he is still attacking women," said the female voice outside. "We think he is hurting them badly, raping and beating them. We think he may eventually kill one of his victims."

"Go to them," shouted Ludmilla, knowing that her next-door neighbor, Maria Illianova, was listening to every word.

"You are the only one who has seen him," said the woman.

Ludmilla sighed, got up on her arthritic legs, and moved slowly to the door. When she got there, she looked down at the two identification cards, but she didn't bend to pick them up.

She opened the door.

Sasha and Elena heard the locks click and watched the door come open. According to their information from the original report of the attack, Ludmilla Henshakayova was a large woman of not yet seventy. The woman before them in a loose-fitting dress was thin and seemed ancient. She looked at Sasha and Elena and then stepped back so they could enter the small apartment.

Sasha paused to pick up their identification cards and hand Elena hers.

The door closed and Ludmilla said, "With two police inside, I can lock it later."

On the television, the laughing man was now interviewing an actor. Ludmilla couldn't remember his name but she recognized him. He sat across from the laughing man, confident, handsome, legs crossed.

"Ludmilla Henshakayova," Elena said gently to get the woman's attention.

"I'm sorry," said Ludmilla. "I suffer from the Russian diseases of fear, loneliness, melancholy, and a desire to forget the past."

The room was not at all what either Elena or Sasha had expected. The neighborhood was nearly a slum and had been for years. Half a block away sat the remains of a building so poorly constructed it had collapsed about four years earlier, killing more than a dozen people.

But this room was immaculate. The walls were clean. Two framed posters of flowers were side by side on one wall. The other walls were bare. The concrete floor was covered by a large, darkly ornate rug, and the chairs and narrow bed in the corner were covered in matching knitted covers of yellow and green. The fourth wall held a full bookcase that stood about six feet high and fourteen feet across. In the corner were two chairs and a table covered with a bright yellow tablecloth. On a polished table in a corner sat the black-and-white television where the laughing man and the movie star were talking.

Both Elena and Sasha saw the low armchair at the window. Elena's aunt had a chair near their window, where Anna Timofeyeva sat for hours, sometimes the whole day, except to do her prescribed walking and to eat a little. Elena sensed her aunt's memories in that chair. Sasha imagined his mother, Lydia, in such a chair, but not for long. Lydia had the patience of a fly. Sasha sensed his mother's fear of loneliness and her ever present impatience. Lydia would not sit still in such a comfortable chair for more than five minutes before she rose and began searching for someone to call, something to do.

"Sit," said Ludmilla.

"May we turn the television off?" said Elena.

"Yes," said Ludmilla, going back to her chair at the window.

Sasha anticipated her, stepped ahead, and turned the chair slightly so it could face the two investigators, who sat in the straight-backed wooden chairs. Sasha glanced out of the window at the cemetery. A trio of crows swooped down on a large tombstone that was leaning decidedly to the right.

"A little girl detective," Ludmilla said with a shake of her head as if she expected no more than madness from the new Russia. "A pretty little girl."

Elena wasn't sure whether she should be flattered or insulted.

"The attack," Elena said.

They had decided that whichever one of them seemed to have the better rapport with the woman would lead the questioning.

Ludmilla now looked at Sasha.

"And a boy detective, too. A boy detective with eyes as old as mine. You know, I used to be a poet. I can show you some of my books, the magazines in which I was published, some posters for readings I did all over the Soviet Union."

She paused and looked up at the two posters on the wall. Sasha and Elena followed her gaze. Indeed, under the flowers both posters carried printed announcements of appearances and readings. One poster was in French. The other was in Russian.

"I no longer write poetry. And then . . ."

She trailed off, pulled her distant memories in, and sat up to say with renewed strength, "Tea?"

"No, thank you," said Elena. "We know it has been a

long time, but we have very little information on the attack."

If it hadn't been for Karpo's notes, the information they had found in the general files would never have led them to this woman. There had been only a brief entry. Ludmilla's name, age, and address. There was also a note on the standard form indicating the location where she was attacked and a description of both the method of attack—knife, sneaking up from behind, hand over the eyes—and the attacker. The attacker's description was simply "Young man, dark hair, brown eyes, khaki jacket. Attempted to take victim's purse. She fought him off."

There were no other entries on the case, and neither Sasha nor Elena thought that there had been any follow-up investigation. It was Karpo's notes that indicated the victim was a highly regarded poet. It was Karpo who had written in his notebook the address of the apartment building in which they now sat. The official report had the wrong address.

"What is he doing to these women?" asked Ludmilla.

"Violent rape," said Elena. "So far he hasn't killed anyone, but . . ."

"I used to be big and strong," said the old woman. "Now I am not as weak as I look, but I have lost my need to write what I see and feel."

"Can you remember the man clearly?"

Ludmilla smiled, rivulets of wrinkles forming around her narrow mouth. There was irony but no mirth in the smile.

"Yes. You want to know what he looked like then and what he looks like now?" she said.

"Now?" asked Tkach. "You've seen him recently?"

"I saw him."

"Did you call the police?" asked Elena.

The smile again.

"Do you think they would care?" she asked. "Do you think they would even write down what I would tell them, an old woman claiming to see the man who attacked her almost ten years ago?"

Both Elena and Sasha knew that the woman was right. In a Moscow gone mad with violence, there was neither time nor inclination to follow up reports about old crimes. There were approximately one hundred thousand policemen in a sprawling city of nine million. Few wanted to be policemen. Even armed with Kalishnikov automatic weapons and wearing bulletproof vests, the police, who worked twelve- or fourteen-hour days, were no match for the new mafias and street gangs who were better armed. The police of Russia, unlike those of America, were permitted to fire on suspects who tried to flee or looked as if they would fire weapons at them. The death rate among criminals was high. Official statistics showed that the Moscow police had fired weapons more than fifteen hundred times in the past year compared to the Los Angeles police, who fired only one hundred fifty times in spite of a much higher rate of violence.

"Where did you see him recently, this man who attacked you?" Elena asked.

Ludmilla looked back at Elena. There was something of herself as a young woman in Elena's face. The silence was very long.

"Would I have to identify him?"

"Possibly," said Sasha. "Probably not, if we can find evidence or find out where he lives. Perhaps we could persuade him to confess to one of the recent attacks."

"You won't do anything," Ludmilla said, eyes scanning the small room from bed to bookshelves to television and then back to the two children who were detectives. "And if you talk to him, he might come and find me. He might kill me. I am resigned, not depressed, and I choose to live a while longer."

"How could he possibly find you? We won't give him your name," said Sasha, tossing back his hair.

"The same way you found me," the old woman said.

"That information is in police records only," said Sasha.

"Exactly," said Ludmilla, leaning forward.

There was a chill in the room. It had been there since they had come in. Elena and Sasha had kept their jackets on, but now they were acutely aware of the heavy chill.

"You mean . . . ?" Sasha began.

Ludmilla closed her eyes and nodded.

"He is a policeman?" said Elena.

"He is a policeman," echoed Ludmilla.

The package had been delivered to Petrovka. It was addressed to Porfiry Petrovich Rostnikov, Office of Special Investigation. Karpo, Iosef, and Paulinin stood looking down at the package. The four people who worked in the mail room had been told to leave.

After the bomber had contacted Rostnikov, the small army of callers had been put into motion and the warnings had begun. People in the energy industry and others even vaguely connected to or supporting nuclear power had been told "penguin," and the callers had checked off the names of everyone they reached. Later Karpo and Iosef would go over the report, providing, of course, that the package they were looking at did not contain a bomb that killed them.

Paulinin was a forensic technician. He had a laboratory on the second underground level of Petrovka and was an expert in everything from examination of bodies to explosives. Most of the officers of Petrovka and all of the scientific employees, including the part-time pathologists who conducted autopsies, shunned Paulinin, who was considered a walking encyclopedia but more than a bit eccentric. He looked rather like a bespectacled, nearsighted monkey with an oversize head topped by wild gray-black hair. His office-laboratory was cluttered with piles of books and objects from past investigations. Here a pistol with the barrel missing. There, on the tottering pile of books on the edge of a desk, some false teeth in a mason jar.

The disheveled scientist adjusted his glasses. He put down the cheap red plastic toolbox he had brought with him, reached into his pocket, and pulled out a pair of rubber gloves in a plastic bag. Paulinin put on the gloves, returned the empty plastic bag to his pocket, and got on his knees before the brown package that looked rather thick to be containing only a five-minute message.

Paulinin appeared to be praying to the package. Around him letters and packages sat in unattended piles. Ancient cubbyholes of various sizes were stuffed with mail.

Paulinin leaned forward and sniffed at the bundle from one corner to another. Then he put his right ear next to the package, not quite touching it. He removed a stethoscope from the red plastic box, put it on with a flourish, and looked into space as he gently listened to the parcel. Next he ran his fingers along the rim of the package, pausing at one point. Still on his knees, he slowly turned the bundle over, touching only the rim. Iosef held his breath as Paulinin began to tap gently at the parcel with his rubber-covered fingers. Then, suddenly, he stood, picked up the package by the edges, and said, "I'd say it contains a single sheet of paper and a solid block of wood, probably birch, judging from its weight. I'll x-ray, then check for fingerprints if I am able to open this and see what else the contents tell me."

Karpo didn't bother to answer. Once the package was in Paulinin's hands, he would do what he wanted with it in his huge, cluttered laboratory in the basement. Karpo had learned that Paulinin was indeed brilliant. He was also, to put the matter kindly, considered to be a bit mad. But it was a madness Karpo had learned not only to accept but to deny. Paulinin was lucid and prone to his own tastes and angers. The anger he sometimes displayed was aimed particularly at all the Petrovka pathologists. He was only a little more tolerant of the so-called forensics experts who at least were not, according to Paulinin, prone to prance like pathology divas. Few things delighted Paulinin more than to be brought a corpse the pathologists had examined and autopsied, for he was always certain of finding something they had overlooked. What he delighted in even more was to be given the corpse first. Such luck came his way only through the Office of Special Investigation and a handful of inspectors in other offices and departments who knew of Paulinin's skills.

Karpo also knew that Paulinin was a lonely man who had made gestures of friendship toward the Vampire. The overtures had been small: a cup of tea in a suspicious beaker in Paulinin's laboratory and, much later, an invitation to share the lunch Paulinin had brought with him that day. Twice now the strange pair had gone out to relatively inexpensive cafeterias for lunch. Paulinin considered Emil Karpo his only friend.

"Come to my laboratory in one hour and forty minutes, Emil Karpo," Paulinin said. "I should have something by then. We can have tea while we talk."

"One hour and forty minutes," Karpo agreed, and scientist and package disappeared through the door.

"What if he blows it up accidentally?" said Iosef.

"Then we shall certainly feel the tremor," Karpo responded with no trace of sarcasm or humor. "If we feel no such tremor and we go to Paulinin's laboratory, you will accept his offer of tea."

"Fine," said Iosef.

"You will not want to accept his offer," Karpo said, "but you will overcome the impulse to refuse."

"I am not expecting *blyeenchyeekee s vahryehn'yehm*, blinis filled with jam. I have drunk suspicious brown water from the bleached skull of an Afghan tribesman and eaten small rodents," said Iosef with a grin. "I was a soldier. We often had such interesting experiences."

"We shall see," said Karpo heading for the door to tell the mail room staff that it was safe to come back.

* * *

The building on Balakava Prospekt in which the Congregation Israel met had been purchased with Israeli money in the form of German deutsche marks. The building was small and the price unreasonable, but it suited the needs of Avrum Belinsky and his small congregation recently decimated by the murders of six of its members. The two-hundred-year-old building had been a Russian Orthodox church. It was basically an anteroom and a large open room. During the Communist reign, the cross on the single turret of the building had been taken down. Then the building had been used for a while as an office of the automobile licensing bureau, then as a meeting hall for party members who also belonged to the construction workers guild, and later as an unsuccessful tourist site where copies of icons were sold and a few hung on the walls.

The church had been purchased from the Russian government by a German businessman who traded a variety of services, primarily intervention with the government and appropriate mafias, to foreign investors for hard currency. He had planned to use the church as a storage space, but it had proved inconvenient. The space was too small, and the traffic was often heavy during the day with no place to park and unload a truck, even a small one, without being noticed. There were too many prying eyes among the neighbors. The businessman decided to move his storage space outside the city. He would have sold the building for half the price he got from the Jews if they had chosen to haggle. Jews were supposed to haggle. The serious Israeli rabbi who spoke perfect Russian had simply asked the price and, in the name of some Russian members of the congregation, purchased the church.

When Avrum moved in, it held nothing more than a small wooden table and a single badly scratched folding chair. The large high-ceilinged room featured a warped wooden floor lying over frozen earth. There was no heat, and the first order of business, after properly blessing the new synagogue, had been to heat the space before the winter came. Building the bema—the small wooden platform where the rabbi conducted the services—was easy. Getting a podium was easy. He had brought his own ark and two Torahs, all relatively new and waiting for the congregation to give them a history of prayer, tears, determination, devotion, and hope. He had no trouble mounting the ark on the wall behind the podium. Even getting chairs had proved far easier than Avrum had anticipated. He bought fifty—the synagogue could hold no more—from a man who claimed to have a right to them since they had been used for Communist neighborhood study meetings and he had been custodian of the building on Narodnaya Prospekt where the meetings had been held for almost half a century. Nor did Belinsky have great trouble attracting a small congregation, which had continued to grow in spite of the first two senseless murders of young men. Only one of the twenty-four people who came when word circulated that a synagogue existed in this part of the city could speak a bit of Yiddish. None could read or write Hebrew. Only two of the males had been circumcised. Few had read the Torah, the first five books of the Bible, from which he would read at each weekly service in Russian and Hebrew. Their sense of the trials of Abraham and Moses were mythic and distant, not powerful lessons in endurance and faith that could sustain their lives.

The greatest problem to overcome among the Russian Jews was that they did not want to be clearly identified as practicing Jews. Anti-Semitism was always an issue, one they had learned to live with by presenting themselves as atheist Soviet citizens who did not practice their religion. Many had changed their names so they would not appear to be Jewish. That Belinsky had been prepared to cope with, and he did so far better than he had anticipated. But he had not been prepared for murder. Perhaps a beating, swastikas on the door, or even a few acts of desecration, but not murder.

Heating had been a serious problem. Belinsky could

not find reasonably honest contractors to do the work. He could tell instantly which ones were frauds, and he knew after a moment or two of questioning which ones were completely unreliable. Finally, though he knew nothing about heating, Belinsky had decided with the help of volunteers, three of whom had now been murdered, to construct his own heating system. He had settled on four metal wood-burning stoves, one to be placed in each corner of the chapel. They would vent through holes made in the roof. He bought the four identical stoves through an old man who was a member of the congregation and refused to tell where he was getting them.

Belinsky had helped build roads, railroad lines, buildings, bunkers, and houses on three kibbutzim. But he knew nothing about heating, the winter had come quickly, and the stoves worked only minimally. Congregants still appeared on Friday nights and Saturday mornings and occasionally for discussions, Hebrew language lessons, and Torah studies, which were conducted during the week, but the wood-burning stoves were far from adequate.

Belinsky had been able to reach all but a few of the remaining members of his congregation to urge them to come to a meeting that night to discuss the killings and to pray for the dead. The congregation barely had a *minion*—the ten men needed to conduct the morning prayers. Fourteen men in the congregation had been bar mitzvahed so that a *minion* was possible. Five of those men were now dead.

Belinsky stood at the closed door of the synagogue to usher each reluctant, frightened, or angry member inside. At eight-thirty, half an hour after he had called for the meeting, he moved down the center aisle past the wooden chairs and up to the bema, where he stood in front of the podium. There were thirty-one people seated before him—young and old, even a few children. There were more people than he expected, even some new faces, which he examined carefully without looking directly at them. The new faces were angry, determined. They were not there to make trouble. They were Jews who had been brought out by the very acts of horror and violence that had been designed to send them hiding in fear. Everyone kept their coats or jackets on. All wore hats or black *kepahs*, which were kept in a wooden box just inside the synagogue door. All who entered the house of worship were required to cover their heads as God had commanded. The rabbi himself wore slacks and a black turtleneck sweater. This was a meeting at which prayers would be said, but it was also a meeting at which work would be discussed. He had decided not to wear his suit and tie.

Belinsky saw eyes looking around but heads not moving. There would be spies in the room, perhaps even the murderers, perhaps the police. There was not a person in the room who did not fear for his life. Yet they had come.

"Chaverim," Belinsky began softly. "Friends. For almost five thousand years, oppressors have risen to murder us by the millions, the dozens, and individually because we are Jews. Sigmund Freud, a practicing Jew, said that the Jews had been the scapegoats of the Western world. He said that there was an animal need in civilizations to have a group to blame for the failure of crops, the outbreak of plagues, and their inability to make a living, and to satisfy their need to feel superior. This anti-Semitism was not only among Christians. It existed thousands of years before the birth of Christ. It was present not only among the ignorant and uneducated but among those who feared the determination of the Jews to survive and even under the worst of circumstances, to prosper and take care of each other. We have been blamed for most of the problems of Western civilization, and we have been hated because God proclaimed us the chosen people. An American poet once wrote, 'How odd of God to choose the Jews.' But through Moses and Abraham he did choose us. He tried us, tested us. We prayed for

protection and salvation, and God always answered and sometimes the answer was no. We have been tested, but we survived. We have our own nation. We have a renewed respect in the world, and with that respect has come fear."

It was at this point that the door opened. Heads turned, almost expecting hooded men with machine guns. Avrum Belinsky looked at the limping policeman who closed the door and quietly moved to a seat at the rear of the small synagogue. He kept his fur hat and his wool-lined coat on.

"The six young men who have been murdered," Belinsky said, looking at Rostnikov, who looked back at the rabbi, "the six young men whose only offense was that they were Jews who wanted to practice their religion will be honored by our continuing to worship. There are those among us who have said we should give up, that they will kill us all, that the police will not find them, probably not even look for them. There are those among us who know that many of the police, many in the procurator general's office and State Security are anti-Semites. But there are some who will honor the law, honor our dead.

"Several weeks ago we held a service for two dead members of our small congregation whose names we inscribed on the plaque that hangs on that wall. On Friday we will hold services honoring four more. We will fight back. We will pray to our Lord to help the police find the murderers. Does anyone wish to speak?"

A thin man in his thirties, clean-shaven, his dark face marked by a broken nose that had never healed properly, stood and said, "I say we arm, every one one of us who does not already have a weapon. I say we should conduct our own search, that we should travel in groups when possible, that we should keep our hands on the triggers of our weapons and have them ready at the slightest sign of danger."

There were murmurs among the congregants; small

arguments began. Belinsky looked at Rostnikov. Guns in the hands of private citizens were against the law, but it was a law increasingly ignored.

A woman's voice said, "If we kill them, we will all be condemned. More people will hate us."

Belinsky nodded, said nothing, and pointed to a man in his sixties, heavyset and wearing a workman's cap, who stood and spoke.

"I'm a clerk, a bookkeeper for a night club where they play loud music, the Rusty Sputnik."

A ripple of laughter crossed the somber room.

"I'm a clerk," the man repeated. "I have always been recognized as a Jew though I never declared or practiced the faith of my fathers and their fathers before them till now. Under the Soviet Union most of us lived as suspicious characters. I have spent my life expecting to be fired, accused, pounced on for no reason other than that I am a Jew. Rabbi Belinsky has given me and my family pride in our identity. I will fight if necessary, though I am only a nearsighted bookkeeper. That's all I have to say."

The man sat. There was no applause, but a general nodding of heads suggested agreement. Belinsky knew that those who were wavering were not going to speak. They had found the courage to come here tonight. They would listen and then they would talk to their families, if they had them, and decide whether to shun the synagogue or join together in determination and fear. Belinsky estimated that at least half of the people sitting in the wooden chairs before him were among the undecided.

Belinsky looked at Rostnikov, whose arms were folded before him. Rostnikov's face showed nothing.

"For those who can attend, funeral services will be held tomorrow for our dead. Their bodies will be here from noon to three, and then we will bury them in the Jewish cemetery."

"What should we do?" asked a woman carrying a sleeping baby.

"I have spent my life fighting," Belinsky said. "Fighting against those who would destroy us, exploit us, enslave us. My father and uncles fought the British. My country and family have fought Arabs who wanted to destroy us. We survive. We prosper. We do this because we are willing to fight and, if necessary, die. Because we are small in number, we survive because we do not compromise in battle. Every Jew is a soldier. I think that those who wish to arm themselves should meet with me for training. I think we should go on meeting, holding services. I am prepared to die for my beliefs. Without beliefs worth dying for we simply pass through life."

With this, Belinsky asked the congregation to rise. He lowered his head and said a prayer in Hebrew. A few in the congregation who had begun Hebrew lessons with the rabbi tried to accompany him. He repeated the prayer in Russian and more voices joined in.

The meeting had ended. Rostnikov stood and waited, putting as much of his weight on his good right leg as he could. He was learning to let his artificial leg help a bit at a time, and each day he believed the pain in what remained of his left leg eased just a bit more as he tried to make the limb of plastic and metal a part of him.

Some congregants stopped to talk to the rabbi, including the young man who had advocated armed defense. Rostnikov couldn't hear them, but he could see that the discussion was animated, passionate. Belinsky shook the hand of the young man and the others. Soon there remained no one but the policeman and the rabbi.

"It's cold in here," Rostnikov said, looking at the four stoves with a pile of wood next to each. "Poor circulation."

"Of that I am aware," said Belinsky. "Correcting the problem is another matter."

Rostnikov's eyes ran up and down the walls.

"With the help of four men and the proper equipment, I believe we could build a duct system with the existing stoves that would effectively heat the building."

"We?" asked Belinsky, moving down the aisle toward the policeman.

Rostnikov shrugged.

"You know about heating?"

"I know plumbing," said Rostnikov. "The principles are not all that dissimilar."

"I'll help and I'll find three others," Belinsky said. "If the materials are available and not ridiculously expensive, we welcome your supervision."

"I know where to obtain the materials reasonably," said Rostnikov. "This will be an interesting challenge."

"And the challenge of finding the murderers?" said Belinsky.

"You can be assured that the less-than-firmly-entrenched current government does not want an international incident over murderous attacks by anti-Semites," said Rostnikov.

"It is impossible to understand the Lord," said Belinsky with a sigh. "Politics, however, I do understand. Expediency triumphs and can be rationalized. It requires no goodwill, only self interest."

"Therefore . . . ?" asked Rostnikov.

"Therefore, I believe at the moment that you will do your best to find the murderers."

"And find a way to heat this building."

Belinsky smiled.

"Perhaps."

"You have something to tell me," said Belinsky.

The two men now stood only a few feet apart.

"One of the four dead men on the embankment was not a Jew."

For an instant, and only an instant, Belinsky looked puzzled.

"All four were of this congregation," said Belinsky.

"One of the murdered men was Igor Mesanovich," said Rostnikov, pulling out a notebook and reading between the tiny drawings. "His family goes back many generations. Before the Revolution, they were practicing members of the Russian Orthodox Church. In fact, according to Mesanovich's brother, who was interviewed a few hours ago by the Saint Petersburg police, they were members of the aristocracy. A few of them were even in the court of the czars. The brother believes that before the Revolution, when much of the family moved to Moscow and lived in this very neighborhood, his family even worshiped in this building."

Rostnikov closed the book and returned it to his pocket.

"Perhaps Mesanovich wanted to be Jewish," said Belinsky. "Some people have a wish to be members of a proud minority. Some Gentiles even believe in the truth of our God."

"But he never told you he wasn't Jewish?" Rostnikov asked.

Belinsky shook his head and said, "He told us his family was originally from Ukraine, a small shtetl."

"We Russians are a people accustomed to lying," said Rostnikov, "lying with such sincerity, conviction, and indignation that we often believe our own lies. I have faced murderers who committed their crime in front of numerous reliable witnesses. The murderers often swore that they had not committed the crime. Their sincerity was convincing. Polygraphs don't work on us. It has taken us almost a thousand years to perfect this art."

"Mesanovich was an infiltrator?" asked Belinsky.

"It is possible," said Rostnikov. "He seems to have belonged to no nationalistic or anti-Semitic organizations. Yet one cannot avoid the possibility that those with whom he conspired distrusted him for some reason, real or imagined, and killed him. In all likelihood he was simply mistaken for a Jew, since he contended that he was one. We are looking into it. So far we have not been able to find Mesanovich's parents here in Moscow. They have not been home when we called, and we have not found out where they might work."

Belinsky's eyes met those of the policeman, and the rabbi made a cautious decision to trust the man.

"Do you have informants within the mafias, the nationalist groups, the hate groups?" asked Belinsky.

Rostnikov shrugged and said, "I have been asked by the director of my office to request that you cease your services and activities until we find the murderers."

"No," said Belinsky firmly.

Rostnikov nodded, having anticipated the answer.

"More may die," said Rostnikov, "as you said."

"We will help God and the police to try to keep that from happening," said the rabbi.

"And I will see what I can do about getting the ducting and tools to heat this place adequately," said Rostnikov.

"Why?" asked Belinsky.

"Because it is cold in here," said Rostnikov. "And because my wife and son are Jews, as will be my grandchildren. Perhaps one day one of them will choose to come here on a winter morning. I should not want them cold."

The rabbi examined his visitor with curiosity.

"One last question," said Rostnikov. "Do you have a favorite color?"

"Yes," the rabbi said. "Two colors, blue and white, the colors of Israel."

"I'm exploring a theory that people often reveal a great deal about themselves from the colors they feel drawn to," said Rostnikov. "It is not my idea but that of a German psychologist who wrote an article I read. It seems reasonable, but the puzzle is what to make of people's choices."

"So, you've not yet drawn any conclusions?"

"About you, yes. You are an ardent Zionist who might well do something dangerous to find these murderers. The colors don't tell me this. They confirm it. My own favorite color seems to tell me nothing about myself. But that is the nature of life."

With that the policeman turned and limped out the door into the snowy night. Belinsky had spent far too much of his time with far too little result keeping the stoves filled with wood. After the funeral he would need to visit each member of the small congregation, not only to help strengthen their resolve but also to urge other Jews to come to stand with them. Belinsky knew he could be very persuasive. That was one of the reasons he had volunteered for this assignment. A horrible irony of the murders could ultimately be that the congregation might grow rather than dwindle, that the money Israel was investing in this congregation would continue to draw those hungry for food and others who shared their outcast state. Belinsky had faith in his God and in his own power of persuasion.

Rostnikov, however, was a nagging puzzle. Belinsky couldn't afford to like the man, yet he was drawn to the detective's apparent openness and odd ideas. In addition, Rostnikov had volunteered to help with the heating system. Belinsky would see if that came to pass. It is easy to make promises and only a little harder to ignore them.

He let the fires die down while he sat in a chair in silent prayer. When he felt the fires were safe, he retrieved his coat from the alcove near the entrance, turned out the light, and locked the door.

He headed toward his small apartment, which was only two blocks away. The streets were empty. It was late and it was cold. There was little for the people of Moscow to do except visit friends, talk and drink tea, read a book, watch television, and produce more Russians.

Avrum Belinsky was less than a block from his apartment building when they appeared. There were three of them. Avrum knew they were there fifteen feet before two of them stepped out of the doorway. He knew there was another one behind. He had seen the one behind in the shadows of a darkened house and been careful not to show in his gait or manner what he had seen.

Belinsky's hand was on the gun in his pocket as he approached the two men who stood before him now, waiting for him to turn around and see that his escape was impossible. But Belinsky didn't want to escape. He continued to walk forward toward the two men, and he didn't look behind him.

FIVE

It was called Trotsky Station by the policemen who worked there and by most of the veterans from other law enforcement agencies who had dealt with or heard about it. Actually this police station, like the other 133 stations in Moscow, had a number. Only the administrators ever used the number. No one was quite sure why it was called Trotsky Station.

The primary tale was that Trotsky and a group of friends had lived for a time in the building. It was certainly old enough. The large stone blocks it was built with probably had been white once. Now they were gray. The stairs to the second floor needed repair. The walls needed plastering and painting, and the heating system was barely functional. The building also had a distinctive, and certainly not pleasant, moldy odor. The floor tiles were loose, and the toilets in the rest room were reluctant at best.

Another reason less often given for the Trotsky name was that those assigned to the district had a reputation for effective brutality. It was said that the major in charge during the 1950s had actually smashed a murder suspect's head with a hammer—a death similar to Trotsky's.

Elena and Sasha sat in the anteroom in front of the office of a Lieutenant Spaskov to whom they had been sent by the clerk downstairs, who sat behind a barred window that made him look more like a prisoner than a police officer. The uniformed man, with an ageless pockmarked face, had barely looked up when they identified themselves.

Sasha had said they wanted to see whoever was in charge of ongoing investigations. When the man behind the bars had asked which investigation, Elena said, "The rapes."

"Which . . . ?" the man had begun, and then he had looked up at them. "Lieutenant Spaskov on the second floor, Room 2. He's in a meeting in his office. I think he'll be done soon."

So they now sat on a wooden bench outside four offices with no names on the doors but numbers over each. They could make out the sound of voices from a few of the offices but no distinct words. In Russia, government officials had learned to keep their voices down and their conversations quiet.

"This is a waste of time," Sasha said.

"You have a better lead?" answered Elena.

"An old woman got a glimpse of a man who tried to rob her ten years ago. He may be the rapist. Now she sees a policeman two or three times in a police car in Leningrad Square and declares it is the man."

"She gave a description," said Elena quietly as she unbuttoned her jacket.

"Which could fit a few million men in Moscow and half or more of the police," he said, slumping on the bench. "I need some coffee."

There were voices in Room 2; one in particular was deep, confident. Occasionally another voice or two would respond.

"How is your aunt?" Sasha said, holding his head, which cried for coffee.

"Anna Timofeyeva is fine," said Elena, looking forward at Room 3, from which no voices came. "She and your mother get along well."

"My mother follows the agreement?" he asked.

"Usually," said Elena. "She comes when she is invited, and when Anna wants her to go, she says she is tired and needs to rest. Your mother is less inclined to follow the rule about not complaining about you, Maya, the children, and the failure of the new Russia to protect her son. She can't stop. Aunt Anna can take more of it than I can. I dread walking down that corridor at night and hearing your mother's voice behind my aunt's door."

"I know how you feel," said Sasha.

"Your mother supports the Nationalist Party," Elena said.

"Just talk," he said, trying to sit upright in the hope that it might ease the tension of his caffeineless headache. "It was probably a bad idea to have her move into your building, but we were desperate."

Elena shrugged and said, "Aunt Anna seems to find your mother amusing and distracting if a bit too loud. Your mother is no fool. She is, however, protectively conditioned to act like one. Eventually the act, if played long enough, becomes reality."

Sasha threw his hair back from his forehead and looked at his partner, who turned her clear, round face to his, prepared for attack.

"You're right," he said.

"She's not allowed in the door without her hearing aid," said Elena, "but I don't think it works properly, or she just has too many years of shouting to overcome her hearing loss."

"Going home to my mother can be depressing," he said, "but she is good with the children. She worries about me. She talks with affection about your aunt."

"But not about me," said Elena.

"She finds you cold and distant," he said, now closing his eyes.

"Perhaps, but I do not want to cultivate too close a relationship to your mother," said Elena as the door to Room 2 opened.

Three uniformed policemen wearing helmets and carrying Kalishnikov automatic rifles stepped out. They were all young. They wore their supposedly bulletproof jackets outside their uniforms. The jackets were of no use against weapons such as the ones they were carrying, and criminals increasingly had weapons far more powerful than those of the police. The jackets were slightly cumbersome, but they were required. The three men, all in their twenties, moved quickly down the hall past the two seated detectives.

A man appeared in the doorway, at least six feet tall, medium build, with thinning dark hair and a mustache, which was common in many officers. At first they grew them thinking it would make them look older. Later some kept them simply because they had grown accustomed to them. It looked good on this man in blue slacks, a blue shirt, and a leather jacket, unzipped.

"Spaskov," he said, introducing himself as the two detectives rose.

Elena and Sasha introduced themselves and showed their cards. Spaskov stepped back so they could enter his office. It was surprisingly large and surprisingly empty—a desk, a chair behind it, four wooden chairs in front of it, nothing on the walls, and a file cabinet in one corner across from the desk on which there sat two wire boxes, both neatly piled with reports. One small, framed photograph and one file were on the desk in front of the chair. There were no windows.

"Would either of you like tea or coffee?" Spaskov said.

"Coffee," said Sasha gratefully.

"Nothing," said Elena.

Spaskov left the office and the two detectives sat in silence till he returned moments later with two white mugs. He handed one to Sasha, who thanked him and immediately took a drink. It was awful—murky, and stale—but it was coffee.

"Frankonovich says you have some information on the rapes," Spaskov said, sitting not behind his desk but at one of the wooden chairs before it. Elena and Sasha pulled up their chairs to face him.

"Most of the attacks came in this district," said Elena.

Spaskov nodded emphatically.

"Brutal," he said. "What he has done ... When I was promoted, Major Lenonov assigned me the case. I interviewed the victims, at least the ones who came forward or were hospitalized and reported by the hospital. Some of them were badly injured, permanently injured. No description. The man is strong, as the report shows. He is probably medium height. There seems to have been no pattern other than the attacks occur at night on women who are alone. Young, old, some girls. I will get you a copy of our file on the case."

Spaskov drank some of the hot coffee from his mug.

"The Office of Special Investigation has been assigned the case," said Tkach. "We have a new lead."

Spaskov was placing his mug on his desk when Sasha spoke. He paused and turned with interest.

"New lead?"

"Witness," said Elena.

Spaskov sat back to listen.

"An old woman was robbed almost ten years ago," said Sasha. "She wasn't raped but she thinks the man was trying to rape her. He hit her on the head from behind, but she fought back, fought him off, got a look at his face. The attack bore striking resemblances to the reported rapes that began four years later."

Spaskov looked incredulous.

"I know," said Sasha, warming his hands on the mug. "The woman is old. The cases may not be related. By now her recollection of the man may be a blur, a confusion. She might identify a perfectly innocent man."

"She claims she has seen the man since," said Elena. "She seems certain."

"Where?" asked Spaskov.

"In a police car," said Sasha.

"She says the man who attacked her was a police officer?" said Spaskov.

"Yes," said Elena. "She says she saw him in a police car

two or three times about three years ago, all around Kievskaya railway station."

Spaskov nodded, finished his coffee, and put the cup down on his battle-scarred desk.

"Does she have a time of day? How good is the identification? I've been in this district almost twenty years. I know every patrol car officer."

"She says it was during the day each time, between three and five," said Elena. "The policeman was dark, wore a cap, had brown eyes and a small white scar on his face."

Spaskov was momentarily lost in thought.

"A number of officers have scars on their faces," he said. "I'll go check immediately, but I think your witness is probably wrong."

Spaskov left again, taking his and Sasha's mugs. He didn't offer more coffee, but what Sasha had taken in was probably enough to tide him over, especially if he could convince Elena to give him three or four of the aspirin she carried in her bag.

Spaskov came back. In his hands was a file, which he handed to Sasha, and a notebook.

"Assignment reports are bulky," he said, sitting. "I copied some of the schedules that might fit. You can look through the whole thing downstairs if you like. If the woman did see her assailant and he was a police officer, there were two regular afternoon patrols in that area, same officers for at least five years. Two of the officers were army veterans, joined the force after your witness was attacked. One of the officers on patrol at that time is dead, died in a car accident while off duty a little over a year ago. He can't have committed the recent rapes, obviously. And the last unlikely suspect is retired now. No scar. He works as a guard at an electronics storage warehouse. I know him well, name is Peotor Grinsk. I can't believe he could be your man, but here is a file photograph of him, which I would like returned."

Spaskov handed the photograph to Elena. Sasha leaned

over to look. The man in the small photograph had nearly blond hair and no scar.

"Peotor is short, stocky, and, as the data in his file shows, he has blue eyes. He is married, married young, has a granddaughter now. But you are welcome to him as a suspect. Now I must go. The men who passed you in the hall are on the way to the home of a known drug dealer. I should be there, though it will be of little use. We have one hundred ten officers in this district and more than seventy thousand citizens, about a quarter of whom seem to be involved in criminal activity of some kind."

Sasha and Elena knew what he meant. The drug dealer would have retained one of the new specialists who might be a lawyer. The specialist would know whom to bribe and who had secrets they would not want revealed. The specialist would have information on members of the police and courts. The drug dealer would probably have connections with a mafia. He would be back in business within a week and spend no more than a night or two in the station's lockup. Sasha and Elena both knew about lockups in Moscow. It would not be a pleasant night or two for the drug dealer, even if he found some guards he could bribe.

"If you need anything more, let me know. I want to catch this rapist. I have a wife and a young daughter. I want him. I want him alone in an interrogation room. But between us, Peotor is not your man, and your witness sounds far from reliable."

Sasha looked at Elena as if the lieutenant's words confirmed his opinion.

"I must leave now," said Spaskov. "You can take the file with you and make a copy. I would like it back."

Sasha and Elena nodded. Nothing they found in the file was very helpful or new. There was a sheet on each victim with a photograph. Some of the women were battered beyond recognition. All looked blank and confused.

None had given a description, only a sense of the man's size and a vague account of a deep voice that might have been purposely disguised.

Nonetheless, they walked the almost eight blocks in the snow to the apartment of Ludmilla Henshakayova and showed her the photograph of Officer Grinsk. The old woman barely glanced at it.

"That's not the man," she said. "I know the man. I'll never forget him. I have seen him. He is a policeman. I told you."

"Anyone could be mistaken," said Elena gently.

Ludmilla looked at the young woman and answered, "About many things, but not about this."

The morning was growing a bit warmer, but it was still cold and white with snow. Sasha and Elena stood in front of Ludmilla's apartment. A trolley bus drove slowly by, its wheels crunching tire patterns in the thin layer of snow that had accumulated since the street was cleared early that morning.

"And now?" asked Sasha.

"You know," she said.

Sasha shook his head and watched the trolley pull away down the street. They would reinterview every victim, try to discover something others had missed, try to build a profile from bits of information, most of which, like Ludmilla's, would be flawed.

Paulinin rubbed his head. His hair was probably in dire need of washing. But Paulinin was only one odd exhibit in this lower-level laboratory of Petrovka. Iosef had heard about the man and about the place, but now that he was actually inside it, the laboratory exceeded even his more extreme imaginings. Large, yes, and amazingly cluttered. Tables filled the room, and to get around you had to walk through a maze of them and past shelves piled with oddities, most of which Iosef could neither absorb nor identify.

There were shelves of glass jars filled with animal organs, probably human. Brains and hearts were the most common. There were pans piled high in a sink. Books and scrawled notes and reports were scattered everywhere, even on the floor near Paulinin's desk in a far rear corner of the room illuminated by about a dozen hanging lightbulbs, all covered with green metal shades that reflected downward. The room was remarkably bright. The curiosities were clearly visible: machines of various sorts; a few of them with spaces for or containing test tubes; a cardboard box of bright, untarnished tools ranging from scalpels to hammers and chisels. Iosef had almost banged into a shelf containing boxes of bones.

Before they had begun, Paulinin had offered Karpo and Iosef some tea. They both accepted and Paulinin poured the liquid from a pot on a hot plate near the sink. The tea was served in glass measuring cups. Iosef tried not to think about how well Paulinin had washed the cup or about what had been in it before the tea.

"Behold," Paulinin said, looking down at the package Karpo and Iosef had retrieved from the mail room. The scientist smiled. "We are dealing with a brilliant technologist. Not a genius. Not as smart as I am, but brilliant, a worthy criminal for a change."

"And what makes you say that?" asked Iosef.

Paulinin looked at Iosef as if he were first noticing the young man.

"You are Rostnikov's son," he said. "I heard you had joined the chaos of mingled purposes teeming over my head, the investigators bumping into one another, contaminating evidence, going to one of those incompetent so-called pathologists with their bodies. Emil Karpo and your father are the only ones who know what they are doing, and sometimes I am not so sure about Rostnikov."

"The package," Iosef said.

"He will learn," said Karpo to Paulinin after drinking some tea.

Iosef drank some tea. It was not nearly as offensive as

he had expected. Perhaps it did not contain the essence of some specimen after all.

"No X rays were possible," said Paulinin. "Can you imagine someone going through the trouble of lining the package with a thin layer of lead, the thickness of a sheet of paper, to prevent X rays? I weighed it to the gram. I smelled it. I calculated contents by density and composition. I did this by inserting a small tube and hypodermic needle into the bottom of the package between the two layers of lead. The tip of the needle just penetrated the envelope. It was a slight risk. I did it inside the bomb squad's iron tub."

Iosef was about to ask what the scientist had discovered, but he saw the warning look on Karpo's pale face and said nothing.

"I was right," said Paulinin. "There is a one-inch-thick block of birch in the package. It is simply wood—nothing attached to it, nothing inside. There are three sheets of paper. And there is a mechanism made of aluminum attached to a claylike substance."

"A bomb," Iosef said before he could stop himself.

Instead of being irritated, Paulinin looked extremely pleased as he turned to the young man.

"No," said Paulinin. "He anticipated the possibility that someone as capable as I might inspect the package. I inserted a fiber-optic probe through the hole I had made with the hypodermic. I probed gently till I saw enough to convince me. It is a fake bomb. The clay is clay. The mechanism is little more than a flimsy mousetrap device set to click when the package is opened."

"A joke?" asked Iosef.

"A challenge," said Paulinin with satisfaction.

Karpo wondered where the scientist had obtained the use of expensive fiber-optic instruments to conduct his probe. The logical conclusion, since Paulinin was almost unfunded, was that he had snuck into a laboratory somewhere.

"I took the fingerprints that were usable from the

package," said Paulinin, "but none of them are the bomber's."

"How can you tell?" asked Iosef.

"Smell it."

Karpo leaned over and smelled the package.

"Do you smell it?" asked Paulinin.

"Something faint," said Karpo. "A powder residue."

Iosef felt like an idiot, but he leaned over and smelled the package. Nothing.

"Latex gloves," said Paulinin. "That's what you smell. He wore lightly powdered latex gloves. The package is safe to open. I should like it back with the original papers inside, after you copy them. They will also contain no fingerprints."

Karpo nodded, finished his tea, and put his cup down on an open spot on the table between a metal object painted black and an empty glass container. Iosef did the same.

"Can you get me anything that's left of the bombs, the previous letter bombs?" asked Paulinin. "I'm sure the bomb squad dolts have destroyed whatever might be of use, and they'd never think of asking me, but there may be something. This man is a worthy opponent."

"We will do what we can," said Karpo.

"Lunch, chess?" said Paulinin.

"Tomorrow, one o'clock," said Karpo.

When they were out in the hall of the lower level of Petrovka and the heavy door to Paulinin's laboratory had slammed shut, sending a metallic echo down the hall, Iosef said, "He's crazy."

"He is also a genius," said Karpo.

Karpo carried the package as they walked.

Within three minutes, they had set the package on the desk of Porfiry Petrovich Rostnikov, who looked up at Karpo, who nodded. It was enough to let Rostnikov know it was safe to open the package.

He did so with the sharp blade of his small pocket knife.

"Fingerprints?" asked Rostnikov.

"Paulinin says there will be none," said Karpo. "Latex gloves."

Iosef stood dumbfounded. On the word of a madman in the basement, his father was opening a package that could explode and kill them all if Paulinin was wrong. Iosef had seen mangled bodies when he was in the army in Afghanistan. He had seen what remained of soldiers and civilians who had stepped on small mines hidden in sand.

Rostnikov reached in and pulled out the contents of the package, laying each piece neatly on the desk—the fake bomb and clay, the thin sheets of lead, the block of birch, and the three sheets of paper. Rostnikov laid the paper before him. The top page was typed and said: "I wonder how many hours and how much sweat were spent before you decided to open this. Probably enough so that it is past today's mail delivery and the letter bomb I sent has already gone off. Meanwhile, enclosed is the declaration to be made on television. I will have made my point if it is delivered to the people of Moscow. I will stop the bombs and I will wait to see what, if anything, will be done. I expect nothing will be done. I expect I will resume my bombing. More will die, more from the hands of those in power than from me."

It was unsigned. Rostnikov handed the letter to Karpo, who read it slowly where he stood.

Rostnikov read the two single-spaced pages titled "Declaration to the People of Russia." The declaration was a demand to dismantle and destroy all nuclear facilities, to clean up all Russian nuclear dump sites, and to cease any nuclear research, whether military, industrial, or medical. The declaration cited examples of the dangers of each and the threat to Russian citizens. The writer was educated, well-informed, and probably as out of touch with reality as Paulinin, Rostnikov concluded.

"Now?" asked Iosef.

"Now," said his father, "we wait for the bomb to go off and the bomber to call me."

"Television?" asked Iosef.

"I will ask," said Rostnikov. "I am confident that the demand to read the declaration will be denied."

"Paulinin would like to examine whatever remnants or traces of past letter bombs exist," said Karpo.

Rostnikov picked up the phone on his desk and pushed three buttons. Pankov answered. Rostnikov asked to speak to the director and was put through immediately.

Karpo and Iosef stood listening as Rostnikov reported on the package and Paulinin's request. Rostnikov listened and then hung up.

"You can pick up the bomb remnants from the bomb squad. They are being informed that they are to cooperate. It is almost certain that the bomber's demands will not be met."

Karpo nodded, turned, and left the office with Iosef right behind.

Rostnikov then ate at his desk, a sandwich prepared by his wife, who had made a request that he would take care of that very evening. Sarah had also prepared a thermos of tepid but sweet tea. Rostnikov had four reasons for eating in today. First, he was waiting for the report of a letter bombing that the bomber had promised. Second, he was waiting for a call from the bomber, who would want to know if Rostnikov had received his package. Third, he was waiting for a call from a former black marketeer who was now a legitimate businessman. The man had promised to find the ducting Rostnikov needed to work on Belinsky's synagogue. The fourth reason for eating at his desk was that it was easier than walking on the artificial leg. He had been getting plenty of practice at doing that. He could use an hour or two seated at his desk.

The phone rang before Rostnikov had finished his sandwich.

* * *

Avrum Belinsky sat reading in a wooden chair that had been placed outside of Rostnikov's office by Akardy Zelach, whose desk was in the room of five cubicles across the hall. Belinsky had not called in advance. He had slept fitfully, dreaming of a war in the streets of small towns, shooting at Syrians, being shot at. Flimsy walls of small one- and two-story buildings crumbled or exploded from shells that would have made small holes or scraped out ruts in larger, more solid buildings of the big cities. He had seen friends die, and he had killed more than once. That was both long ago and not long ago in his memory.

Avrum had come to Petrovka after his morning prayers. It had been a long journey with a stop at the synagogue to see if it was still there. It was. Untouched. But a truck was waiting at the door when he arrived, and a man sat in the cab of the truck, a burly man with a coat and cap and a scarf around his neck. The man was smoking and looking lost in thoughts or memories. The motor was not running.

Belinsky had approached the truck and startled the driver, who rolled down his window, no mean feat in this weather and considering the age of the truck.

"Belinsky?" asked the driver in a rasp of a voice that suggested a tonsillectomy had been botched in his childhood.

"Yes."

The man rolled the window up, got out of the truck, and closed the door with a slam.

"I knocked," he said.

"It's still early."

"I have many things to do," said the truck driver, who was thin and much older than he had first appeared. "Are you strong?"

"Reasonably," said Belinsky.

"Good. This isn't one of those days you can't work?" asked the man, holding back a sniffle. His nose was quite red.

"No," said Belinsky. "That's Friday night and Saturday."

"Good. Yuri has a sore back. He's my helper. He's good for nothing, but he's strong and he's my sister's son," said the driver. "Let's go."

The driver moved to the rear of the truck, pulled out a ring of keys, and opened the padlock. Belinsky stood back and watched as the doors squeaked open to reveal shiny aluminum sheets of various sizes and a variety of joints and angles.

"Let's go," the man said with resignation, and driver and rabbi slowly began to move the metal into the small synagogue.

It was especially slow because the driver was old and the rabbi probably should have been in a hospital.

That had been several hours ago. At Petrovka, Avrum asked to see Rostnikov. The young uniformed man at the guard cage looked at him with less than respect when he said his name was Rabbi Belinsky. The guard made a call and apparently got Zelach, who told the guard to let the rabbi in.

A second guard, who was supposed to be outside the cage, arms at the ready, had come into the cage to warm up a bit, though it was not particularly warm there. The second guard, who looked younger than the first, stepped out and pointed toward the entrance of the U-shaped building. The courtyard was a white rolling garden of snow hills. A wind, chill and whistling low, swirled around the U, sending up puffs of snow.

The lobby of Petrovka was dark. There was a desk inside with another uniformed man. This man was older than the guards and wore a brown uniform and no hat. His head was practically shaved at the sides, and his short brown hair was brushed back. Behind him stood a uniformed guard carrying Kalishnikov automatic weapons. Belinsky recognized the guns. He had seen them in the hands of the PLO, Syrians, Lebanese. Uzis against Kalishnikovs. Belinsky told himself that was another place and time. This was a new Russia. Another armed guard stood at a stairway nearby.

All three armed guards looked at Belinsky, though they pretended not to. Four people came down the stairs arguing. All were in their forties or fifties; only one wore a uniform. It was a military uniform. The military man was doing all the talking. Emphatic, certain, loud, confident, he spoke slowly while the others listened with respect.

"Yulia Piskovaya," said the military man in disgust. "We bring the case against Yulia Piskovaya. She spends eleven years as a court stenographer and then, suddenly, she's a judge. How do you talk to someone like that?"

"She'll find him guilty," one of the other men said wearily. " She finds everyone guilty. Don't worry, Constantin."

"I don't like dealing with fools," the older, disgusted man said.

They passed and Avrum turned his attention back to the man with short hair behind the desk.

"Someone will be down for you," said the man, writing in the ledger before him. "Belinsky, David."

"Avrum," the rabbi corrected.

"Abe-ra-ham," the guard strung out flatly, but making clear what he thought of the Jewish name. "To see Inspector Rostnikov. He is expecting you?"

"He will not be surprised," said Belinsky, feeling dizzy but not showing it.

The man grunted, examined the rabbi, and went back to his book, pretending to work.

Akardy Zelach was there soon after, awkwardly greeting Belinsky and just as awkwardly asking if it was all right to walk up since there was a problem with the elevators. He didn't add that there was always a problem with the elevators.

Though it became an ordeal, Belinsky kept pace with the detective, who fortunately did not move quickly. Then they were in the hallway, and Zelach was fetching a

chair and asking him if he wanted some coffee. Belinsky
declined and Zelach hesitated for a moment, unsure of
what he should do next, watch the visitor or go back to
his desk. He knew better than to discuss what little he
knew of the murders with the rabbi. All clergymen made
Zelach uncomfortable. His father, who died when
Akardy was a boy, had hated all religions but his own.
He was a loyal and unthinking Communist policeman
who believed Stalin was a god to be worshiped. Zelach's
father saved his greatest venom for the Jews, and his
mother made it clear, through her silence, that she agreed
with her husband. She had feared his rages and did her
best to agree with his frequent and fervent lectures on
everything from collective farming to Jews. Gradually,
because her husband was smarter than she, she came to
share his prejudices, though she'd had none when she
had married.

Even before the Soviet Union ended and the Communists fell into disgrace, Zelach's mother had returned
to the Russian Orthodox Church and had told her son
that his father had been right about most things, except
Stalin: He was no god, but a mass murderer. Years later
Akardy, who admittedly was slow, was just beginning to
reconcile the differences between his dead father and his
living mother and what he had learned of tolerance from
Rostnikov and his coworkers in the Office of Special
Investigation.

Zelach disappeared across the hall.

The blow to his neck had been the worst, Belinsky
decided as he sat waiting. His neck was sore to the touch,
and it had throbbed when he was helping the truck driver.
The cut on his chest was certainly worthy of a long line
of stitches. There were a few other lesser injuries, and
there was a possibility that the small finger on his right
hand was broken. He had packed it in snow, taped it, and
taken some codeine pills that he had stored in a drawer in
his small room. The wound on his chest he had treated by
a thorough cleaning with soap and water and then

stinging peroxide. The wound appeared to be clean. He had taped it neatly, expertly, probably better than would have been done in a Russian hospital. He would bear a scar, but that did not bother him. It would join the other scars both inside and outside his firm body. The tape had probably loosened a bit from the hour or so of moving metal and parts from the truck, but it would hold till he could re-dress it. It was his neck that troubled him most. Turning it was painful. The man had hit him hard but didn't know what he was doing. If Avrum had delivered such a blow, he would have done it correctly, and his opponent would be dead.

What had happened was curious. So curious that Avrum had lain awake most of the night waiting for the dawn thinking about the event, doing his best to ignore his pain.

Avrum had kept walking toward the two young men in front of him. Before he had reached them, the two stood together to block the sidewalk and the one on the right said, "Jew, if you live through this night, you are to take yourself and the rest of your filth out of Moscow. You are to sell your church to anyone foolish enough to buy it. We will probably let you live so you can do this, but we can't guarantee it."

Belinsky stopped about five feet before them, sensing the man coming from behind, moving slowly. The young man before him was talking loudly and rapidly to cover the approach of the assailant behind, who tried not to make sounds in the snow.

Belinsky stood, listening both to the young man and to the slight sound behind him. He watched the eyes of the man who wasn't talking. It was dark but there was enough light to see the man's eyes. Both young men wore scarves around their faces like masks, an indication to Belinsky that they might seriously be considering letting him live, but unable to identify his attackers. Even as he spun and squatted, he wondered why he wasn't dead. Why he hadn't been shot like the others.

The man behind Belinsky was big, bigger than the other two, and older. Belinsky plunged his right fist into the man's stomach, but the man didn't go down. The attacker swung his right fist, catching Avrum in the neck. The pain was swift and electric. The rabbi thought he might pass out, but his life might well depend on staying awake. His second strike at the older man was with the heel of his left hand into the big man's nose. The nose broke. Belinsky had been weakened by the blow to his neck and had not struck hard enough to drive the broken bones into the attacker's brain, but he had done enough damage to send the groaning man to his knees.

It had all happened quickly, before the other two, the ones who had blocked his way, could react. They had assumed the smaller rabbi would put up little resistance to Georgi. Georgi was big, strong, and unafraid. Now he lay in the snow holding his hand to his face to slow the flow of blood from his nose. What they saw made them cautious and gave Belinsky an instant in which to turn as the young man who had spoken, Yevgeny Tutsolov, struck out with a slash of his knife. The cut had gone through Belinsky's coat and shirt and across his chest.

Belinsky felt a sudden chill race along his fresh wound. He kicked out at the kneecap of the man who had slashed him. The blow was high. The kneecap did not break, but the man staggered back with a scream of pain. That left the silent man standing before the rabbi, trembling with fright, a pistol in his hand. Belinsky could see in the man's eyes that he was going to shoot, but the man had made a mistake. He was no more than two feet away. Avrum stepped swiftly to his right and with a chop brought his right hand down on Leonid Sharvotz's wrist. Leonid let out a gasp and dropped the gun in a knee-high bank of snow.

A first-floor light went on in the building next to which they were fighting. A woman's face appeared, squinting at the window, wiping away a small circle of frost so that she could see what was going on. The three men fled in different directions. The one he had kicked above the knee hopped rather than ran. Belinsky could have caught him, but the rabbi had no idea of how serious his chest wound might be, how much blood he had lost. The one whose nose he had broken was far down the street, and Avrum could see a trail of blood in the light from the woman's window. His eyes turned to hers, and the woman backed away quickly and turned off her light.

Avrum went to the snowbank where the gun had fallen, picked up a handful of snow, and pressed it through the tear in his clothes onto his bleeding chest. He groped in the bank for a few seconds, found the weapon—a Glock 9mm, model 17. Avrum had seen them before. There were few weapons that Avrum had not seen. He pocketed the Glock and walked home, but not too fast, as he continued to press the freshest snow he could find against his wound. To run or even walk quickly would make his heart beat faster and the blood flow more rapidly. He made it home, teeth tight, a prayer in his mind, and deadbolted the door.

His clothes were ruined. Even his pants were covered with blood. He washed and treated himself, relieved that the chest wound was not deeper, took the codeine, and lay in his bed with a small light on next to him.

Why hadn't they simply killed him as they had killed the others?

The question jabbed at him through the night and the pain till the relief of his morning prayers.

And now he sat waiting to tell his story to the police; the Glock he had taken taped under his small dresser. He had called his Israeli contact before he came, had called from an outdoor phone, told her what had happened and described his attackers. She had seemed more puzzled than Avrum that he was still alive. She promised to get orders and suggested that he call back late that afternoon. He agreed.

Now he sat waiting while Rostnikov talked on the phone.

* * *

A few hours earlier Oleg Selski had finished his breakfast: a bowl of barley soup, some bread, and a cup of strong, hot tea. Oleg was a man of average height and weight, forty-five yeas old, with a head full of hair that always needed cutting and a wife and a ten-year-old daughter.

Oleg was an editor of *Izvestia* who had grown comfortable with the new openness of Russia. His job was no longer simply a bore, concerned with only the rote tasks of editing and selecting stories to be published after approval, of course, by the senior editor from the Party. That had changed. Though it had lost millions of readers to the newer, bolder Russian newspapers, *Izvestia* had also been liberated, and Oleg had found causes, crusades, and corruption. His salary had increased, not enough to make him and his family financially secure, but enough to give them some comforts. All in all, life was good for Oleg Selski.

He was just finishing the last of his bread when Katrina, his daughter, came in with a letter. Selski occasionally received letters at home from his brother in Volgograd or from sources who didn't want to write to him at the news office.

This letter was a bit bigger than the rest.

"Can I open it?" Katrina asked.

Oleg threw the last of his bread into his mouth and washed it down with the last of his tea. He smiled at his daughter, pigtailed, in her blue-and-white dress, her pink face aglow.

And then something struck Oleg. He wanted to speak, but he choked and spat out bread. He could be wrong, must be wrong. His instincts were not always right, but he was a cautious man who had learned how to survive.

Katrina, a smile on her face, was already opening the letter when he finally shouted no. His shout startled the girl, who dropped the half-opened letter to the floor, where it instantly exploded.

SIX

THE CALL ROSTNIKOV WAS TAKING WAS FROM THE bomber. Emil Karpo was listening in on the phone in his cubicle across the hall. Iosef stood next to Karpo drinking coffee and waiting. There was a definite winter wind rattling the window in the next cubicle, the one that had belonged to Iosef's father before he had moved across the hall.

"Did it happen?" asked the bomber.

"It happened," said Rostnikov, calmly sitting up in his chair and doodling on his pad of paper.

"Do you want to know why he opened the letter?"

"Yes," said Rostnikov, drawing a cube on top of another cube. He knew he would draw a simple bird inside each cube, but he had no idea why.

"He's not on your list," said the bomber smugly.

A car horn beeped angrily over the phone.

"I'm calling from a pay phone. I'll make this short and be gone before you get here if you even have access to the technology for locating where I am."

"Your reason for selecting Oleg Selski?" Rostnikov asked calmly.

"His newspaper, instead of spewing Communist lies, now spews capitalist ones," said the bomber. "He has approved stories, editorials about the need for nuclear power plants. Chernobyl is operating again, a bomb far more destructive than any I have sent, destined to go off again, and he approved."

"So you sent him a bomb?"

"Yes."

"I assume that means anyone in Moscow could receive a bomb if they believe in or use nuclear energy," said Rostnikov.

"Chernobyl is still operating," said the bomber excitedly. "And yes, you are right. Even you, you are helping them by trying to catch me instead of helping me. You could get a bomb. The package I sent you could just as well have been a bomb. Any policeman could get one. You can't protect the entire city. Did you read my statement?"

"Yes," said Rostnikov. "I gave it to my superior with your demand."

"What did you think of it?"

"Well written but trite," said Rostnikov. "If any station carried it, viewers would be bored after the first paragraph. There is not a citizen who has not been brought up on the simplicities of propaganda."

"I know," said the bomber soberly. "But I owe it to my father. I owe it to the victims. I owe it to my mother. I am the last in my family. The name dies with me."

"You plan to die soon?" asked Rostnikov.

"Slowly, gradually, like my father unless you catch me first, in which case I will kill myself," he said.

"The letter bomb you sent today," Rostnikov said, easing his new leg into a less uncomfortable position, "it was not opened by Selski. It was opened by his ten-year-old daughter. Would you like to know what happened to her?"

Silence from the bomber.

"She started to open the letter," Rostnikov continued. "Her father suspected something. He told her to drop it. She is in the hospital. Critical but expected to live. She lost her toes and part of her right foot. Her father was unharmed. Tell me, what is your favorite color?"

"My fav—I have none. The girl will live?"

"So I am told."

"This is not a trick?"

"No," said Rostnikov.

"I believe you," the bomber answered so softly that the inspector could barely hear him.

"Your statement will not be read on television," said Rostnikov.

Silence from the bomber. Then he hung up.

"Come in, Emil," Rostnikov said to Karpo on the other end of the line. He looked at his watch. It was still early. School would not be out for hours. He had told Sarah that he was taking the girls after school.

The door to the office opened. Karpo and Iosef entered. Iosef closed the door and said, "There's a man waiting to see you in the hall."

"I know," said Rostnikov, looking at the notes he had written on his pad. The pad also contained a diagram of the large room of Belinsky's synagogue. While he was talking, Rostnikov had made drawings, in pencil so he could erase them, of possible configurations of tubing.

"The tape worked?"

"Perfectly," said Karpo, holding up a cassette.

Karpo stood at near attention, hands folded before him. Iosef, almost as tall as the pale man at his side, looked around the room and then at his father. Something more than anger paled his face.

"So, what do we know now?" said Rostnikov. "Iosef?"

"We're dealing with an educated psychopath," he said. "He thinks nuclear energy is killing us all, so he takes the ironic position that if he kills those who produce it or support it, he is making a statement against self-annihilation. The irony is that he would, if he lived and wasn't caught, eventually murder most of the population of Russia. At least that would be his goal. I say, find him, kill him on the spot."

"A soldier's answer," said Rostnikov.

"I was a soldier. I saw what terrorists and lunatics can do," answered Iosef.

"Emil?" Rostnikov asked, now looking at the impassive man before him.

"First, the bomber is on our contact list. He himself has something to do with nuclear energy. He knew that if Oleg Selski had been on the list, he would not have allowed his daughter to open the letter. The bomber's father was involved in some aspect of the production or use of nuclear energy. He may have been a scientist or a technician, but well educated, judging from his son's speech and his proclamation. The father died as a result of nuclear accident or contamination, or at least his son believes so. He is probably right. In spite of this, the bomber also works or worked in nuclear energy research, production, or technology, probably studied the field because of his father. The bomber has radiation poisoning or believes he does and wishes to make a statement before his death. He lives with his mother, is probably around forty-five."

"Do you think he will stop now that he has almost killed the child?" asked Rostnikov, looking at his son.

"No," said Iosef. "He will believe that he must continue, that he has more reason now because he won't want the girl's injuries to be meaningless, especially in light of the director's refusal to try to get his proclamation read on television."

Rostnikov shook his head and said, "First a soldier. Then a playwright and actor. Now a policeman. An interesting combination of talents. Karpo, what do you propose doing?"

"Checking hospitals and physicians for men being treated for radiation poisoning," Karpo replied. "See if any names coincide with those on our call list. Check with all Moscow corporations or government agencies dealing with nuclear materials. Review every person on our contact list."

"There are many?" asked Rostnikov.

"Seven hundred and twenty-seven," said Karpo. "We can begin to check immediately."

"What, I wonder, is the bomber's favorite color?" Rostnikov mused, staring down at his drawing of birds inside of cubes. "If he calls again, I'll ask him again, but I think I know the answer."

"Which is?" asked Iosef.

"He considers himself a dead man. He gets satisfaction from nothing but his crusade and self-pity. I believe we are looking for a gray man, a very gray man."

Rostnikov had not bothered to tell Karpo to make a copy of the cassette of the bomber's call. He knew he would have one on his desk by the time his visitor left. Nor did he suggest to Karpo that Paulinin listen to the tape. He was sure the detective would arrange it immediately.

When his visitor left, Rostnikov would report to Yakovlev and then follow some leads on the murder of the Jews after getting a report on the Shy One, the rapist, from Sasha and Elena. It was a busy day, but he had promises to keep.

Rostnikov picked up the phone, dialed two numbers, and told Zelach to come in and bring the man waiting in the hall.

Moments later Zelach and Belinsky entered and Zelach closed the door.

"What happened?" asked Rostnikov, pointing to his chairs.

Belinsky sat. Zelach hesitated and then sat also.

"I was attacked last night by three men," he said. "I can give you descriptions of all three, poor ones of two of them and a precise one of the third. The third man has a badly broken nose. One of the other two men will be walking with a limp for some time. The last will have a stiff wrist for at least a week."

"You can give the descriptions to Inspector Zelach when we finish. Are you badly hurt?" asked Rostnikov.

"I shall have another scar," said Belinsky, touching his chest. "Each one with its own history to remind me that I and my people must remain forever and always alert."

Rostnikov nodded in understanding. He, too, had such scars, as did Zelach.

"They had weapons?" Rostnikov asked.

"Yes," said Belinsky, saying nothing about the Glock hidden in his room.

"Then I assume we both have the same question," said Rostnikov.

Zelach looked decidedly puzzled when Rostnikov turned his eyes on him to see if he understood.

"Why didn't they simply kill me like the others?" asked Belinsky.

Rostnikov nodded again. "Anti-Semites who have not hesitated to murder six others do not kill you, a rabbi. What did they say?"

"That we should get out," said Belinsky.

"Name-calling?"

"Almost none, but there was no time," said the rabbi, whose neck was throbbing. He had looked in the mirror before coming. His neck was purple. He covered it with a scarf, which he still wore over his second coat. The first coat, his better and warmer one, had been cut to uselessness the night before. Even with a sweater, the short brown coat he now wore was not warm enough for the cold weather.

"They said—" Rostnikov began.

"Only one spoke," said Belinsky.

"*He said*," Rostnikov corrected, "get out. Out of where? Russia? Moscow? Did you have any sense of what he meant? Was he talking of all Jews?"

Belinsky started to shake his head, but the pain in his neck stopped him, and he said "No" and then amended that to "Maybe."

"Maybe?" Rostnikov repeated.

"I think he wanted us out of the way. We were standing in his way," said Belinsky, trying to remember.

The rabbi sat firm, upright, not ignoring the sense that blood had begun to seep slowly through the bandage and tape on his chest. He should, he knew, be lying down quietly, letting the wound close and begin to heal, but there was much to do. He would finish here, go to his room, change his dressing, and lie on his back quietly.

Rostnikov looked at Zelach, who clearly had no ideas. Rostnikov was aware that Zelach's mother loved him, cared for him, was grateful to Rostnikov for his confidence in a son she knew was less than bright. But Zelach's mother was, Porfiry Petrovich knew, a quiet bigot. A word here, a word there had made that evident. Akardy Zelach simply accepted the prejudices of his mother, although little in his life bore out the distrust his mother expressed. Every day bore out his experience that crime, violence, and evil appeared in all groups, among all people, as did kindness and a love of family and a respect for the law, no matter how confusing that law might be. Rostnikov preferred not to consider the dilemma.

"You have any suggestions or ideas, Akardy?" Rostnikov asked.

The Jew looked at the slouching, uncomfortable man in the chair next to him. There was nothing in the Jew's eyes to indicate anything but interest in what Zelach might say. Suddenly Zelach got an idea.

"Mesanovich," he said, almost without thought. "The one who died on the embankment, the one who wasn't a Jew."

Rostnikov smiled. Avrum Belinsky shrugged, though it brought on a wince of pain, which he disguised by gently biting his lower lip as if in thought.

"You want a doctor?" Rostnikov said.

"I know where I can get one of my people if necessary," said Belinsky. "I made a mistake last night. It will not happen again."

"Mistake?" asked Zelach before he could stop himself.

"The rabbi thinks he should have killed the three men," said Rostnikov. "Am I correct?"

"Yes," said Belinsky, rising from his chair. He had

considered using the gun in his pocket during the attack but had been confident that he could defend himself without it and create a sense of fear in his attackers without killing them. "I'll not make that mistake again if I have the opportunity."

The detective and the rabbi looked at each other, and both knew that there was no chance of changing the other's mind. Belinsky turned toward the door, forcing himself to walk deliberately. He paused, turned, and said, "The materials for the heating arrived."

"Eight o'clock tonight?" asked Rostnikov.

"Yes," said Belinsky. "You'll need help. I can get some of my congregants, and I will be there."

"You are in no condition to help, but be there," said Rostnikov. "I need only two of your people, the stronger the better. I'll recruit others."

"It will be," said Belinsky.

The rabbi went out the door and closed it. Rostnikov began to adjust his artificial leg.

"What do you have planned for tonight?" asked Rostnikov.

"Tonight?" asked Zelach. "Dinner. Television."

"How would you like to learn the profession of heating engineer?" Rostnikov proposed. "It will be something to fall back on in times of trouble."

Zelach was confused but said he would be willing to learn if Inspector Rostnikov thought it a good idea.

"Eight o'clock," said Rostnikov. "At the synagogue."

Zelach nodded a confused yes.

"Mesanovich is a good idea," Rostnikov said. "Let's go."

Zelach tried not to beam. He couldn't remember ever having been praised for an idea before by anyone but his mother. His mother. What would she think about his working for Jews, and for nothing? He would, when he had the chance, call her and tell her he was working very late, directly with Porfiry Petrovich. She would only ask if it was dangerous and tell him she would have something for him to eat when he came home.

Akardy Zelach was in a very good mood.

Legwork. The process was essentially the same for the police in every country in the world. Knock on doors of people who might but probably didn't have information. Interview past victims who had probably told all that they knew. Reexamine any evidence that they might possess.

"A waste of time," said Sasha to Elena as they stood waiting in the small outer office of the International Arab Export Corporation. The woman, well groomed and definitely not an Arab, had come into the office from the offices beyond a door and asked if she could help them.

Elena had asked if it might be possible to talk to Valeria Petrosyan for a moment or two. Both detectives showed their police cards. The woman examined them carefully and clasped her hands together before her.

"About what?" she said.

"We believe she witnessed an automobile accident a few weeks ago," said Sasha. "Hit-and-run. We want to know if the man we have arrested might be the person we are looking for. Of course, we don't know how good a look she had at him. It will only take a few minutes. We show her the photograph, ask her a few questions."

Sasha was smiling at the woman, his best boyish smile.

"I should ask Mr. Mogabi," she said, "but he's in a meeting."

Sasha and Elena knew they could simply demand to see the woman they sought, but then she would have to answer questions from her employers, questions she would probably not wish to answer.

"All right," the woman said. "I'll send her out."

The room they waited in was small but spotless. There were high-quality reproductions of French impressionist paintings on the walls—a Monet on one wall, two

Monets and a Renoir on the other. The floor was carpeted—gray and clean. The four chairs were gray fabric and chrome.

They had already interviewed four victims of the rapist. Since all of the crimes had occurred in the same general area, the women did not live outside of a manageable circle. Some of the victims did not have phones or did not choose to answer. The detectives had trudged to apartments, and since a number of the victims were retired, Sasha and Elena had found them at home. The first two had answered questions but had been of no help other than to confirm the method of the rapist and his strength. They had not seen him, had heard only a raspy voice, probably disguised, and had been beaten. One of the two suffered severe hearing loss from the attack, and her deafness and size reminded Sasha of his mother. The third woman they found at home simply refused to talk to the detectives. She was younger than the first two, probably about sixty. She had suffered a broken skull and had since experienced blinding headaches that forced her to lie on the floor of her small bathroom in darkness for hours at a time. This she did not tell the detectives. All she said was that she would not talk about the incident.

The fourth woman had tried to be helpful. She was the youngest of the lot, in her twenties, pretty, dark, worked in the Hotel Russia, where they tracked her down. She had been a young teen when she was attacked. Sasha had told her employer a tale similar to the one he had just told the woman at the International Arab Export Corporation. The girl's name was Alexandra. She cleaned rooms. The most striking thing about her was her thick glasses, which she took off to speak. The rapist had hit her across the forehead. A week later her eyesight began to deteriorate. The doctors thought it would continue till she went blind, but the deterioration had suddenly stopped. The girl hoped it would not start again. She, too, had been of little help other than to confirm what the others had said. She explained that for years she had tried either to remember details of that night or to forget the event entirely. Neither effort had been successful.

"I'll bet this place is a front," said Sasha, looking around the little room.

"Front?"

"Weapons, drugs, something," he said.

"Then they probably have the room bugged and are listening to what you're saying right now," replied Elena sarcastically.

"Probably," said Sasha, as the inner office door opened and a woman in her late forties came out. She was tall and wore a dark suit with a white blouse. Her dark hair was brushed upward off her neck and sat stylishly on her head. Her makeup was light and she was distinctly pretty.

"Dark hair," said Elena softly to Sasha. "They are all gray or have dark hair. I wonder if the gray ones had dark hair when they were attacked. I wonder if they were all as slender as this one and the one at the hotel."

They knew they had to go back and check.

"Valeria Petrosyan," the woman said warily.

"Can we go out in the corridor to talk for a moment and show you something?" asked Elena, trying to convey the need for more privacy.

"If you wish," said Valeria.

The three moved into the broad hallway of the seven-story building, where dozens upon dozens of Communist Party offices had been vacated and converted shortly after Yeltsin came to power.

"You are not here to talk about any accident," Valeria said, looking from one to the other of the two young people before her. "I witnessed no accident."

"You were attacked and raped four years ago near the Kropotkinskaya metro station," said Elena.

"I thought so," the woman said with a sigh. "I have told the police all I know, I told them when it happened. I lost a husband because of what happened that night. That was the one good thing about it. The rest . . . Please make this quick. My employers are engaged in a very sensitive business and . . ."

Sasha looked at Elena with satisfaction and turned to Valeria.

"Please, just tell us once more what you remember of that night," said Elena.

"You know I don't want to remember," the woman said, her voice deep, controlled. "But there are things one cannot forget. As I told the police, I was on my way home from working late. My husband was supposed to meet me at the metro and walk home with me. He wasn't there. He was off somewhere getting drunk in his cab. I walked two blocks. There wasn't much traffic. Some cars. Few people. There was a slight rain. I didn't hear the man coming. Cars were going by when he pushed me into the doorway, holding me around the neck from behind. He warned me not to make a sound or he would kill me. He showed me a knife. He opened the door. It was a government building. The light had been unscrewed in the entryway. That's what the police told me later. He threw me down, kissed my neck, punched me hard in my back, and kept warning me to be quiet while he lifted my dress and pulled down my panties. It was fast. It was painful. I know I whimpered. He told me not to turn around when he let me go, not to look at him or he would kill me. He made me say I understood. Then he got up and went out the door. I turned and saw him. He was taller than you." She looked at Sasha. "Well built, wearing a blue jacket and pants, a stripe on the pants. I think his hair was dark."

"You saw him?" asked Elena.

The tall woman nodded.

"A uniform?" asked Sasha.

"I told the police that I thought it was a policeman's uniform, but I wasn't sure," Valeria said softly.

"You didn't see his face," said Elena.

"A bit of profile, but it was raining and I had been raped. My eyes were full of tears. I couldn't identify him and I only had the sense when he paused for an instant that he had a white scar right here."

Valeria touched a spot just to the left of her nose.

"That's all I know," she said. "All I remember. Believe me. I have tried. I want him caught. If it were possible, I would like to personally kill him. I believe I could do it."

"I believe you could," said Sasha.

"Now, if there's nothing—" she began, but Elena cut her off with, "And you told this same story to the police when it happened?"

"Probably the same words," Valeria said. "Now, I should like to get back to work before I get questioned by my supervisor. I need this job. I have a child."

"Not . . . ?" Sasha began.

"No, not from the rape," she said. "Before—he was an infant when it happened."

"Thank you," said Elena as Valeria turned to the door and said, "You'll tell me if you catch him."

"Yes," said Elena.

A few minutes later Sasha and Elena stood on the street. The snow was still heavy but the sidewalk was clear. Only a touch of new snow had fallen during the night, but the temperature had dropped. Sasha shuffled from one foot to the other.

"She told the police," Elena said. "Why isn't it in the report?"

"I have one idea," said Sasha.

"What?"

"The old woman was right. The rapist is a policeman. He has access to the files and removed any references to his description, probably weeks or months after the reports were filed."

"So," said Elena, "we look for a well-built policeman with a scar next to his nose?"

"First, we talk to the other victims and see what else they said that may have been removed from the files."

Elena nodded.

"Tea?" she asked.

Sasha nodded an emphatic yes.

Iosef looked at the list before him on his desk and waited for the sound of Elena returning to the office. The list was long and the question seemed to take a while for each government office and business to answer.

Karpo was not in his cubbyhole. He was down in Paulinin's laboratory. Paulinin had called about a half hour earlier saying he had more information. Iosef did not want to go back into the mixture of acid smells and staleness. Iosef had asked Karpo if it would be all right for him to stay at his desk and start making the calls.

"Paulinin may have information that will help with the calls," Karpo had said, a pale, somber figure in black standing in Iosef's doorway.

"If he does," said Iosef, "I'll call back the ones I reach."

Karpo had nodded and Iosef knew he thought the son of Porfiry Petrovich Rostnikov was simply trying to avoid the man known in Petrovka as the Mad Scientist of the Underground.

"As you wish," Karpo had said, and left.

Iosef was on his eleventh call.

"Hello," he said when a woman answered, "Karkov Enterprises."

"I am a deputy inspector in the Office of Special Investigation," he said. "My name is Iosef Rostnikov. I wish to talk to someone in charge who has been with your company the longest time."

"Give me a number I can call to verify who you are," the woman said.

Iosef gave his number. She called back.

"Sergei," she said. "He was here when we were still part of the Bureau of Energy. You are a policeman?"

"I am," said Iosef. "If you'd like to call back again and confirm at a different number . . . ?"

He looked at his watch. The list was long.

"No," she said. "But we have new partners in the company, French. I don't want to lose my job."

"I understand," Iosef said. "I'll make it clear to Sergei that I insisted on talking to him."

The woman said nothing more. There was a click and a buzz. After about ten seconds a man's voice came on, high and reedy like a clarinet.

"Sergei Ivanovich," he said.

"Deputy Inspector Rostnikov," said Iosef. "I have a few questions to ask you."

"About?"

"Do you have any current employee who is suffering from an illness related to exposure to nuclear materials?" asked Iosef.

"Why?" answered the man nervously.

"It relates to an important investigation," said Iosef, finding himself doodling in the margins of the list. He stopped doodling, realizing he was doing what his father did, only Iosef wrote names, ornately. He had written "Elena" four times with curlicues. He also realized that he had doodled with a pen and not a pencil.

"It is his business," said Sergei with the reedy voice. "If he would rather the world not know . . ."

"It is a murder case," said Iosef. "We don't plan to harass innocent people."

Sergei paused, coughed, thought.

"Hell," he said finally. "I'll be seventy years old. They're going to boot me out on a pension I can't live on anyway as soon as they're sure they don't need my memory anymore. It's almost all on computers now. Then—"

"The sick person," Iosef reminded gently.

"We had two," said Sergei. "Last year. Oriana died. She and Alexi had accidentally been exposed to an improperly sealed container from Iran. The radiation dose was high. She was dead of radiation poisoning within three months. She was young, a very good worker. It's all in the records, the reports I was assigned to fill out and submit to the Nuclear Power Committee where someone in the Kremlin probably filed it without reading it."

"Alexi?" asked Iosef, looking again at the long list.

"He was across the room," said Sergei. "Lower dose. Still high. He has not looked well since a few weeks after the accident. His behavior changed. He was always a little sullen. Didn't talk much. Like his father. Then he stopped talking to almost everyone, and he has been missing a lot of days, calling in ill. He's going to his own doctors if he is going."

"Alexi's last name?"

"Alexi Monochov," he said instantly. "He's not here today. Called in sick. He doesn't get paid when he's sick, but he doesn't seem to mind. Lives with his mother and sister. I think they have money. They have a good address. I don't believe in God. I lived my whole life under the godlessness of Communism. Even became a Party member. But there can be coincidental ironies that make you wonder, don't you think?"

Iosef had the definite belief that Sergei of the reedy voice had very little to do at work and welcomed a caller, any caller.

"Yes," said Iosef.

"It is an irony that Alexi's father died of the same thing that may be killing his son," said the man.

Iosef stopped doodling Elena's name.

"His father died of radiation poisoning?"

"Yes," said Sergei. "Caused a prostate cancer. Monochov was brilliant. Moody. Thought he wasn't sufficiently appreciated, that others above him were getting credit for his work. To tell the truth, he was right. That was a long time ago. We weren't so careful then. Deaths were almost common. Then his son comes to work here. Almost as brilliant as the father. And he may be dying of the same malady. Good thing Monochov isn't married and doesn't have a son."

"His address," said Iosef.

Without hesitation Sergei Ivanovich gave an address on Chekhov Prospekt.

"When Monochov returns," said Iosef, "we would prefer that you not tell him about this call."

"I haven't exchanged ten words with him in over a year," said the old man. "I doubt if he'll tell you much."

Iosef paused and then decided to ask a question, which well might be a bad idea, but Sergei was a talker.

"Do you think Alexi Monochov could make a bomb?"

Sergei laughed and said, "Anything from a hydrogen bomb to a shrapnel bomb the size of a pen. It's his specialty, detonation. It was his father's, too."

"*Spahseebah*," said Iosef, keeping calm. "Thank you. And remember . . ."

"I won't tell anyone you called," the old man said. "I hope Alexi isn't in trouble. I can't say I like him, but he's been through enough."

Iosef hung up and looked down at the notes he had just taken. It looked good. It looked like a possible match. He had no trouble finding Alexi Monochov's name on the list of those to be called if the bomber threatened another attack.

The door to the offices opened. Iosef heard footsteps and Karpo appeared at the door.

"I think we may have a good lead," Iosef said, trying to remain calm.

"Alexi Monochov," said Karpo before Iosef could say the name.

Karpo had sat listening to Paulinin without saying a word. Paulinin had much to say.

Karpo had, at the scientist's insistence, sat on a wooden stool while Paulinin displayed the fragments of letter bombs on a wooden table he had cleared. The various shapes, some no more than the size of a fingernail, were back in zippered see-through plastic bags. It looked like a jigsaw puzzle.

"Fragments," said Paulinin with satisfaction, pointing

at the pieces laid out neatly in front of him. "But a piece here, a piece there, some tentative conclusions. If only the dolts who had collected all this had been more careful, but that would be asking too much . . ."

Paulinin paused, patted down his mat of hair, looked at Karpo, and waited. It was like a magician's act. Paulinin had something to say, but he would say it in his own way, in his own time, knowing that Karpo would be one of the few people, perhaps the only one, to appreciate what he had done.

"Conclusions?" Karpo prompted.

"Fragments," Paulinin repeated. "On one thin piece of metal a strange letter is stamped. At first glance it looks like random scratches. It is incomplete, but I recognized it and matched it. It is Arabic."

Paulinin pointed to one of his exhibits. Karpo looked. There was a small piece of paper and an even smaller darkened and jagged piece of metal. No scratches were clearly visible, but Karpo had learned to trust the scientist.

"Second," said Paulinin, "some of the more recent bombs, particularly the one you brought today, had a similar odor, a residue of chemicals. I found traces, traces so small that I needed the electron microscope when everyone was out of the lab upstairs."

Paulinin was not supposed to use the more sophisticated equipment in the forensic laboratory almost directly above him. Normally he prided himself on what he could discover more from a small piece of dust or a charred strip of human flesh with the equipment in his cluttered laboratory. Paulinin had no friends in the forensic laboratory. They resented his success and his air of superiority, and they were more than just uncomfortable with his air of near madness. Paulinin had unkind words to say about all of them, but his favorite target was the pathologists. Paulinin frequently took bodies when autopsies were completed and discovered crucial evidence the highly respected specialists had missed.

"The trace proved to be from a plastique-style explosive that the military and even terrorists stopped using long ago," said Paulinin. "Too volatile. More terrorists than victims died from their ignorance of the sensitive explosive. Iran still has some. Hammas uses it sometimes in Israel. They don't care if the carrier dies. In fact, that's the point."

"And here? In Moscow?" asked Karpo, knowing when he had heard a cue.

"Three laboratories worked on stabilizing the explosive as long ago as the 1950s," said Paulinin. "I made some calls. One man was working on such a stabilization using a particular aluminum alloy from Iran. The man was also working on development of nuclear weaponry. He died almost twenty years ago, radiation poisoning. I knew him slightly from conferences. He was less a fool than most."

There was silence. Paulinin smiled, the corners of his thin mouth coming up at the corners. He looked more constipated than pleased, but Karpo had come to know the man well.

"Then he is not the one we're looking for," said Karpo.

"He had a son," said Paulinin, springing his surprise. "His son is an engineer, more a technologist than a scientist. He works in the same laboratory where his father worked. I have encountered him, too, at a few conferences. He lacks his father's skills, but . . ."

"And the name of this man and the laboratory?" asked Karpo.

"Alexi Monochov, Karkov Enterprises," Paulinin said. "If he is still there."

The man known as the Vampire was wearing his coat, as black as the rest of his clothing.

"Yes," said Iosef, in awe when Karpo uttered the name he himself was about to speak. "Did he turn himself in?"

"No," said Karpo.

Iosef got up and followed Karpo to the door and out into the corridor, putting his coat on as they walked.

Twenty minutes later, the two detectives were in the outer lobby of a fashionable apartment building on Chekhov Prospekt. More buildings at this level were hiring doormen, many of whom were former policemen or even former KGB agents. The pay for protecting the tenants from the rash of thieves was better than government pay, though it could be dangerous. Such doormen were always armed. Not long ago a doorman had been confronted by a gang of four children who entered at night. One of the children had an automatic weapon that looked like an old machine gun from an American gangster movie. The doorman had shot the twelve-year-old, whose weapon misfired, and the other three children had fled. The twelve-year-old had survived the wound, refused to name his partners, and boasted that they had planned to terrorize the building apartment by apartment, tearing out telephones so the police couldn't be called and taking what they wanted. That attack, and most other attempts, failures and successes, had come at night, though daylight apartment robberies were no longer unheard of.

However, this building had no doorman on duty. Instead of ringing the bell to the Monochov apartment, Karpo took a black leather pouch out of his pocket. The rectangular pouch was about two inches wide and about a quarter of an inch thick. Karpo's long fingers extracted two small metal tools. One was no more than a bent piece of metal; the other, the size of a small pencil, came to a sharp point. Using both tools, Karpo opened the lock within a minute.

Iosef noted the procedure as one he hoped to be able to perform in the not-too-distant future.

The inner lobby was small, tiled, empty. It was late morning. People who worked were at their jobs. People who didn't were in their apartments or out shopping. People in buildings like this, Iosef thought as he followed Karpo to the elevator standing open before them, had the money to shop.

The Monochov apartment was on the eighth floor. The two men approached it at a normal pace. Before the end of the Soviet Union, Karpo had not carried a weapon unless he knew he was likely to run into armed resistance on a case. Now he wore a holster under his coat, and in the holster was a SIG Sauer P 226 that could deliver sixteen 9mm rounds rapid-fire with great accuracy. It was also the safest handgun. The loaded and uncocked gun put the hammer in register with the safety intercept notch, so firing was possible only when the trigger was pulled. It could not go off accidentally. Karpo had the weapon nearby all the time, on duty and off. Armed resistance roamed the streets. Iosef's weapon, a .32 Smith & Wesson, was also under his coat. Karpo didn't reach for his gun. Iosef followed his lead.

There was a knocker, silver plated and well polished, on the door. Karpo knocked. There was an immediate bustle inside and then the sound of footsteps.

"Who is it?" asked a woman.

"Police," said Karpo. "Open the door immediately."

The door did not open immediately.

"How do I know you're really the police?" she asked.

Even a newcomer like Iosef knew the drill, which might or might not work. He pulled out his plastic identification card and slid it under the door. He knocked on the bottom of the door so the woman would look down.

They could hear her moving. Silence. Then the door opened to reveal a very frightened looking woman in her seventies wearing a long-sleeved green dress, her white hair tied in a bun atop her head. She held Iosef's identification card in her hand.

"You really are police?" she asked, looking at Karpo in fear and then over at Iosef, who smiled.

The young detective was good-looking, amber-haired, and had a good smile with even, white teeth. He took the card from her hand and pocketed it.

"Alexi Monochov," Karpo said, stepping in with Iosef at his side.

Karpo closed the door.

"Alexi's in trouble, isn't he?" she asked.

Her face was pink and her gray eyes showed a new fear.

"You are his mother?" asked Karpo.

"Yes."

"We would like to speak to him," said Iosef.

"Speak to . . ." the woman began, and seemed to lose track of what was happening.

"Some questions," said Iosef.

The woman backed up slowly as if she were being attacked. She backed into a large living room with solid French style furniture. Lots of wood and soft cushions. There was an Oriental rug on the floor.

"Alexi isn't here," she said. "He's at work."

"He called in sick," Iosef said.

"Maybe he went to the doctor," she said. "He's been complaining about a sore stomach. He doesn't tell me everything. He is in trouble?"

"His doctor's name?" asked Karpo.

"I don't know. He's never told me. He doesn't talk to me or his sister much. My daughter's not here. She's at work. She helps at a school."

"When your son left this morning," said Karpo, "did he have anything with him?"

"His briefcase," she said. "I don't know why he would need his briefcase to see the doctor."

"Did he do anything unusual?" asked Karpo.

"Yes," she said, looking down. "He kissed my forehead. He never does that."

"We would like to see his room," said Karpo.

"Which one?" she asked. "The workroom is locked. Only Alexi has a key. His bedroom is open."

"Show us the workroom," said Iosef.

"It's locked," she said.

"Please," said Iosef. "Show us."

She sighed deeply and looked around the room before speaking again.

"Alexi won't like this," she said.

"We'll talk to him," said Iosef.

The woman turned and led them through the living room to a hallway with a polished wood floor. There were four doors. She stopped at the last one. Karpo looked at the lock, took out his tools, and went to work.

"Alexi won't like this at all," she said. "No one is allowed in his workroom. No one. Ever."

The lock was good. It took Karpo almost two minutes to open it while Iosef and the woman watched. Then Karpo motioned for the others to move away. They did and so did he. He reached over, turned the handle, and the door swung open. There was no bomb triggered to the door, though there might be a delayed one. They stood back for a full minute, and then Karpo went into the room. Iosef and the woman were right behind him.

"I've never been in here before," the woman said.

"Don't touch anything," Karpo ordered, looking around the small, windowless room. There were shelves up to the ceiling filled with neatly arranged materials. On the opposite wall was a large cabinet, its doors closed. In front of them was a table covered with carefully laid out tools, empty mailing cartons, large brown envelopes, and a box of disposable latex gloves. The two policemen had no doubt about what they were looking at.

On the wall over the worktable was the framed photograph of a somber man in profile.

"That's my husband," the woman said, and then she glanced at the large picture next to the photograph of the man. The second picture looked as if it had been taken from a newspaper. It showed a large mushroom cloud.

On the table directly in front of them was a handwritten note on a sheet of lined legal-size paper. It was held down by a small pliers.

Karpo and Iosef moved forward and began to read the note without touching it. It was addressed to the police and began, "There are duplicate copies of this statement in the mail to a newspaper and a television station in

Moscow and to the bureaus of two newspapers, one American and one British. Since I will be dead along with many others when you read this . . ."

Iosef blocked the old woman from the note, but she tried to push past him.

"What is it? This is my house. Alexi is my son. Where is he?"

SEVEN

GALINA PANISHKOYA GAVE EACH OF HER GRAND-daughters a hug. The twelve-year-old began to cry. The seven-year-old held back and then ran into her grand-mother's arms. The trio stood together weeping.

Rostnikov took a seat in the small room. His choices were limited to one of four identical wooden chairs, all very old and scratched. The only other furniture in the room was a wooden dining room table that definitely did not match the chairs. There was a single window with bars. The view from the window was an empty square courtyard below and dozens of similar windows with bars around the courtyard of the square red building. The courtyard was where the prisoners were permitted to exercise twice a day.

The women's prison was north of the city and required both a metro ride to the Outer Ring Circle and then a bus ride to the prison. Rostnikov had not told the woman that he was bringing the girls. Too many bureaucratic problems were possible—delays without explanation, excuses without substance. But Rostnikov knew a few people in the prison office and was on cordial terms with the warden.

Galina Panishkoya was sixty-six years old. She looked like she should have been wearing a babushka and warm coat, not a loose-fitting dress that served as a uniform. When Rostnikov had talked her into giving him the gun in her hand almost two years earlier in the back room of

State Store 31, she had been sitting on a stool holding a frightened young employee at gunpoint and looking down from time to time at the manager, whom she had shot. It had all been a blur to Galina. There had been a food riot over cheese supplies. People had tried to grab the cheese, and Galina, after hesitating, had joined in. The manager had pulled out a gun, a 7.65mm Hege, Wlam model, the one with the Pegasus in a circle on the grip. Rostnikov knew it was quite a fickle and dangerous weapon.

Rostnikov had explained to the woman who sat on a stool that day, gun in hand, with the body of store manager Herman Koruk on the floor beside her in a pool of blood and a sobbing young girl in a white smock splattered with small drops of blood cowering against the wall, what the mythical Pegasus was.

Galina didn't quite remember exactly how she got the gun from the manager. Perhaps she thought he was going to kill her or someone else. All the woman knew was that she had two hungry granddaughters at home she had to take care of. The girls' mother had long ago departed, as had their father.

Now Galina was in prison for murder. The trial had been quick, coming just as the Soviet Union was about to end. The judge had been in fear of losing his job and had come down with a firm sentence, though he spared her life. Galina was to be in prison for the rest of her days. Now Rostnikov and his wife were trying to get her another trial or parole. Iosef had a friend from his army days who was one of the new lawyers. He was working on the case. It looked promising, but he offered the woman no guarantees.

When he had first met Galina in the back of State Store 31, the first thing she had asked him was about the leg he dragged behind him. Now, as she sat in one of the chairs, an arm around a granddaughter on either side, she said, "*Spahseebah*," unable to keep the tears from her eyes.

Rostnikov nodded.

"You're walking better," she said.

"He has a new plastic leg," the younger girl said.

Rostnikov rolled up his pant leg to reveal the creation.

"Take it off for her," said the younger girl.

The older girl tapped her sister on the head.

"That won't be necessary," said Galina with a smile. "I have seen men with one leg before."

"How does it go, Galina Panishkoya?" asked Rostnikov.

The woman shrugged and pulled her granddaughters even closer to her.

"*Bweet zayela*, every day life has challenged me, but I work and I eat. I'm making dresses here," she said, "all the same kind, like this one. I am useful. I don't have to stand. I used to work at the Panyushkin dress factory, but that was long ago."

Rostnikov knew this, but he nodded as if it were new information.

"The light is not always good here," she said. "But they let us read. They gave me reading glasses. I read better now."

Rostnikov shifted his weight and pulled a tattered paperback from his pocket. He put it on the table in front of Galina. It was an Ed McBain novel called *Mischief*. Porfiry Petrovich had read it three times.

"Thank you," Galina said, looking at the book.

"Galina Panishkoya," he said, "you still don't remember what happened that day in the store on Arbat Street?"

"No," the woman said. She could pull her grandchildren no closer but she tried. "Not clearly."

It was the right answer. The woman had always said she didn't remember getting the gun or firing the shot. There was no doubt that she had done it, but Iosef's friend, the lawyer, said that there was something called "temporary insanity" in the United States and other countries. Galina Panishkoya had ample reason to go insane that day. With the legal system still in post-Soviet chaos and no one knowing what laws to follow, the lawyer was trying to schedule a hearing with a sympathetic chief district judge, one of the new ones who might be willing to blame the Communist system for the woman's temporary madness. The judge who sentenced Galina had been fired in disgrace. The trial had been a typical mockery, with the old woman sitting in a cage in the middle of the small dirty courtroom and being referred to by her own appointed lawyer as "the criminal being tried." Things were different now. A well-timed request for a new trial before an election might be effective. Then, possibly with a *vzyatka*, an unofficial payment for services, including the judge's, a new trial could be scheduled. There was even the possibility, though Iosef's lawyer friend held out only a little hope, that a high enough judge might be willing simply to free the woman on the grounds that she may, in fact, not have fired the shot at all but picked up the weapon in a state of complete confusion. Such a ruling, however, would take a bribe far beyond what Rostnikov and his wife could come up with. Still, the possibility existed.

"Porfiry Petrovich," the woman said meekly, "please thank your wife for taking in my granddaughters."

"It is our pleasure," the detective said. "It has been good to have children in the apartment."

"He lifts weights on bars," said the older girl proudly.

"And he fixes toilets," said the younger one. "And tonight he's going to fix some heating thing for some Jews."

"Jews?" asked Galina. "You are going to work for Jews?"

"Mrs. Rostnikov is Jewish," said the older girl.

"She's Jewish?" asked Galina, looking at the detective. He nodded.

"So many new things have come to me at such an old age," the woman said, shaking her head as a male guard entered the room to indicate that the visit was over.

The woman and the detective both stood slowly, each for a different reason. The girls gave their grandmother hugs and kisses. Then the guard ushered them into the

hall when Rostnikov motioned for him to do so. Rostnikov stood facing the woman who, he had noticed, now
had a full set of teeth. When she had gone into prison,
she had the brown minimum of teeth common in Soviet
citizens. Rostnikov had arranged through a charitable
fund he had once dealt with to have them removed and a
false set fitted.

"You will bring them back?" she said, holding her
hands together in a gesture of near prayer.

"I will," he said.

"Can you, might you, bring your wife so I can thank
her personally?"

"I will try," he said. "Are you giving up hope,
Galina?"

"No," she said with a little smile. "I miss my girls. I
want to be out of here, but I am at peace and the
other women look at me as a grandmother. I am safe. I
don't think about hope. I make dresses. I read. I'm fed. I
remember the good things outside, what few there were."

"You have grown more articulate in prison," said Rostnikov with his own smile.

"I know what 'articulate' means," she said with something of the same pride her granddaughter had shown in
Porfiry Petrovich's artificial leg. "Thank you."

Rostnikov said nothing. He moved past her and
touched her arm as he walked out the door into the
hallway.

The policeman was still in uniform when he got home.
His daughter came rushing to him in her nightshirt, and
he picked her up as his wife moved to the center of the
room with a resigned smile.

The policeman didn't remove his black jacket. He
scooped the giggling child up in his arms and threw her
into the air. Not too high. Not high enough to frighten
her, but enough to make her giggle even more and to
make her yellow curls bounce. She was a little *alionshka*,
a fair-haired beauty.

"She heard you at the door," his wife said. "She came flying out of her bed past me. I don't understand how she could have heard. Maybe she just sensed it."

The policeman nuzzled the child's neck and asked her what she had done that day. It was a mistake. The girl was almost eight and could talk nonstop. Sometimes she made sense.

"She should get to sleep," his wife said.

He nodded and held the little girl in his arms as she spoke. He grinned with love as he moved past his wife, pausing to give her a kiss on the nose. The policeman's wife smiled, but it wasn't a sincere smile. She hoped he didn't notice.

"Hungry?" she called as he took the little girl to the bedroom.

"Starving," he said.

"I have chicken," his wife said.

"Amazing," he said from the small bed in the corner, where he placed his daughter. This had always been the child's bed. When she was an infant, they had pushed the bed against the wall and set up a trio of high-backed chairs on the other side. The head- and footboards of the bed were old but made of sturdy wood. The child, still talking, took her stuffed clown, Petya, into her arms.

The policeman gently touched the child's lips to let her know it was time to stop talking. She yawned as he leaned over to kiss her.

"You will be home when I wake up?" she asked sleepily.

"For a little while," he said. "But don't try to get up early. I won't leave without talking to you."

"You promise me?"

"I promise you," he said.

He left the room, moving around his and his wife's bed, and closed the door. There was enough light from the window to keep the bedroom from being completely dark. Almost directly outside of the second-story apartment was a street lamp.

While his wife prepared his dinner, the policeman walked back to the apartment door and took off his jacket.

"I'm sorry I'm so late," he called as quietly as he could across the small living room into the kitchen area.

The house smelled of chicken and he was hungry.

His wife made a sound but asked nothing. It was as he hung up his jacket that he noticed the blood on the left sleeve. How could he have missed the blood? He had checked in the car mirror and washed himself at the station. Was he growing careless? What would his wife have thought had she seen the blood? Had she seen it? She would think, he concluded, that he was a policeman and it is not unusual for a policeman to be in contact with blood from time to time.

His wife, whose name was Svetlana, was not the kind to ask questions. She had never been a beauty. Too thin. Almost no breasts. But her skin had always been smooth and clean and her eyes a perfect blue. Her hair was cut short. It was blond, a dark blond, but still . . .

The policeman spat on his hand and wiped the spot away with his fingers. Now his jacket was relatively free of blood, but his fingers were a watery red. He moved across the room to the sink behind his wife and washed his hands.

Svetlana was a good wife, a quiet wife. She used to ask about his days, but he had never told her much, and as the years went on, he told her less and she asked less. Instead, at the dinner table they talked of her day, which consisted of taking care of their daughter and trying to edit technical manuscripts at the kitchen table. Svetlana was educated, far more than her husband, though she was careful not to show it. Her editing brought in much-needed extra money. But she didn't talk much about her work. She talked about their daughter and any visitors they had, including his sister. She talked about how she had gotten food for the day. She talked a bit about the news and who was sick and who was well. More and more she talked with her head just a little bit down, not quite looking him in the eyes. He noticed, but he said nothing.

After dinner, if it was not too late, they watched a little television sitting next to each other. They made love infrequently, but when they did, it was gentle and sad and he was careful with her as if she mighty easily bruise or break. There was no passion in their coupling. There had never really been much, but in the beginning it had been better. Now she had no desire.

Tonight it was too late to watch television and he was tired. When they entered the bedroom quietly, they could hear their daughter's even breathing. The room, like the apartment, was just a bit cold. He was a big man and didn't mind the cold. But she was thin and wore a sweater to bed.

He whispered to her that the chicken had been delicious and kissed her on the cheek. Light from the street lamp created shadows in the room. Either one of them could have pulled the curtain, but neither did and neither wanted to. They lay in the bed, eyes closed, pretending to fall instantly asleep.

Tonight he had raped his twelfth woman. She had been tall and he had seen her from the front as he had passed her in the car. She had seemed pretty in the lights of the street and in the headlights of his car. Too much makeup but pretty and no more than forty. Her coat was warm and heavy and she wore red boots. The coat had a hood, which she wore over the back of her head of dark hair.

He had followed her from the Polezhayavskaya metro station. He had almost missed her. He had hoped she wasn't too skinny beneath that coat, that she had big breasts or at least full ones. When the street was clear of traffic, he had turned off his lights and followed her slowly. She did not seem to be aware that the car was behind her. She turned into a small street and he followed, pulling the car to the curb behind her. This street was dark and empty. Had she turned around, he would

have, as he had done before, simply identified himself as
a policeman and suggested that it was late and he should
escort her home, which was exactly what he would have
done unless she had refused his offer. In either case, she
would have been safe.

But he had gotten out of the car quietly, not closing the
door all the way, and quickly followed the woman, who
did not look back. He had attacked her from behind as he
had all the others except the first, the old woman who had
seen him, the old woman he hadn't raped.

Tonight had been a different experience. He had grabbed
the tall woman from behind, hand over her mouth, knife
to her throat. She had not struggled as he pushed her into
a doorway and ordered her to put her hands on the wall
and lean over. He had whispered to her that if she turned
around and looked at him, she would die. If she did as
she was told, she would live.

The woman had not wept and had not struggled. He
had reached under her coat and pulled down her skirt and
ripped off her panties. She did not move. He had his erec-
tion, had it almost before he had spotted the woman.
Now he slipped on the condom and tried to enter her. She
was tight and dry. He had told her to loosen up. She had
not done so or could not. She did not plead. She did
nothing but comply. She did not beg. She did not have
the look of a prostitute, but maybe she was an expensive
one. Yet her apparent indifference angered him, and it
was only with great effort that he began to enter her. He
didn't get far.

He had stepped back in failure and fury and struck the
woman on the side of the head with his fist. She had gone
to the ground huddled in a fetal ball, her panties in the
snow, her hands over her head. Still she didn't whimper
or beg. He went mad and began to hit her with both fists,
kicking her as he buttoned his pants. It was he who made
the noise.

He heard a car. It was a block or so away, but it
seemed to be coming toward them. He left her lying there

after warning her not to move. She remained perfectly motionless and at that instant he thought he may have killed her. The last he had seen of her was her still body and her red boots.

Now, lying in bed next to his wife, he thought it definitely possible that he had murdered the woman. She had made him lose his sanity for perhaps a minute. She had been nothing but a stiff log. His frustration had turned to fury. She might be lying dead in that doorway.

He was not exactly frightened. He was confident that he could continue to control the situation, especially if the woman was not dead. He should have paused to check, but the car had been coming and he had run back to his own vehicle, continuing to button his pants as he hurried.

He had long ago stopped trying to understand what he was doing or why. It simply came to him from time to time that he had to find some woman alone, to attack her, humiliate her. He would feel a surge of power when he entered her and for hours later, remembering her pleas, her weeping, her fear. But tonight had been different. Tonight had been very bad and unsatisfying.

He had placed his holster and handgun on the high shelf near the apartment door. He had placed his watch on the table next to the bed. The dials glowed in the darkness. He lay on his side watching them, watching the second hand, trying to hypnotize himself into sleep.

It took only ten minutes before he was snoring gently.

His wife, however, now that he was asleep, rolled on her back and looked out the window toward the light. She had a vivid imagination, which she kept to herself, and she was a careful observer. She had seen her husband wipe something from his jacket and then immediately move to the sink to wash his hands as he made very small talk about visiting her mother on his next day off.

She got up slowly, quietly, and tiptoed across the room. She listened to his gentle snoring, knowing it was real. Normally she was lulled by the duet of her husband's gentle snore and her child's more subtle breathing, but for months it had been more difficult to hear this music of the night. One instrument was flat.

She opened the door and stepped into the living room, closing the bedroom door almost all the way behind her. There was a window in the living room, too, but the light was not as bright as in the bedroom. She moved in faint shadows to the front door and turned on the small overhead light they seldom used. Then she pulled the sleeve of her husband's jacket into the light and looked at it carefully. The stain was faint where he had attempted to remove it, but he had done so hurriedly. She could see it. She was not sure what it meant. He was a policeman. He had no reason to hide a bloody spot on his sleeve. It was not the first time he had come home with a sign of what he did to earn a living. Once he had a broken hand. Another time, a deep bandaged gash on his forehead. She shivered inside her sweater, turned off the light, and went quietly back to bed.

She slept little that night.

Yevgeny Tutsolov went over all of the mistakes he had made as he sat in the one-room apartment he shared with Leonid Sharvotz. At the moment he was sitting, alone in his underwear, applying compresses to his aching leg where the rabbi had kicked him.

It had been a disaster, a farce.

The towel was cool. He took it off and limped to the small stove in the corner, where he kept the water just below boiling. He dipped the towel in the hot water and wrung some of the water back into the pot. His hands burned, but that would pass quickly. He limped back to his chair and placed the towel on the black-blue-yellow patch above his right knee.

The television was on in front of him. The picture was terrible and the show boring, but Yevgeny liked the sound of other human voices when he was alone. He had no great love for humanity as a whole or for his supposed friends in particular, but he did not like to be alone with his own thoughts.

He had killed six people. Five of them had been Jews. He felt no remorse, not even for Igor Mesanovich. Igor was a fool, not because he wanted to get out of the plot but because he wanted the killing of the Jews to stop. He wanted to find another way. Yevgeny was the smartest of the group, the leader. He had decided early that there was no other way. He knew, in fact, that there were certainly other ways, but he couldn't think of any that made sense, and once he had killed the first two Jews, they really had no choice.

Georgi lived across the way in a building identical to the one Yevgeny and Leonid lived in. They were outside of Moscow in one of the "new" planned apartments near the airport. From the moment the buildings had been completed sometime in the 1950s, they had ceased to be new and had begun crumbling. Shoddy plumbing, heating, insulation, and wiring were more than problems. They were disasters.

Yevgeny was almost thirty. Georgi was almost fifty. He should have been the leader, but he was stupid, *khitry*, clever but stupid. Yevgeny was beginning to think that he himself was, while not stupid, careless. What would it have hurt to take the money from the bodies of the Jews? Yevgeny needed money. His job in the hotel laundry paid barely enough to live on even when combined with what Leonid made working as a perfume salesman in the giant GUM department store. GUM had made a miraculous comeback with the arrival of capitalism, and the perfume shop had done more than respectable sales with both tourists and the nouveau riche, who were mostly into illegal enterprises. Leonid was a good salesman. He was boyish, handsome, and looked like an aristocrat, which, in fact, he was.

Yevgeny hadn't taken the money from the dead Jews and Igor because he and the others had decided the killings had to look like anti-Semitic attacks on members of the growing congregation. Leonid and Georgi had no great fondness for Jews, but neither did they have sufficient animosity to kill or even attack them. They were more concerned about survival. Igor had actually grown to like many of the Jews with whom he had dealt as he passed himself off as one of them.

The most immediate problem, however, was that they had not anticipated the young rabbi's ability not only to defend himself but to attack them when he was cornered. Georgi had suffered a badly broken nose, which had been hastily taped by a nurse Yevgeny had been seeing. The nurse thought they might eventually live together, even consider marrying. Yevgeny had said it was definitely an idea for the near future, when he finished his current business venture. Yevgeny had no plans to marry the woman, who was well built, loaned him money, and was ten years his senior.

After treating the broken nose, the nurse had said that Georgi had almost been killed. If a little more pressure had been put into the blow, broken bone would have penetrated his brain. Yevgeny had said his friend and he had gotten into a fight with some drunken street toughs who had attacked them. The nurse acted as if she accepted the explanation. Yevgeny was handsome, confident, and a pleasure in her bed the infrequent times they wound up there.

Mistakes, problems. Now the Jews would be more determined to stay. They had to be driven out. Perhaps Yevgeny and his friends simply should have murdered the rabbi, but these people were determined. Another rabbi would be sent from Israel, and the next one would probably come with protection.

The wound in his shoulder, which he had treated himself, did not bother Yevgeny, though his arm had been stiff in the morning. The woman at the top of the embankment had been a very poor shot, lucky to even graze his shoulder. But, on the other hand, she might have been lucky enough to kill him.

He was sure that he had hit her with his single shot, but, truth be told, Yevgeny was not a particularly good shot either. This was all new to him. He was a poor laundry worker and a mediocre murderer. His ancestors, he had told Leonid, would have handled this better. His great-great-grandfather and those of Leonid, Georgi, and Igor were trained warriors who had gone to their execution wordlessly, with courage, but that was more than a century ago. With the Revolution, families like theirs had buried their aristocratic heritage and embraced Communism. Some of them even believed in it.

He had to leave for work in an hour. He would do his best to hide the limp he would certainly have. He would give the same excuse to the laundry manager that he had given to his nurse. The manager, a woman, tall, a little older than he with short, straight, dyed blond hair, was always well groomed and handsome if not traditionally pretty. Yevgeny did not quite hate her, but he certainly resented her and her attitude.

If he could get past the problems, and he was determined to do so no matter how many Jews had to be killed, he would no longer need this job. Yevgeny would no longer need Russia.

The idea came to him as a burst of pain shot through his sore leg. A bomb. If murder did not budge these stubborn Jews, the destruction or at least partial destruction of their place of worship would certainly force them to move, at least temporarily. And if a few more Jews died in the process, it wouldn't hinder Yevgeny and his fellows in attaining their goals.

Yevgeny knew nothing of bombs, but Leonid had studied mechanical engineering. He knew something of such things. They would discuss it tonight. Georgi might be able to help get the materials Leonid would need if Leonid had any idea of how to make a bomb.

The Jews might be determined, but so was Yevgeny. The Jews had their congregation and place of worship to protect. Yevgeny was after much higher stakes.

He took off the now cool wet towel and tested his leg. It hurt. It really hurt. What kind of rabbi were they dealing with?

Yevgeny forced himself to dress in the same slacks and heavy wool shirt he had worn the day before. In five minutes, slowed by pain, he was dressed, hair brushed, teeth brushed, black shoes brushed and polished. He knew it would be agony to pull his far-from-new black galoshes on, but he had only one pair of decent shoes, so he went through the agony, after which he stood panting and biting his lower lip for about fifteen seconds before putting on his coat and hat and turning off the television.

He had killed and had discovered that he had no regrets and no remorse, not even over Igor. Yevgeny knew he could kill again, and he now wanted to, not just for the sake of the plan but to see the rabbi dead. He wanted the confident Jew standing in front of him, knowing he was going to die, and Yevgeny wanted to pull the trigger and watch the man fall.

Yevgeny turned off the television and went to work.

Alexi Monochov had been standing across the street under the marquee of the Rossia Cinema when the two men came out of the Pushkin Square metro station. Alexi had been waiting for them. There was no doubt that they were policemen. They had the air of confidence and determination that such people had even when unwarranted. He could not get a close look, and even with his glasses, he was not able to tell much about them other than one was tall, thin, and dressed in black and the other was younger and stocky, not stocky like Alexi but a solid stocky. Still, Alexi was some distance away, and there was some frost on his glasses, so he may have been imagining things, but he had not imagined that Rostnikov now knew too much and that it was no longer safe to remain at home. Thus, he had prepared the note for the police and had carefully packed his briefcase, which he held in his gloved right hand as he crossed Pushkin Street to get a better look at the two men who entered his apartment building.

Alexi had gotten out of the apartment with only about fifteen minutes to spare. He hadn't really expected them to come so soon, but fortunately he had taken no chances.

Alexi had adjusted his glasses, plunged one hand in his pocket, firmly grasped the briefcase in his other hand, and looked up at the apartment, guessing when his mother would open the door, when the policemen would discover his workshop, when they would be picking up the note. Would they come running out of the building? Would they make a call or two and then begin a useless search? He didn't guess. He waited.

For the last few days the ache in his groin had turned to real pain, not searing, screaming pain, but pain. The pain, he had been told, would grow worse. He knew what could be done to slow the process, but a cure or a remission was out of the question. Alexi was dying as his father had died, but he would not go in quiet darkness as his father had.

The policemen were inside for less than fifteen minutes. When they came out, a plastic bag in the hand of the younger, stocky one, they did not hurry. The tall, gaunt one set the pace, steady, serious. Alexi began to walk in their direction on his side of the street. He bumped into an old woman whose head was down against the wind. He did not bother to apologize. His head was down, too, but he was watching the two men and for an instant could see their faces.

The taller man was as pale as the snow, as white as his clothes were dark. The stocky young man held the clear plastic bag firmly as they moved toward the corner.

He watched the two men go down into the metro and then Alexi wandered. He could have gone to the small hotel room he had rented two days earlier, but he preferred the cold air that numbed his body, forcing him from feeling to thought.

Problems could arise. The material in his briefcase was

volatile, powerful, and of only acceptable quality, though Alexi had carefully prepared the device.

He still had time to make his call, plenty of time. He stopped at a phone and was informed that Rostnikov was not in, but that he could speak to an inspector in the Office of Special Investigation. The woman who answered next identified herself as Inspector Timofeyeva and said Rostnikov might not be back that day but was expected the following day. Alexi asked if he could make an appointment. The woman asked if she could help him.

Alexi declined to tell her what it was about but did say that he had information on the bomber and that he was a State Security agent. "My superiors think that if Chief Inspector Rostnikov and I share our information on the bomber, we may prevent more injury to civilians."

"Your name?" said Elena. "Perhaps I could take the information."

"My name is Leo Horv," said Alexi soberly. "I must get my information directly to Inspector Rostnikov—and only to him—as soon as possible. The fewer people who know about this, the better. There is a chance that the bomber may be getting information directly from State Security. There is also a chance that we are dealing not with an individual but with a conspiracy. If you or Inspector Rostnikov would like, I can have my superior call him back to confirm our desire to cooperate."

"I suggest you call in the morning," Elena said, holding back a yawn. "I'll leave a message that you will be calling."

"Thank you," Alexi said, and hung up.

It had been easier than he had expected. The woman had asked few questions and seemed to have something else on her mind. The real question was whether Rostnikov would accept his story, be tempted by possible evidence from State Security and the chance of conspiracy.

Thousands, maybe tens of thousands, including Alexi Monochov, were dying, carelessly murdered, and the police could be tempted by the opportunity to catch the killers of a worthless businessman.

The briefcase in his hand was light, much lighter than one might imagine, considering it contained enough explosives to destroy at least a huge government building or a block of small houses. The case also contained a razor, a change of socks and underwear, and a notebook on which he intended to go over his plan through most of the night, making sure he anticipated all likely problems and as many unlikely ones as possible.

Alexi doubted he would eat. His appetite had begun leaving him months earlier, and now he felt hardly any need for food. He had lost weight, but not nearly as much as he had expected and nowhere near as much as his father had lost before he died.

Alexi walked through snow and cold trying to focus only on what he planned to do, trying to avoid thinking about his mother and his sister. The note would explain. What had happened to his father would explain.

He did not regret what he was about to do. Many would say that innocent people had died, but Alexi knew that there were no innocent people where he was going in the morning. There were only those who chose to ignore the horrible reality.

Alexi had no illusions. He had told Rostnikov. He would not change the determination of the people of the world to destroy themselves. But what he could do, perhaps, was make a statement, a statement so big that it could not be ignored, a statement that would ignite debate and perhaps, just perhaps, cause people to think about what they were doing.

At worst, his action would be a gesture of anger so great that it simply could not be ignored. For days it would be discussed around the world. At best, it would inspire others to action.

There was absolutely no way the world could ignore the total destruction of Petrovka, the central headquarters of the Moscow police.

EIGHT

MARIA INSPENSKAYA INSPECTED THE CARD IN HER hand and looked over at the man whose photograph appeared in the corner. She double-checked the data, though she knew she had made no mistakes, and placed the card in the laminating machine in the corner of the small garage.

It was cold in the garage, but Alexi didn't care. He watched Maria, in her extrathick wool sweater, move from the photo machine, where she had taken his picture, to the printing machine and computer, and now, finally, to the laminating machine.

The entire process would take about an hour. Alexi didn't mind. He didn't mind the cold either, and had refused Maria Inspenskaya's offer of tea, which she drank from a mug printed with blue letters in English. Alexi's English was barely passable, but he knew the words on the mug were THE GRATEFUL DEAD.

Maria made strange humming sounds as she worked. She was short, probably in her fifties. Her relucent hair was brushed straight back and tied in a rubber band. Her glasses were the thickest Alexi had ever seen.

Maria was well known among criminals and businessmen who needed expert false identification. She did not advertise and she kept no samples in her garage. Were she to be caught by the police, she would claim that her only job was to make photo identification cards for pets. She had samples of those and photographs of dogs, cats,

139

and birds tacked to the walls. In truth, Maria disliked all animals. It wasn't just her allergies. They consumed food humans could use. They befouled the streets. They were coddled by their owners. Maria had received nothing in her life that might reasonably be called coddling.

Alexi had heard of her while eavesdropping on a conversation on Gorky Street. One man had been telling another that he could get a proper ID from a woman named Maria. He had given the other man Maria's number, and Alexi had remembered it and written it down. That had been more than a year ago, before Alexi had made his plans. He had simply stored the information, as he had so much other data gathered in likely and unlikely places.

At first the woman had been wary, fearing that Alexi's call might be a police trap, but finally during their phone conversation, Maria had agreed to meet Alexi at a stand-up snack bar not far from the garage.

He didn't look like a policeman. Alexi was short, balding, sober, and willing to pay in American dollars far above the already high asking price. His willingness to pay so much for a card had worried Maria a bit, as did the kind of card he wanted, but she was convinced that she was dealing with a depressed, determined individual who was not an informer or a policeman.

Alexi was well dressed, well spoken, polite. He had given her five hundred-dollar bills in advance.

When they had reached the garage, Maria had turned on the lights and gone to a desk. She pulled out a deep drawer. Inside the drawer was a bag that could be dropped into the sewer through a hole in the wooden floor if danger threatened. She had forgotten the bag the day before—a mistake she vowed not to make again. Her mind had been on a knight's gambit she had witnessed earlier.

"I know I've got at least three," she had said as she rummaged and Alexi stood waiting, briefcase in hand.

At last she had come up with what she was looking for. She took Alexi's photo, a bright light in his face as he sat on a metal bench. She told him not to smile.

Now she was putting the finishing touches on the card, trimming the plastic lamination.

Maria handed the card to Alexi, who examined it carefully and handed Maria an additional two hundred dollars, which she stuffed into the pocket of her pants. She had to lift several layers of sweater to reach the pocket.

She had no idea what the punishment would be if she were ever caught, particularly if she were caught making a card like this one. Chances were good that with former clients acting as intermediaries she would be able to bribe her way out of conviction and punishment, but you could never tell. She had, however, been unable to resist' all that American cash.

Maria was accustomed to dealing with odd, nervous, cold, and ranting men. There was no type she hadn't seen. Few of her clients were women, but the women tended to be quiet and look determined and guilty.

The man who had just given her seven hundred dollars for less than an hour of work was one of the oddest she'd seen. She had learned her craft working as a preparer of identification cards for railway employees. When her ulcers had caused her to lose too many hours, Maria had been dismissed. It had proved the luckiest thing in her bleak life. The first false identification card had not been her idea but that of a former railway worker with whom she had become friends of a sort. He needed identification for his brother to get a job with a new American business opening a branch in Moscow. Maria had done a more than adequate but makeshift job without the proper equipment, but now she had cash hidden away and a well-equipped garage. She could afford a good private doctor to treat her ulcer, and she had a warm room and enough money to indulge in her passion, chess, which she played at her neighborhood club every day, sometimes for many hours as she and the others sipped hot tea and contemplated their moves.

Maria's prize possession was a trophy for a tournament victory, a team victory. The tournament had been held in Tbilisi in 1987.

While she had been preparing the identification card for the man with little hair, she had the uneasy feeling that he was insane. She had dealt with people who seemed insane, but this one was different. Fleetingly she thought that he might be considering killing her when he had what he wanted. But seven hundred American dollars had quieted her fear, that and the small pistol in her pocket. When she had taken his money and handed him the card, Maria kept her hand in her pocket, grasping the gun.

But the man had done nothing. He had said nothing. He pocketed the card, shifted the weight of his briefcase, and left the garage.

When she was sure the man was gone, she turned off her machines, closed her bag of identification cards, zipped it, and hurried out, turning off the lights and locking the door behind her. If she hurried, there was a chance she could witness at least part of the game between Ivan Ivanovich Presoka and whoever might have the privilege of playing against him. The ancient Presoka played only in the mornings. He was not well enough to do more. But he was still brilliant. His hands might have a bit of a tremor, but his mind was as keen as when he had been a ten-year-old boy wonder.

Maria didn't give another thought to the man for whom she had just made a State Security Agency identification.

The pile of neat dark green files was manageable, fifteen in all. It included all the information on each of the women attacked by the serial rapist. It also included several other files that were not connected to the case but, according to the computer, had sufficient similarities to be examined. They sat in Sasha's cubicle, he on one side of the small desk, she on the other. Each took one pile. They were both tired, but for vastly different reasons. Both had been at the former church where the makeshift Jewish temple now existed. Both, along with Iosef, Zelach, Belinsky, and a few members of his congregation, had, under the direction of Porfiry Petrovich, spent five hours the night before installing a heating system. Rostnikov, who had read a book on the subject, did much of the heavier lifting. The book was badly out-of-date, but so was the system they installed.

It had gone smoothly, and the skill of Iosef and Belinsky with tools borrowed by Rostnikov had been a key to their success. When they were finished, Rostnikov had told them that Belinsky should expect some problems, but they could be remedied. He suggested that the rabbi find some place to store the leftover sheets and scraps of metal and the various screws and joints in case they were needed later.

It was late, and in spite of the heavy labor, they were cold when they were finished. The system was now being turned on. It didn't look too bad, and Belinsky was already working on ways to cover and decorate the exposed metal tunnel that ran around the room.

Iosef asked Elena if he could take her home so they could talk on the way. She agreed and they were the first to leave. They went to Iosef's small apartment, which he shared with an actor who was touring with a new play. Elena had called her aunt, who sounded fully awake, and said she had no idea yet when she would be home. There had been something in Elena's voice that she knew her aunt, the former procurator, would pick up. Then there had been tea. There had been talk. There had been kisses and then the cool sheet of Iosef's narrow bed.

The fact that he had condoms in the drawer of the little table next to the bed could have meant many things. Elena was a policewoman. She couldn't help considering (*a*) there were many young women who had been in this bed, (b) he had been confident that Elena would be there and had prepared, or (c) Iosef was, in general, simply prepared and properly cautious.

She stayed the night, and it was he who talked of marriage as he gently rubbed her nipples in the dim light he had left on when they undressed and went to bed. Elena wasn't sure. They made love twice. First, when they went to bed. Second, when they awakened early in the morning. Both times were wonderful for Elena, but she couldn't tell what they meant, though he proposed again.

She wanted time to think about it. They had not known each other long, and they had shared few talks like this. She knew that the first night they met Iosef had told his mother he planned to marry Elena.

She slept little and had no time to change her clothes before meeting Sasha at Petrovka.

Sasha had experienced as little sleep as his partner but for quite a different reason. After they had finished the duct work at the temple, Sasha had lingered, wanting to talk, not wanting to go home, but everyone had left quickly. They were tired. It was late.

When he got home, Maya greeted him with a screaming baby in her arms. He looked around for his mother. She wasn't there. Pulcharia was probably in the next room asleep, but Maya was desperately trying to soothe the crying baby. Maya looked exhausted. There was darkness under her beautiful eyes, and strands of hair had escaped the brush.

"He has a temperature," she said. "He is hot."

Sasha, still in his coat, reached over to the crying baby in his wife's arms and touched his forehead. Very hot.

"He is coughing," Maya said. "I couldn't wake Pulcharia and take him to the doctor. I didn't know how to reach you, and I couldn't take your mother coming over, though I would have called her if you hadn't come soon."

Beneath the tone of concern for the child there was a hint of the anger he would have to face when the baby had been taken care of, anger at his being off somewhere helping Rostnikov on some church repairs.

Still wearing his coat, Sasha went to the address book on the table near the phone. It was very late, but the baby was very sick. He called. The doctor was home and sounded quite awake.

He was not a pediatrician, but he was Sarah Rostnikov's cousin Leon. He was the one to whom Porfiry Petrovich's people turned when they needed medical care, and he had given what he could, protecting them from the horrors of Moscow hospital care.

The conversation was brief. They were to meet at a nearby hospital with which Sarah's cousin was affiliated. He would be there in half an hour.

One of them had to stay with Pulcharia. One of them had to take the baby. They both knew which one. Maya continued to try to soothe the child as she dressed him warmly while Sasha went back to the street in hope of finding a cab. It took him ten minutes, and he had to show his badge through the closed window when a cab finally stopped.

The cab driver rolled down the window, and Sasha explained his situation. The cab driver was a Lithuanian who had come to Moscow as an engineer and stayed as a cab driver. The pay was better if one included the tips, particularly from foreigners in search of food, drink, gambling, and companionship. Even after the payoff to the mafia that protected him, Max made a far better living than he had as an engineer. There were too many people now claiming to be engineers and no one to hire them. Max had been on his way to the Hotel Russia when Sasha stopped him. Taking the woman and child to the hospital and waiting for them would cost him.

It would also cost Sasha far more than he could afford, but he didn't consider that. He got in the cab and guided it to his building, where he told Max to wait for Maya and the baby.

Maya was packed and ready. The baby was still crying and coughing.

"The cab is downstairs," he said. "He'll wait for you at the hospital. Please call me if anything . . ."

He hurried to the bedroom, made his way in darkness to the dresser, pulled out the cash they had been saving, and brought it to Maya, who handed him the baby while she tucked away the money. He kissed the baby and his wife. She turned her cheek to him and left.

He sat for ten minutes before taking off his coat and hanging it up and then he sat again. There would be nothing on television at this hour. He had a newspaper but he had read it during the day. He couldn't concentrate on a book. There was some cold coffee left. He heated it and drank a cup while he sat at the wooden table worrying, weary and feeling more than just a bit sorry for himself.

Maya did not call. She simply showed up back at the apartment three hours later, baby asleep in her embrace. Sasha had fallen into a restless sleep at the table with his head on his arms.

He looked up for answers, waiting for her to gently put the baby in bed.

"A virus," she said. "Not diphtheria."

There was a vast outbreak of diphtheria in Russia, and not only diphtheria. In Moscow alone more than a dozen people had died the year before of dysentery, an illness that could be easily cured. Measles was becoming a common occurrence.

"I have medicine. They gave him an injection. We'll keep him cool. Give him medicine. The doctor will call in the morning. If he is worse, we'll have to take him to a private hospital."

There was no way they could afford a private hospital.

Sasha moved to take Maya in his arms. She didn't stop him but neither did she respond. He expected her to cry but she was silent.

"I waited for you," she said evenly. "Hours."

"I told you," he whispered, kissing the top of her heard. "Porfiry Petrovich asked for volunteers to put a heating system into a church."

Sasha didn't add that it was a Jewish "church." He might tell her that later.

"Telephone," she said. "You should have called. You should check on your family. I should know exactly where you are. You were needed. You didn't want to come home."

Since she was absolutely right, Sasha protested vigorously and sincerely. He apologized, explained, took the blame and responsibility, and promised this had been a lesson to him.

"Your mother called," Maya went on. "I told her everything was fine. I couldn't handle her and the children."

"I understand," said Sasha sincerely.

They opened the bed in the living room, leaving a small light on as they lay down and listened to the baby's labored breathing.

They had two hours of semirest. Pulcharia roused them early asking for breakfast. Wearily they got up. The baby still slept. Maya felt his forehead.

"Cooler," she said, "much cooler."

Sasha smiled and Maya smiled back.

Maya had an appointment with Sarah Rostnikov's cousin Leon for later that morning. Her plan was to take both the baby and Pulcharia with her. Maya called her office as soon as it was open and explained the situation. The secretary said that she understood and that Maya should, if possible, call back to let her know how the baby was doing. Unfortunately the new boss was not as understanding. He was a widower in his sixties who had never had any children. But he did have a roving eye and hands. More than once he had made overtures to Maya: a touch, coming too close behind her, a whispered comment whose intent was clear. Maya had managed to avoid all of this. Sasha knew nothing about it. Now her boss would have a small weapon to use against her.

Maya decided to worry about that later. In the United States, she knew, there were laws about sexual harassment at work, but there was nothing like that in Russia. It was considered part of the business world and had been for centuries. Now there were even embarrassing shows in which young women seeking office jobs would get made up, put on revealing dresses, and perform onstage, singing songs, smiling, parading for men who might hire them as receptionists or even as computer technicians.

Now Sasha blinked and sipped his coffee to stay awake while he and Elena sat before the files, reluctant to begin.

Elena had gone through two files and Sasha one when Pankov called to inform them that there appeared to have been another attack the night before in District 37. He gave Elena, who had answered the phone, the number of the woman who had been attacked. He also made it clear that he had informed Inspector Rostnikov. Director Yakovlev, according to Pankov, was concerned that the story was about to get out to the media in general.

"And," said Pankov nervously, "he would appreciate your putting in as much time and effort as necessary to bring this case to a satisfactory conclusion as quickly as possible."

Pankov gave Elena the name and telephone number of the latest victim, Magda Stern. The name touched something in Elena's memory.

"Magda Stern," Pankov said, "is a reporter for Moscow Television News."

Pankov hung up. Elena relayed the information to Sasha, who wearily reached for the next file with one hand and his cup of terrible, tepid coffee with the other.

"You or me?" he asked.

She understood and dialed the number Pankov had given her for Magda Stern. There was no answer. Elena hung up and found Moscow Television News in the phone directory. She made the call, identified herself, and asked for Magda Stern. She was put through almost immediately.

"I'm calling about the incident last night," said Elena carefully while Sasha paused to listen. Elena identified herself as an inspector in the Office of Special Investigation.

"The attempted rape," Magda Stern said.

"Yes," said Elena. "We know you reported the incident and were interviewed by the police last night. We will have the report in the next few minutes. We take this very seriously and would like to talk to you. We would like to meet you at the station today."

"No," said Magda Stern firmly. "I will come to you. I would prefer, if at all possible, that people here know nothing about the incident."

Elena immediately agreed, and the reporter said she would be on her way to Petrovka within half an hour.

Elena called both the guard station and the uniformed officer at the check-in desk in the lobby to ask that they admit Magda Stern and let her or Sasha know when she arrived.

And then back to the stacks.

When they were finished with their first run-through—they planned to switch files with each other and go through them again—the phone rang and Magda Stern's arrival was announced. Elena asked if one of the National Police meeting rooms was available. The man in the lobby said he didn't know; the room log was somewhere upstairs at the moment. So they would conduct the interview in their cubbyhole office. Fortunately Karpo, Iosef, and Zelach were all out, ensuring some degree of privacy.

The two inspectors gathered the green file folders and put them neatly into the empty bottom drawer of Sasha's desk. Then they went downstairs. The lobby was crowded this morning. People, about two-thirds of them in uniform, moved about in clusters, talking softly as they passed the trio of watchful armed officers.

Magda Stern was easy to spot. She was taller than most of the men. And she was striking. Were she a bit younger, Elena thought, she might have a career as a model somewhere in Western Europe or even the United States. But there was a determined look on the woman's face that told Elena she was probably not model material. It wasn't just what had happened to her last night. The look was something Elena was sure had been with the woman for some time. She herself had a bit of it, and her aunt, before her illness, had had it, too.

The two detectives greeted the woman, who was wearing a green suit under her tan leather coat. Her hair was short, dark, nothing out of place. And she wore tinted glasses. She shook the detectives' hands firmly and followed them up the stairs.

"The elevators are not particularly trustworthy," Sasha explained.

Magda Stern did not respond. Elena noticed that the woman was wearing stylish red boots, probably from the Czech Republic or the West.

When they entered Sasha's cubicle, he offered the woman coffee or tea. She refused with a gesture. They sat on the three chairs in the tiny space. Sasha moved his chair around to sit next to Elena and avoid the impression that he was in charge. In some situations the image of command might be valuable. In this case, without a word, Elena and Sasha knew that Elena should lead the way.

The woman did not take off her coat.

"You wouldn't be talking to me and I wouldn't be here if I were an individual case," Magda Stern said. "We're talking about a man who has attacked other women."

"Yes," said Elena. She could now see that heavy makeup covered most of the bruises on the woman's face, and the tinted glasses probably covered more. Only a red bump on her forehead refused to be hidden. "You've been seen by a doctor?"

"Do you have the report on my attack?" she replied.

"Not yet," said Sasha.

"It indicates my injuries, but it does not contain the

essential information," Magda Stern said, sitting with her back straight, her long legs planted firmly on the floor.

"Essential information?" asked Elena.

"My injuries," the woman said, "are accurately documented in the report. Concussion, bruises, one rib cracked. It is tightly taped. I have been feeling a mild to intense dizziness since the attack and will see a physician in whom I have some trust later today."

Sasha was amazed, but he hid his amazement. The woman looked fine except for the bruise.

"I do not intend to give my attacker, should he see me, the satisfaction of knowing the extent of my injuries. I do not intend to have any of my coworkers find out what happened. Both of these considerations, however, I will forgo if it helps to catch the *bastard*."

She had used the English word. The Russian language has a wide variety of insults, many of them quite colorful, but the recent style was to pick up insults from the French and Americans. It suggested that the person being insulted did not deserve the Russian language.

"You withheld essential information in your report to the police last night?" said Elena.

"Yes," Magda answered, her voice even.

"Why?" asked Elena.

"Because the person who attacked me was a policeman," she said. "And I did not trust the two uniformed men who questioned me at the hospital emergency room. Neither was the one who attacked me, but the report might be seen by him, and the danger to me would be very great."

"But you'll tell us?" asked Elena.

"Someone must be told and you are not part of the regular National Police or the district police. I am well aware of the reputation and success of your office. Your director, Colonel Snitkonoy . . ."

"He's a general now," said Sasha. "And he is in charge of security at the Hermitage in Saint Petersburg."

Elena gave Sasha a look of gentle reproof. Had he not

been so weary, he would never have said what he had, but it was too late, and perhaps it would give the newswoman some confidence in their openness.

"And who has replaced him?" Magda asked.

"You'll have to call the office directly for that information," said Elena.

Magda nodded.

Sasha wanted to hurry the woman. He was tired. He was on the verge of his old irritability. He knew his usual charm would be of no use on Magda Stern.

"The man who attacked you was a police officer?" asked Elena to return to the subject.

"I recognized the uniform, the shoes," Magda Stern said. "And once, as he hit me, I rolled into the doorway onto a small bank of snow and got a glance at his face. I'm confident he was unaware that I saw him. I think if he knew, he would have killed me. I covered up as best I could and refused to be intimidated. He tried to rape me but I tightened up. You understand?"

Elena nodded. She understood.

"He grew angry and hit me some more, but he never fully penetrated," Magda said. "He was frightened away by a car coming down the street. I kept my face down, but I turned just enough to see him get into a police car and drive away."

Elena and Sasha looked at each other.

"Anything else?"

"He dropped his condom. I pointed it out to the police when they came. I called from my apartment. A car came quickly and took me to the hospital."

"You can describe your attacker?" asked Elena.

"I can describe him. I would definitely recognize him."

The next step was clear. There was no need for the two detectives to even discuss it. They would bring their information to Rostnikov and ask him to arrange a gathering of every uniformed officer in the Trotsky Station district, which covered the area where Magda lived. If that failed to yield the attacker, they would go through every one of the more than one hundred districts and every officer assigned to Petrovka itself.

They explained their plan to Magda Stern, who immediately agreed. She asked only that the two officers be efficient and take as little of her time as possible. However, whatever time it took, she would devote to catching the man who had attacked her.

They would also try to convince Ludmilla Henshaka-yova, the old woman who had fought off the would-be rapist almost a decade ago. There was a chance that if Magda identified him, the old woman might confirm the identification, even though it had been many years since the night she had seen him.

The call came within half an hour not from Rostnikov but from Director Yakovlev. Rostnikov had suggested that it come from the highest authority. As little as Yakovlev liked doing things that might someday have political repercussions, he agreed with Rostnikov and made the call to District 37, Trotsky Station.

Lieutenant Valentin Spaskov, with whom Elena and Sasha had met the day before, took the call from Director Yakovlev and assured him he would see to it that all uniformed officers under his command would be present at noon. He would pass this on to Major Lenonov, his immediate superior and the head of the district station. Off-duty officers would be called in.

Igor Yakovlev thanked the lieutenant and hung up.

The director of the Office of Special Investigation had not told Spaskov the reason for the gathering, but there was only one conclusion Spaskov could draw. The woman he had attacked the night before had seen him and was willing to identify him. Lieutenant Valentin Spaskov was determined that such an identification would not be made. He would set up the meeting, but he would not be present, nor would the major. Valentin, second in command of the station, a twenty-year veteran, would be occupied at the Ministry of the Interior. He and the major were certainly above suspicion.

When he hung up the phone, Spaskov ordered his hands not to shake, ordered his brow and the pits of his arms not to sweat. They refused to obey, so he sat in his small office waiting for the tremor to stop as he thought.

He could be identified. It was possible the two young inspectors could even find sufficient evidence, by going back through the files, that someone had altered the information on each attack and that the alteration had begun at Trotsky Station. He had been careful, but he and the major, along with the three officers who did most of the paperwork, would be the most likely suspects.

Valentin knew that if he escaped identification this time he should stop the attacks. Eventually he would make another mistake. He would have to stop. He thought of his wife and of his daughter, and he told himself again that he had to stop.

But a wordless voice that communicated to him with only impulses and vague feelings told Valentin that he could not stop, that if they did not catch him this time he would wait a week, possibly a month, and then the compulsion would once again be too great. It would swell within him, driving him half mad, though only his victims would know that. He would have to attack again and again. The only difference was that now he knew that he would have to kill any future victims, and he would have to find and kill the woman he had attacked the night before so that she could not identify him.

Getting her identity from the two inspectors, Tkach and Timofeyeva, would not be difficult, and finding her would not be difficult. There wold be no point in trying to make it look like an accident. It would come too close after her visit to the police with the information that she could identify him.

He would have to protect himself and his family.

Valentin had killed before. Not any of his rape victims—he had not wanted them to die. He had not even wanted them to suffer, but the need had been there so long and it had grown within him.

He had killed at least two members of a local gang of teens and young men in their twenties. It had happened during a raid. The gang had been responsible for extortion and murder. The major had sent an armed squad in bulletproof vests with automatic weapons to bring the gang in for questioning. He had also made it clear to Valentin in private that he was certain the gang would resist arrest. Valentin had understood and he had conveyed to his squad of six that resistance was to be expected and that if he began firing, they should do the same.

In fact, when the squad had gone through the door, one of the gang, a scrawny mad-looking kid with an orange mohawk, had reached for a gun in his pocket. Nine members of the gang had died in the spray of bullets that followed. The youngest was fourteen. The oldest was twenty-three, the leader. Four of the gang had not been in the room, but afterward, when they heard what had happened, they disappeared, knowing that the police had marked them for death.

The only other time he had killed had been when he was on patrol a dozen years earlier. He and his partner spotted a man being beaten. They had stopped their car, pulled their weapons, and ordered the man doing the beating to stop. He paid no attention. The victim was old. The man doing the beating was no more than forty and huge.

The policemen repeated their order for him to stop. He continued the beating and both officers were sure that he would soon kill the old man. Valentin had hit the big brute in the head with his pistol. The man turned in pain and anger and hit Valentin with his fist. Valentin had gone down shooting. He fired all the bullets in his gun, and the huge man fell dead against his whimpering victim, who turned out to be his father.

Valentin still carried a scar on his upper lip from the dead man's blow. It was shortly after this that he had made his first attack. The victim was an old woman who had seen his face and would certainly remember his scar. He had grown a mustache to cover the scar and managed to resist attacking another woman for almost four years. When he did resume, he made sure that his victims didn't see him.

Now killing would be necessary, and it would start with the woman last night, the woman whose name, he would soon learn, was Magda Stern. Before he even arranged the gathering of his officers, he knew where she worked and where she lived.

He called in Sergeant Koffeyanovich and told him that there would be some people coming and that all officers should be gathered in the meeting room. They should come whether or not they were ill or off duty. Those who did not show up, if any, should have their names and addresses turned over to the inspectors who would be arriving soon. Meanwhile the sergeant should give the lieutenant's apology that he and the major were not available to help them, since both he and Major Lenonov were at an important meeting at the Ministry of the Interior.

The sergeant, a veteran near retirement, simply said *da* and left the office. Spaskov called a friend in the Ministry of the Interior and requested a few minutes of his time for some advice. The flattered friend immediately agreed. Spaskov had more than enough cases in the district about which he could ask advice.

As he put on his coat to leave, Spaskov debated how and where he would kill the woman. He decided it would be with a knife on the street as quickly and quietly as possible. He would wear gloves, take her purse, remove her money, and drop the purse in the street no more than a block from the stabbing.

Perhaps it would be taken for coincidence, but probably not.

A number of journalists who had attacked mafias, corrupt officials, and politicians of the right had, over the past year, been threatened, terrorized in their homes. One popular television journalist had even been shot down.

Perhaps the investigating officer, who if Spaskov had his way, would be him, would accept the crime as a chance robbery or a politically motivated assault.

At this point, Spaskov had no choice.

The couple, probably in their late fifties, sat straight-backed next to each other as if they were about to have their photograph taken. The man was tall, lean, and clean-shaven, with dark thick gray-flecked hair. He wore a spotless pair of dark trousers, a blue shirt, and a dark pullover sweater. The woman at his side had hair cut short and growing gray much faster than that of her husband. She was less thin than he and bore an air of confident superiority.

Rostnikov and Zelach sat across from them drinking tea. The apartment looked like something preserved from a previous century, from the well-polished old furniture and sparkling tea service to the chairs that would have seemed at home in an aristocrat's parlor. Iosef had seen such things in history books that illustrated the decadence of a previous age. And the walls. On one wall was a framed double-eagle-head flag from the czarist era. Next to it was a portrait of a man in uniform, his dark hair parted in the middle, his mustache finely groomed. A white sash ran across the man's chest and he wore three medals. His look was one of determination, not unlike that of the man who sat before the two detectives.

Zelach did his best not to be intimidated by this proud couple who looked at him with critical eyes. He almost managed to give the appearance of confidence.

Rostnikov, on the other hand, noted the frayed quality of the man's trousers, the patched corners of the pillows on the sofa, and the very slightly odd angle of the tea table leg that looked as if it had been repaired one time too many, and said, "Remarkable." He moved awkwardly, his new leg only partially cooperative. "Who is the man in the painting?"

They were in the apartment of Anya and Ivan Mesanovich. It was their son who had been shot with the three Jews on the embankment.

"That," said Ivan with pride, "is my great-great-grandfather, Pavel Pestel."

"Captain Pavel Pestel," his wife corrected. "A cavalry officer who also served, for a brief time, as a member of the czarina's guard."

"Your name is not Pestel," Rostnikov said conversationally, turning from the portrait to look at the couple.

"There was an incident," the man said. "My grandfather was impelled by circumstances to change his name and move to Moscow."

Rostnikov said nothing more on the topic. He turned to the subject of his visit, the couple's dead son. As he did so, he noted that Zelach had finished his tea and was awkwardly balancing the empty cup and saucer on his broad knee.

"When did your son tell you he was interested in becoming a Jew?" asked Rostnikov, knowing the question would be likely to elicit some emotional reaction.

"He was not interested in becoming a Jew," said the woman firmly. "Through two generations, in spite of the Communist doctrine of atheism, my husband's family and my own have never deserted our religion nor our belief in and hope for the return of the monarchy. We want a country ruled by those bred to rule rather than louts who claim to be working for the people but are actually mad with their own power."

"We are not fools, Inspector," the man said. "My father was a precision machinist and a member of the Communist Party. I was a machinist and a Party member. My son was the best machinist of us all, but our dreams fascinated him."

"Hypnotized him," Anya corrected.

"The past," said Rostnikov.

"Our heritage," said Ivan. "We have our heritage. For my wife and me it is a symbol of our . . ."

"Superiority?" said Rostnikov.

"Yes," said the man, meeting Rostnikov's eyes.

"So you don't know why he spent so much time with the Jews, even went to services?"

"No," said Ivan.

Anya nodded in agreement.

"Since I never had the opportunity to meet your son," said Rostnikov, "you must tell me: Is it at all possible that he would join the Jews to gain information about them for some organization to which he belonged?"

"Igor belonged to no organization," said the woman. "He had a few friends, recent friends, but he didn't believe in organizations."

"Did he talk about the Jews?" Rostnikov asked, finishing his tea and handing the cup and saucer to the woman. He nodded at Zelach to do the same.

"We didn't know what he was doing," said the man.

"He did say once," the woman recalled, "that he thought the Jews, who had been supposedly chosen by their God, had the longest history of suffering of any people on earth. The comment came, as I recall, when my husband commented on a news report about Israel. I argued with some vigor that the Russian people had suffered as much as the Jews."

"You had this conversation recently?" asked Rostnikov.

"A few days before he was murdered," said Ivan, head up. "We want the murderer caught. If the state does not execute him when he is caught, I will execute him. If the state does not find him, I will find him."

Rostnikov believed him, at least believed that the proud man would try to see that a life was taken for the life of his son.

"Igor was our only child," the woman said, touching her husband's arm lightly.

"Can you tell us about his friends? Names? Addresses?" asked Rostnikov, notebook out. "Perhaps they can help."

The woman gave them two names, Yevgeny Tutsolov and Leonid Sharvotz. She didn't know where they lived, but she had the impression that they lived together. She also remembered that Igor had said that his friends' families had originally come from Saint Petersburg, as had theirs.

"We never saw his friends," said the man. "My wife and I suggested that he invite them here. He never brought them. I'm surprised my wife remembered their names. I am not good with names and numbers. But I remember faces."

He looked up at the portrait of his great-great-grandfather and then back at Porfiry Petrovich.

"May we see his room?" asked Rostnikov.

It was a polite question to grieving parents. In fact, Rostnikov needed no authority other than his own to search the house.

"Yes," said Ivan Mesanovich, pointing to a door over his right shoulder.

"Please," said the woman. "Do not change anything. We want to keep it as it is for a while."

Rostnikov nodded. He had the sense that it would be a long time before the woman would bring herself to change the room. This was a family that worshiped the shrine of a lost aristocracy. They would worship both the memory and the room of their dead son, keep it neat, clean, a memorial. He had seen such things before.

Zelach followed Porfiry Petrovich, who limped into the dead man's room. It was small. It was neat. There was a chest of drawers, a small closet, and a neatly made-up bed with two pillows. The pillowcases were completely unwrinkled. Above the head of the bed hung a framed photograph. Rostnikov recognized the building in the photograph. Zelach thought it familiar.

"The Hermitage," Anya Mesanovich said from the doorway.

"Has it been up long?" asked Rostnikov.

"Less than a year," she said. "Before that there was a large poster of a woman in a bathing suit. He said her name was Demi Moore. She was an American actress. He knew we didn't like it, but we never tried to get him to take it down. And then, one day, it was gone and the Hermitage was there."

Her last words were said with pride.

"We will be gentle, and quick," said Rostnikov. "You may certainly watch."

She did, from the doorway. Zelach was uncomfortable but he did his job, going through the chest of drawers while Rostnikov took the closet so that he would probably not have to bend down. There wasn't much in the closet. The dead man had few clothes. What he had was clean and relatively unfrayed, but there was little. Zelach found the same in the drawers. In the bottom drawer he found a book. He showed it to Rostnikov, who took it. It was thin but in good shape, quite old, and in French. The title, as far as Rostnikov could tell, was *Lost Treasures of the Czars*.

"May we borrow this?" asked Rostnikov, knowing, once again, that he really didn't need their permission.

"You'll bring it back?" asked the woman.

"In two or three days," said Rostnikov. "I give you my word."

"And what is your word worth?" asked Ivan, suddenly appearing in the doorway, showing a tinge of anger at the violation of his only son's room.

"In my work," said Rostnikov, handing the book to Zelach, "it is all I have."

When they got back to Petrovka, Rostnikov settled behind his desk, Zelach across from him. Rostnikov was turning the pages of the book, looking at the pictures, understanding only a drop of the text.

"Well?" Rostnikov asked.

Zelach didn't know what to say.

"What did you think?" Rostnikov prompted.

"I don't know," said Zelach.

"What do you think we should do now?" Rostnikov persisted, still thumbing pages.

"Interrogate the dead man's friends?" said Zelach.

"Precisely," said Rostnikov. "What did we see at the Mesanovich apartment?"

"Old things," said Zelach, knowing there was something Rostnikov hoped he had observed, but not sure of what it was. "An old banner, an old portrait, old furniture, that book, the photograph over the bed."

"Excellent," said Rostnikov, reaching for the phone.

It took him only ten minutes to get through to Saint Petersburg, another five minutes to locate the security office, and another seven minutes before General Snitkonoy came on the line, his voice as deep and confident as ever.

"Inspector Rostnikov," he said.

"General," answered Rostnikov. "May I congratulate you on both your promotion and the responsibility the state has given you."

"Thank you," said the Gray Wolfhound. "You have a purpose other than social in calling?"

"If you would be so good as to help me with a case," said Rostnikov, watching Zelach's puzzled face and shifting his false leg by dragging it across the floor under his desk.

"Of course," said the general.

"Pavel Pestel," said Rostnikov. He spelled out the name. "Supposedly a member of the czarina's guard, an army officer, probably in the 1850s or 1860s. Whatever can be discovered."

"I will have a good man on it right away," said Snitkonoy. "What has he to do with the Hermitage?"

"I don't know," said Rostnikov. "Maybe nothing."

"I shall have someone call you back," said the general.

"Thank you, General," said Rostnikov, hanging up.

Although Zelach said nothing, the look on his face said "I don't understand."

"See if you can find Tkach," suggested Rostnikov, returning to his book. "He reads French."

Zelach got up.

"After General Snitkonoy's people call back with the information, we will visit the two friends of the dead man as you suggested," said Rostnikov.

Zelach's look of confusion turned to one of slight satisfaction as he left the room.

Tkach and Elena Timofeyeva had just returned from Trotsky Station, where Magda Stern had been unable to identify any officer as the one who attacked her the night before. None even looked like a possibility. The men, about half in uniform and half in civilian clothes because they were supposedly off duty, filed out disgruntled, tired, and puzzled.

They would move on to another station or two the next day. Elena was setting it up. They would start with those nearest the District 37 and work their way out. On the way back to the station, Elena had come up with a plan. It had been a good one, but one that would keep Sasha away from home for a number of nights. He had told her his plight, and she had suggested that they go to Porfiry Petrovich.

So, when he entered Rostnikov's office, the senior inspector looked up and said, "No luck."

"No," said Tkach, who then told Rostnikov the plan.

"Sounds good," said Rostnikov.

"The baby is sick," said Tkach. "I have to be home. Maya is already . . . upset."

Rostnikov nodded in understanding and said he would assign someone else to work with Elena at night. And then he handed the book to Sasha.

"Read it, please," said Rostnikov.

"Now?" asked Sasha.

"Sit. Read. Summarize for me as you go along. The book is not long."

Sasha had just started reading when the phone rang. Rostnikov picked it up.

"Inspector Rostnikov?"

"Yes."

"This is Leo Horv, State Security. I would like a few minutes of your time this afternoon. It is a matter of importance. I believe we have some information on the bomber."

"So I was informed by Inspector Timofeyeva. Would two o'clock be acceptable?" asked Rostnikov.

"Two o'clock," the man said, and hung up.

Rostnikov looked at the phone and then began drawing on his pad, a cage with a faceless man inside, while Sasha went on reading and summarizing.

Sasha had almost finished the book when the phone rang. Sasha placed the open book on his lap and rubbed his forehead wearily. The call was from a civilian who identified himself as one of the historians of the Hermitage.

Rostnikov took notes as the man spoke, and made no sound as the man gave him far more information than he probably needed. The conversation, almost completely one-sided, lasted a little more than twenty minutes. When it was over, Rostnikov looked up from his notes at Sasha, who seemed to have fallen asleep.

"Sasha," he said.

Tkach was immediately awake, brushing the hair from his eyes and ready to continue his reading.

"Go back to what you were reading about the gold wolf," Rostnikov said, looking at his notes. "Translate every word. Then go home and get some sleep, be with your family."

Sasha did not argue. He found the section Rostnikov wanted and translated it word for word as best he could.

* * *

The afternoon before, when Rostnikov had brought the girls back home from visiting their grandmother, Sarah Rostnikov listened to them as they sat around the table. The girls were more animated than Sarah had ever seen them. They spoke of their visit. They told of how Inspector Rostnikov had promised to see what he could do about getting their grandmother out of prison. They both emphasized that he made no promises, but that he said he would try.

Sarah smiled. The girls ignored the tea she had placed before each of them, though they had finished the cookie they had each been given.

The pain had come back, perhaps ten minutes earlier. Sarah showed no outward signs but continued to smile and listen. The pains had grown more frequent. They had started recently, months after her cousin Leon was reasonably certain that the delicate surgery had been successful. But then, about two weeks ago, the head pains had come. Not really headaches but pains. At first they lasted only a few seconds, but now they were getting longer. At first she told herself they had nothing to do with the surgery she had undergone, that this was something entirely different. But the last three times the head pain had come there had been slight tremors in both her hands. She hid her hands in her pockets or, as she did now, under the table.

The girls talked.

Suddenly the pain stopped and perhaps a second later the tremors stopped, too. It had felt as if someone had stuck an electric probe into her head with no warning and then, suddenly, pulled it out.

She would have to do something about it. She knew she would. She had promised herself the day before that the next time it happened, she would call Leon. If it was serious, she would think of a way to tell Porfiry Petrovich, and she would ask him to do whatever he could to free the girls' grandmother. It wasn't that Sarah had not grown to love them. She had. But Sarah Rostnikov had the distinct fear that a time might come when she would be unable to take care of them.

Sarah did not usually procrastinate. She kept her promises to others and to herself. It was one of the many traits of his wife that Rostnikov admired. Since he had met her, when she was just a young girl, she had been resolute. Although she could easily have hidden the fact that she was Jewish, she would quickly proclaim her heritage whenever the word *Jew* came up in conversation. She tolerated no injustice at work, though a bit of such tolerance would have saved her job on two occasions. In both cases, the injustice had not been to her but to coworkers. Sarah's sympathy for the girls' grandmother was very strong.

She decided not to wait. When the girls had left for school this morning, at least an hour after Rostnikov had left, she reached for the phone, first to call her job to say she was ill, and second to call Leon.

It was difficult in both cases to keep her voice steady. It was even more difficult to keep the phone from falling from her trembling hands.

NINE

THE CALL ANNOUNCING PORFIRY PETROVICH'S VISI-
tor came exactly on the hour. State Security Agent Leo
Horv showed his identification card at the Petrovka guard
station, where the young uniformed officer with pink
cold cheeks looked at it and called the lobby check-in
desk. Sergeant Sismikov answered in a bored, deep voice
that let the guard know that the sergeant was warm
enough to be bored. Sismikov checked his appointment
log and told the guard to send Agent Horv in.

Since the State Security agent wasn't carrying anything, there was nothing to be searched. Nonetheless,
Sismikov, who was the size of the Kremlin cannon,
asked if Agent Horv would please pass through the metal
detector.

Horv smiled and readily agreed. The machine was
extremely sensitive. Still, it did not screech.

Horv made his way up the stairs, found Rostnikov's
office, and stepped in.

He hadn't been prepared for what he saw.

The box of a man behind the desk rose awkwardly
with a smile of greeting and held out his hand. Horv took
it and looked at the other two men in the room. The
unkempt one seated to his right wearing a blue smock
examined the guest as if he were a specimen. He was
introduced as Technician Paulinin, and the gaunt man in
black was introduced as Inspector Karpo. The newcomer
recognized him as one of the two men who had entered

his apartment the day before. He had carefully removed all photographs of himself, but had she kept one somewhere? Did this blank-faced, erect man recognize him?

There was an empty seat between Paulinin and Karpo. Rostnikov, sitting awkwardly, held out his hand, palm up, to suggest that the State Security agent have a seat.

He sat and said, "I suppose you want to get straight to business. All right. I'll tell you why I am here."

"I think that first Citizen Paulinin would like to see the bomb," said Rostnikov conversationally, folding his hands on the desk in front of him. "Would you like some tea, Alexi Monochov?"

Alexi sat back, trying to hide his confusion.

"I recognized your voice from our telephone conversations," said Rostnikov, "but, even more compelling, was the fact that Inspector Karpo has been to your apartment. He has seen your photograph, an old photograph, but it is you. Your mother gave it to him. Well?"

"I'm here to . . ." Alexi began.

"No, I'm sorry. I was asking about the tea," said Rostnikov.

"No tea," said Alexi eyeing the men.

The two flanking him looked like variations of madness. Karpo sat rigidly, unblinkingly examining him. Paulinin looked as if he were suffering from some slight malady that made it difficult for him to sit still.

"Then, may we see the bomb?" asked Rostnikov. "I don't know much about bombs, but I do know that making one with the use of almost no metal, particularly for the detonator, is quite an achievement."

Confused, trying to regain his determination, Alexi opened his coat to reveal the deep-pocketed black nylon belt strapped to his stomach. There was only one wire coming from it. Alexi held up his hands now to show that the wire was attached to a small, polished wooden device in his hand.

Paulinin put on his glasses and scratched his chin. He asked Alexi what kind of explosive he was using.

No harm at this point. Alexi told him.

Paulinin nodded in admiration.

"Good choice," said the scientist. "The wire. Why wasn't that detected downstairs?"

"It contains no metal," said Alexi. "No more questions."

"I'm sorry, but I have one," said Rostnikov. "Forgive me for asking, but it is my job. How do we know you really have a bomb?"

"You will find that out soon enough," said Alexi, avoiding the examination by Paulinin with the thick glasses. This was not going at all the way he had expected. Why had Rostnikov let Alexi come up knowing that he most likely carried a bomb?

"Ah," said Rostnikov. "You mean to . . . ?"

"Yes," said Alexi, trying to sound firmly resolved.

"But first you have something to say," said Rostnikov.

"You counted on that."

"Certainly," said Rostnikov. "If you simply meant to set off a bomb that would destroy part—"

"All," Alexi amended.

"—all of this building," Rostnikov went on, "you would simply have done so without getting a false identification and going through the risk of getting caught."

"When we finish talking," Alexi said, his thumb on the button of the device, "we all die."

"I would assume that would be one of the results if you detonate your bomb," Rostnikov agreed. "But before you do so, there is something I'd like to tell you."

Paulinin had leaned forward and Alexi turned to look at the eyes behind the spectacles of the scientist. He saw no fear. He turned to Karpo, who betrayed no emotion. Did no one in this room fear death? Alexi felt dizzy. He would have liked some water, even warm water, but there was no way he could ask. Maybe he should have accepted the tea. But it might have been drugged or even poisoned. His mouth was dry, very dry, and things were not going according to plan.

"Did I ever ask you in our phone conversations what your favorite color is?" asked Rostnikov, pushing a thick folder across the desk and nodding at Alexi to look at it.

Alexi cautiously took his free hand out of his pocket and leaned over to open the file.

"Photographs of the survivors of your bombs," said Rostnikov.

"Gray," said Alexi, looking at the photographs of the maimed and the blind. "My favorite color is gray."

"There are before-and-after photographs where we could get them," said Rostnikov. "They are in the back. My staff ran something through the computer. You would understand how it worked. I am not a man of science. If you set off your bomb and it is as powerful as Paulinin here suggests, you will kill between one hundred and two hundred people at this time of day. A little more than half will leave wives and children. The total number of children under the age of sixteen left without a father will be about one hundred and ten. Alexi Monochov, because your father died and you believe you are dying, that is not a good enough reason for what you plan to do."

"Hundreds of thousands have died," Alexi answered with passion, putting his free hand back in his pocket, holding up the hand with the wired plunger. "The world should be made aware of the horrors of nuclear power. It will destroy Russia. It will destroy the world. It won't even need a bomb to do it. Do you know how Russia's nuclear materials and weapons are stored and protected?"

"Yes," said Paulinin.

Alexi turned, surprised by the scientist's high-pitched voice. But Paulinin wasn't finished.

"Nuclear storage areas are protected by young soldiers in ramshackle sheds with padlocks on their doors that can be picked in about thirty seconds or cut off in about two or three. Of course, there are a few better-protected facilities, but they, like the others, are subject to theft through attack or, more often, bribery of key guards."

"Yes," said Alexi.

"And you are making it better by bombing people," said Rostnikov.

"Yes," said Alexi with conviction. "Everyone who creates, protects, or condones nuclear development—nuclear death—should be destroyed as an example."

"So," said Rostnikov, leaning farther over his desk, lowering his voice, and focusing on the face of the bomber, "almost everybody deserves to join you in death."

"Almost everybody," said Alexi, nodding.

"But you haven't the time to do it because you are dying," said Rostnikov.

"That is right," said Alexi. "I want to speak."

Rostnikov nodded, giving the bomber his full attention.

"I have left notes with the media again, sent them out of the country. The world will know what has happened here today. I have also sent my greatest achievement in the mail to someone whose death will draw even more attention."

"And you think this will make the world wake up and begin a program of ceasing the creation and use of nuclear weapons. . . ."

"Any nuclear creation is dangerous. Don't you understand?"

Alexi tried to stop the tears beginning in the corners of his eyes. What good did it do to kill men like this? They seemed unafraid of what he was about to do, while Alexi mourned and feared the death that would come to him in minutes.

"No," said Rostnikov. "I find it difficult to imagine that the Chinese would be swayed in any way by what you plan to do. I think the Americans would use it for propaganda to try to get us to gain more government control of storage. It would not affect the Americans at all. Of course, this is just my opinion."

"It is worth trying," said Alexi. "It will be the largest gesture of its kind. It may well start an international movement so powerful that governments will be unable to ignore it."

"I doubt that," said Rostnikov. "But, since none of us will be here to see it, we will never know. I talked to a psychiatrist about you. An American, by phone. Gave her your profile. She does this for the FBI. Would you like to know what she said?"

"No," said Alexi, holding the wired detonator menacingly.

"Since I am about to be blown to pieces—with the exception of my left leg, which is already gone—I think it would be unreasonable of you not to allow me a few minutes to say what I wish. You've spoken and, given the circumstances, can speak again."

"Talk, quickly," said Alexi.

"Well, she says you are afraid of dying and want to show control by maiming or condemning to broken lives or even death those who might survive you. Nuclear energy is an excuse."

"It killed my father. It is killing me," Alexi insisted, partially rising from his chair.

"You are not dying, Alexi Monochov," said Rostnikov. "Look at the back of the file before you. We found your appointment notes, went to the hospital where you were diagnosed, got the X rays and test results, and sent them to the Americans, who examined them. You went to incompetent doctors at an incompetent hospital."

"As are most in Russia," said Paulinin.

"You have an infection, Alexi," said Rostnikov. "A prostate infection. It can be controlled with daily medication. It is not cancerous. Your life, except for the bomb strapped to your stomach, is in no impending danger."

"You're lying," said Alexi, examining each of the faces around him. He could see no trace of a lie, but they were trained to deceive. His eyes scanned the desk as if it might hold some answer, but all it held was the file folder of photographs of his victims. He flipped open the file and in the back found the medical reports.

"Had the hospital continued to treat you," said Rostnikov, "they may very well have killed you, but that is really of no consequence now. If you set off this bomb, the American psychiatrist will issue a joint statement with the director of the Institute of Psychosis here in Moscow. You will be remembered briefly as a dying lunatic who vindictively took the lives of innocent people."

"But you will all die, too," said Alexi. "You let me in here knowing you could die, probably would die."

"You and your family live well," said Rostnikov, ignoring the observation.

"What?" said Alexi, even more bewildered.

"Your father did not have much money. You do not earn much money. Your sister's salary is more pitiful than a policeman's, and your mother comes from a poor family."

"What has that . . . ?" Alexi began.

"Your father got the money by blackmailing important officials involved in corruption in nuclear production," came the voice at Alexi's right.

Alexi turned to the technician, the scientist who looked more mad than Alexi felt.

"Rumor, a word here and there," said Paulinin. "Gossip in the halls of meetings of scientists. I seldom go to such things. The pompous asses there make me bilious."

"Give us the names and tell us where the evidence is against these people," said Rostnikov. "That will accomplish more than what you plan."

"If I do that, my mother and sister will be reduced to poverty," he said.

"Then," said Rostnikov, sitting back in his chair with a deep sigh, "you are a hypocrite."

"You are in no position to call me names," said Alexi. "You're twisting things."

"I am giving you the opportunity to live and provide that life with a meaningful act against those who abuse the very creation you are willing to kill for. I am giving you the opportunity to speak out at a public trial where the criminals your father confronted can be denounced," said Rostnikov. "Would you like to see my artificial leg?"

"What?" asked Alexi, sitting back in complete confusion.

"I'm reaching down for it," said Rostnikov. "Don't panic. I'm not reaching for a weapon. If it were simply a matter of shooting you and taking our chances, Inspector Karpo, to your left, would have done so minutes ago. Ah, here."

Rostnikov put his prosthetic leg on the desk. It made a clunking sound.

"Marvel of science," said Rostnikov, admiring the leg. "Prosthetics. They're improving them all the time."

"Made by people with no knowledge of human anatomy," said Paulinin with disgust.

Alexi was in total confusion as he looked at the leg on the table before him. No one in the room seemed the least bit afraid except Alexi, who now believed that he might well not be dying.

"I don't want to see your wooden leg," Alexi said, staring right at the prosthesis.

"It's not just wood," said Rostnikov. "It has, in fact, almost no wood. It is metal and plastic. The plastic, as you can see, is made to somewhat approximate the color of human skin, but what is the point of that, I ask you? Anyone looking at it can see it is artificial. I believe in facing the truth, Alexi Monochov."

As the bomber continued to stare in fascination, Paulinin made a gesture to Karpo. He mimed putting his hand in his pocket. Karpo's nod was so slight that only the scientist caught it. Rostnikov's eyes were looking at the artificial part of his anatomy.

Alexi was hypnotized by the leg before him, confused

by the apparent fact that he was not going to die. This was going all wrong.

"No," he said, sitting down. "No more talk."

"The photograph," Paulinin said.

"Ah, yes, the photograph," said Rostnikov. "I think this will interest you."

Rostnikov pulled an eight-by-ten out of his drawer and reached over his artificial leg to place the photo face-down in front of the perplexed bomber.

"You are all crazy," said Alexi.

"You don't include yourself?" asked Rostnikov.

"I . . . I . . . It doesn't matter."

Alexi took his hand out of his pocket and reached for the photograph. The next instant was a sudden shock. Something grabbed his left hand as he reached forward. Then there was pain up his right arm as it was pulled behind him.

Karpo ignored the detonator button in Alexi's right hand and put the confused man in handcuffs behind his back while Paulinin reached into Alexi's left pocket and came up with a small black plastic box the size of a key-chain flashlight with a black button. Paulinin smiled in triumph and unstrapped the explosives from Alexi Monochov's body. Alexi didn't struggle, but Karpo still pressed down, holding him in place. Paulinin continued to search Alexi and then said, "Nothing."

Rostnikov nodded.

"I assume I may have all this for further study," asked Paulinin, examining the explosive loot in his hands as he moved away from Alexi to his chair.

"Of course," said Rostnikov.

"How did you know?" asked Alexi, looking at Rostnikov.

"I had no idea," said Rostnikov. "It was Technician Paulinin. My hope was to persuade you with the truth, Alexi. You are not dying or even seriously ill. My hope was to get you to give us the names and the evidence your father had collected. That was my hope, that and your fear of dying once you knew you were not ill. That and the opportunity in open court to make whatever kind of political or environmental statement you might choose. I don't think you would have pushed that button. But, just in case, Technician Paulinin was here to insure that you wouldn't."

Rostnikov turned to the scientist, who gently patted the strap-on bomb on his lap.

"First," said Paulinin, obviously delighted with himself, "you supposedly have a wire attached to the detonator you held in your right hand. The metal detectors downstairs didn't perceive it. They are very delicate. The police are very paranoid. But it was possible you had another means of using the detonator, though I wondered why a man with your abilities—and I don't give out compliments easily; you may ask Inspector Karpo—a man with your abilities should have such a primitive detonation device as a simple plunger and encased wire. It was for dramatic effect, perhaps? It could have been compressed air, but that would require more pressure than that simple wire and plunger could guarantee. It would require that your detonator be so delicate that it could have gone off simply while you walked or took the bus or metro here. Second, you are left-handed. Your watch is on your right wrist. You kept your left hand in your pocket. An odd thing to do under the circumstances, unless you had something in the pocket. Conclusion: the real detonator, a remote, was in your favored hand in your pocket ready to be pressed should someone manage to grab your right hand held high with a dramatic though false detonation device."

"You could have been wrong," said Alexi, head down, weeping. "I had it planned."

"Your false detonator is attached to a screw," said Paulinin. "A plastic screw to help insure that you could get through metal detectors. The screw is attached to the pouch. I know of no detonation device that would simply be triggered by a current through a plastic screw, though there are instances—"

"Paulinin," Rostnikov interrupted, retrieving his leg from the table. "You are better than Sherlock Holmes."

"Who is that?" asked the scientist warily.

"It is of no importance," said Rostnikov. "I have paid you the highest of compliments. You are free to leave with your plunder."

Paulinin did something with his face that may have been a smile and then he left the room. When the door closed, there was silence broken only by Alexi's sobs. Karpo stood behind the seated man, looking at Rostnikov for instruction.

Rostnikov motioned with his hand for Karpo to release Alexi. Karpo did so, though he remained standing behind the bomber.

"Give us the names of the people your father was blackmailing," said Rostnikov. "Give us the evidence. Tell us who you sent that last bomb to. Regain your dignity. By the time the world's media receives your letter, they will know Petrovka has not been destroyed. Your letter will go in the garbage with the other eccentric letters of the day. You've killed only one person to this point. If you must die, you can now do so without taking any lives and with some pride in what you have done to bring criminals to justice."

"They are rich," Alexi said, wiping his eyes on his sleeve. "These men. They are powerful. They'll bribe their way out of trouble."

Rostnikov shrugged. Alexi had a point.

"Perhaps," Porfiry Petrovich said, "but this is a new Russia. No one knows what a court will do, especially in a high-profile case. Bribery might be difficult and dangerous to a judge or anyone else in the government."

"You will take care of my mother and sister?" Alexi said, feeling the cuffs digging into his wrists.

"No," said Rostnikov. "There is nothing I can do. We

have no budget for such things. They will have to get along as best they can."

"I expected you to lie," said Alexi.

Rostnikov shrugged again.

"I'll tell you," Alexi said with a sigh. "But it may be too late to stop the bomb I delivered before I came here, my backup bomb."

There was silence—a long silence broken only by a pair of footsteps in the hall passing the office.

"And where is this second bomb?" Rostnikov prompted.

"Probably in the hands of whoever is the director of the FBI in the American embassy," said Alexi. "The detonation device is delicate. Even a strong vibration will set it off. The box is small and looks like it might contain a pen-and-pencil set."

"They will catch it," said Rostnikov. "They'll be suspicious."

"It was delivered by hand, by a man in uniform, me," said Alexi. "I informed the guard at the door that it was from you. I came here directly after I delivered it and changed my clothes."

Rostnikov reached for his phone and pulled an address book from his drawer. Rostnikov was terrible with numbers of any kind, particularly phone numbers. He had, on occasion, been known to forget his own home number. He found the American embassy number, called and asked for Agent Craig Hamilton, said it was urgent, and identified himself as he watched Alexi Monochov looking at the face-down photograph he had been reaching for when Karpo grabbed his hand.

Rostnikov stretched across the desk, holding the phone to his ear, and turned over the photograph so the handcuffed prisoner could see it.

The man in the photograph was massive. He wore a pleasant smile and a sweat suit. There was something written on the photograph.

"Alexiev," said Rostnikov, waiting for Craig Hamilton to come on the line. "The greatest of all Olympic lifters."

Monochov looked baffled.

"Alexiev," said Rostnikov, shaking his head. First Paulinin didn't know who Sherlock Holmes was and now the bomber didn't recognize the man whom Rostnikov and almost any Russian over the age of thirty would recognize.

"I sent him no bomb," Alexi said.

Rostnikov shook his head and then heard Craig Hamilton's calm voice. The two men spoke in English.

"A package was delivered to your office about half an hour ago," Rostnikov said. "You've obviously not opened it or you wouldn't be answering the phone. It's from the bomber, supposedly from me. Small, about the size of a pen-and-pencil box."

"The nearest bomb expert we have is in Frankfurt," said Hamilton. "The soonest we could get him here would be in ten hours. I doubt if we have ten hours. I'm evacuating the building when we hang up. If you've got someone who can disarm the bomb, send them over. I'll be nearby to let them in."

Hamilton hung up without another word and so did Rostnikov.

"Now," he said, nodding to Karpo, who sat down and took out his black leather-covered notebook. "We will talk about corruption and evidence, and those of us who believe in the possibility of a deity will pray that we can deal with your bomb without any deaths. The Americans have no bomb expert."

"I could tell them," said Alexi, his voice breaking.

"I believe you could," said Rostnikov, "but I'm not prepared to trust you. Alexi Monochov, your record leaves much to be desired."

Rostnikov knew he could call the military bomb squad, who might or might not succeed. Their practical experience was very limited, and their record, like that of Alexi Monochov, left something to be desired.

"Paulinin and I will go," said Karpo. "Paulinin will welcome the challenge."

"You will die," said Alexi Monochov simply.

"We shall see," said Karpo.

"With the deputy inspector's permission," said Karpo, "I will ask Technician Paulinin."

Rostnikov looked up at the two men. Paulinin was brilliant but emotional and definitely more than just a bit mad, but he had disarmed Monochov, and if there was such a thing as genius, Paulinin surely qualified. As for Karpo, there was no doubt that he cared little if he lived or died, but there was no chance of his panicking, and he seemed to have a rapport with Paulinin. In addition, Karpo had some experience with bombs. He had almost been killed by a terrorist bomb in Red Square four years ago. The major damage had been to his left arm, which had taken surgery and a year to heal. The incident had prompted Karpo to learn what he could about bombs.

"You have my permission," said Rostnikov. "Emil."

"Yes?"

"I want you back alive," Rostnikov said.

Karpo nodded and looked down at Alexi, who was still weeping.

"You can leave Alexi with me," said Rostnikov.

Karpo nodded and left the room.

"They will die," said Alexi, growing a bit more calm when the door was closed.

"Let us both hope that they do not," said Rostnikov.

The plan was breaking down. Not all district stations had a time or even a place where all the officers could be brought together. Elena and Sasha could gather officers on each shift, but that would require Magda Stern to be at each gathering. It could take days. It could take weeks. And what if he wasn't from the adjoining districts? Maybe he was from farther out. Maybe he wasn't even a police officer.

Magda Stern had said that not only was he in uniform but he got into a police car after attacking her. Could it have been a car disguised to look like a police car? That was possible.

As for current photographs of the officers in each district, some stations had a full set, some had a few, and some had only old ones. Elena suggested that they methodically take photographs of every officer from top to bottom, starting with Trotsky Station. If an officer was home sick, they would go to his home.

"It could take months," said Sasha, holding his forehead. "I need aspirin."

They were seated in Elena's cubbyhole office. Sasha sat across from her. The desk between them was very small.

"You have another idea?" she asked.

"We are already trying my idea," he said as Elena dug into her drawer and came up with a small, white plastic container with a red top. She handed it to Sasha, who opened it and gulped three white capsules dry. He coughed, swallowed, and managed to get them down. He returned the container to Elena. There were only two pills left.

"Do you have any other ideas?" she asked.

"You have a camera?"

"Yes," she said.

"Film?"

"We will talk to Porfiry Petrovich about buying and processing the film," she said, the idea taking shape as she spoke.

"By the time he gets permission for such a purchase, if he even agrees with the plan, six more women could be raped and beaten, possibly murdered."

"I say we try," said Elena.

"So do I," came a voice from the open entryway to the cubicle.

Iosef Rostnikov wore slacks, a white shirt and a sweater, and held a coat over his arm. He was smiling at Elena. Sasha, head in pain but feeling perhaps a bit better, looked at Elena, who was trying to hide a smile.

With all that is happening, am I not to be spared this maudlin mating ritual? Sasha mused.

"In fact," Iosef went on, "I'll supply the film. Japanese. Black-and-white. 800 ISO. You won't even need a flash."

"Just time," said Sasha. "Where did you get enough film for this?"

"A donation when I worked at the theater before I became a policeman," he said, stepping into the small room. "From a man who described himself as a business-man. Foreign accent. Very good clothes. Came to see me after a show. Shook my hand. Said he liked my work. The next day a carton of film was at the theater with a Japanese camera, a Nikon. I think the man was a gang-ster. The camera and the film are in my closet."

"A waste of time," said Sasha.

"A dead end," said Elena, looking up at Iosef with a smile.

"A red herring," said Iosef.

"Doomed to failure," Elena came back.

"Preposterous idea," Iosef agreed.

"As much chance as a cooked chicken," said Elena.

"A completely—" Iosef began, but was interrupted by Sasha, who almost shouted, "All right. We use Iosef's film. But we are going ahead with my plan."

"At this point," said Elena, "we have no choice."

"And I will add my camera to Elena's so you can both go out at the same time," said Iosef.

Sasha shrugged, tossing his head back, closing his eyes. Elena looked up at Iosef more guardedly than she had a moment earlier.

Elena Timofeyeva had come to work exhausted. She had taken three aspirin before she even left home. Iosef was pushing gently for marriage, but pushing nonetheless.

Last night in his bed they had talked, held each other and talked. Elena had gotten up at four in the morning. Her hope had been to get into the pull-out bed in her aunt's living room before her aunt rose. If she hurried,

which she had done, she would even have time for up to
two and a half hours of sleep.

However, when she had returned to the apartment she
shared with Anna Timofeyeva, the former powerful
deputy procurator for Moscow who was now an invalid
who read and looked out windows, she was not alone in
the living room. It was just after dawn and she needed
that sleep, but Lydia Tkach, Sasha's deaf, shrill mother
was there, at the table, across from Anna. Anna was
drinking her tea and listening. Lydia was ignoring her tea
and talking.

Anna was a heavy woman given to gray dresses. She
had no children, had never married, and had had only
three affairs in her life, all brief, all long ago, before she
was her niece's age. Anna kept herself clean and her
rapidly graying hair neatly brushed and cut short. In her
aunt, who had suffered two heart attacks, one major,
Elena always saw her future self. It depressed her. To
marry Iosef and turn into her aunt or even her mother
back in Odessa was something she preferred not to con-
template. Elena knew she had a pretty, clear-skinned face
and that she was smart and intuitive, better at her job than
Sasha, who had been an investigator for almost a decade.
But Iosef. He was bright, creative. His mother was still a
beauty. His father, Porfiry Petrovich, was no beauty, but
he had a confident, resigned power and great loyalty to
those who worked with him.

Bakunin, Anna Timofeyeva's orange cat, leapt off
Anna's lap and ran to Elena, who reached down to stroke
her as she greeted her aunt and the rapidly talking visitor.

Anna looked up at her niece and shared an almost un-
detectable look that said "I am trapped. What can I do?"

"I know I said I would not complain," said Lydia
loudly, holding up her hands. She was as frail in appearance as Anna was solid, though it was Lydia who was by
far the more healthy of the pair. "And this is not techni-
cally a complaint. I leave it to Elena if this is a complaint.

Who should know better than Elena what my son goes through each day? He is my only child."

"Elena has worked all night," said Anna. "I think she needs some rest. Elya, go into my bedroom and use my bed. Lydia and I will do our best to be quiet."

Elena nodded her head in appreciation. Later, when she got up and before she left, she would make herself something to eat. There wasn't much. Some tea, bread, cheese, a bloodred sausage whose origins it was best not to question. There was also half of a sad, small cabbage.

"Elena," Lydia said, touching her bird breast with her fist somewhere in the vicinity of where people thought the human heart resided. "Tell me, before you sleep. Honestly. My grandchild, Illya, is ill. My daughter-in-law does not tell me, does not call me. My own son doesn't call me."

"He's been very busy," Elena said. "We have a serial rapist."

"Rapists!" Lydia cried. "Murderers. Rapists. Sasha's been wounded more than once, beaten by car thieves, lunatics. Fine, that is what he wants to do, I can't stop him. But I should see my grandchildren when I want to. I have nothing to do anymore. No job. I can take care of them. They don't need day care. You have to pay for day care. And the little one is sick. My daughter-in-law doesn't like me."

I wonder why? thought Elena in resignation as she moved back to the kitchen area to prepare an awkward sandwich with two crumbling slices of bread. Elena looked at her aunt, who was close to having enough of Lydia for the day. Lydia Tkach, Elena knew, was a very mixed blessing. When she wasn't decrying the offenses of her son, the police, her daughter-in-law, her low pension, and the chill in her apartment down the hall or recounting with fondness the protection they all had under Communism, Lydia Tkach was surprisingly good company. She was bright, well-read, could handle a computer with great skill, played chess at the same level as

Anna, and was more than willing to run small errands or just sit at the window with Anna looking at the mothers with their children in the snow of the courtyard.

But Lydia was not abiding by the rules that Anna had instituted when Sasha had approached her. A rift would surely come between Anna and Sasha's mother. Elena hoped that her aunt could remain calm when she became inflexibly firm.

Elena was sipping her tea and listening to Lydia talk about the reunification of the Soviet Union.

"Belarus first," she said. "Then Ukraine. My daughter-in-law is from Ukraine. Then the southern states. The Soviet Union will be reborn. A world power. Dangerous criminal gangs with machine guns will be executed. The ruble will rise. Pensions will be worth something again to you and me, Anna Timofeyeva."

"It will not happen," said Anna. "Communism is dead. All parties, especially the Communists and extremists, are afraid of thoughts like those you have just expressed. The new Communist Party and the Nationalists are forcing displays, false hopes."

"You were a Communist," said Lydia.

"I am still," said Anna. "I believe in what we did. What I did. It failed not because it was a bankrupt idea, but because of Russian corruption, the weakness and greed of human beings who get even a small fistful of power. I worked with them. I prosecuted them. These new Communists are vultures preying on dead hopes and memories."

"Emil Karpo says the same thing," Elena said, slicing off a piece of cabbage that did not taste quite good but wasn't bad enough to discard. Elena was too hungry. She was on a diet, like the Americans, but it did little. Her problem wasn't an excess of food. There was no excess of food. Her problem was genetic.

"Emil Karpo is a madman," Lydia said, folding her arms and looking at the two other women for contradiction.

Neither responded, though from what Elena had said,

Anna was convinced that since the end of the Soviet Union and the death in the crossfire of a street battle of Mathilde Verson, Karpo had become suicidal. She had seen many like that, disillusioned, confused. Karpo was a pencil wound tight with twine. He would never actually consider suicide, but he would and had taken chances that might well be considered very dangerous and fool-hardy, though Karpo was no fool.

Elena was concerned whenever she was teamed with the Vampire. He didn't talk very much, even less than when she had first met him, before Mathilde's death. He remained focused and knew what he was doing. She knew she could learn a great deal from him and she did, but if he was going to risk his life unnecessarily, she did not want to be with him. She didn't want Iosef with him either, but Iosef seemed to welcome the partnership. They made a strange pair, the straight, gaunt man in black with his black hair brushed straight back from a receding hairline and the brawny, handsome, and usually smiling ex-soldier, playwright, and actor who preferred light colors and worried little about his bushy auburn hair that held just a touch of the red of his mother's.

Whatever love was, and Elena was not at all sure, she believed she loved Iosef Rostnikov. They had made love. It had been good. He had proposed frequently. She had told him of her experiences, down to the last affair with the married Cuban police officer who probably only wanted information from her. She had been far from promiscuous in her life. The graduate student engineer in the United States. The Canadian policeman she met in Boston. Iosef responded with careful references to his experience in Afghanistan, experience he had tried to deal with as a playwright and actor, and had failed.

They had been lying in his bed, naked, on their backs, looking up at the ceiling, a small light casting steady shadows.

"I was a murderer. I murdered the innocent during the war," he had said. "I confess, too, that I did not like the

Afghans. They are surly, nomadic people who kill each
other over whether Allah wants them to cut their toenails
or something. It was their land, but they killed my fellow
soldiers, my friends. Some of our men hated me since I
was considered Jewish. I fought with them. But I killed
our enemies, the Afghans—even women and children.
And I will live with that and dream about it and continue
to wake up nights sweating and weeping."

"But you seem so cheerful," Elena said.

"That is the irony," said Iosef. "I get that from my
father. I find life interesting, a moment-to-moment
adventure. My guilt I save for my dreams."

"And you can do that?" she said.

"Much of the time," Iosef answered. "Not always. So
you see, your confession, though I respect it, is pale compared to mine. You require no forgiveness. I deserve
none."

"So, do you agree, Elena?" Lydia Tkach said.

"Agree?" Elena asked, half asleep and drawn from her
memory of the night with Iosef.

"That Sasha deserves an office job," Lydia shouted.
"He has a mother, a wife, and two small children, and he
is always depressed."

In fact, Elena did agree, but it did not pay to give
Lydia ammunition if she were again to approach Rostnikov, whom she blamed for the dangers her son had
been subjected to.

"I am going to see Rostnikov again," Lydia said with
determination, folding her hands on the table resolutely
when Elena simply shrugged and took a bite of her sandwich. "Porfiry Petrovich has been promoted. Now he can
do this."

"Does Sasha want a desk job?" Anna said.

Lydia paused for a moment and then answered, "Of
course. It is his responsibility. With all the crime now,
why would anyone want to be a police officer?"

"Lydia," Anna reminded her guest, "Elena is a police
officer."

"I know that," said Lydia impatiently. "She is alone. No responsibilities. She is not depressed."

Anna nodded once to acknowledge the statement without agreeing or disagreeing.

When Elena was finished eating and cleaning her plate and utensils, Anna said she was growing tired. The hint did not work on Lydia, who was looking off into a corner of the room considering another assault on the injustice of human existence in general and specific humans in particular.

"My mother was raped and killed," Lydia said, still looking at the wall, her voice so uncharacteristically low that Elena almost missed the words. "I was a little girl. During the famine. Five soldiers, drunken soldiers, came to our house in the village. They were our soldiers. They raped and killed her. I was too young and scrawny to bother with. I remember one rapist was a man in a brown uniform who got down from his horse and pushed us both into the house. My father was gone, in the same army as the men who attacked my mother. My father was dead when it happened, but we didn't find that out for a long time, my baby brother and I. I have no idea how old the killers were. I don't even remember their faces. Afterward, I took care of my brother. A cousin of my father barely kept us from starving."

Lydia stopped as if coming out of a dream and looked around at Anna and Elena.

"I don't know why I told you that," she said.

Both Anna and Elena knew.

"I've never told anyone before," Lydia went on, talking almost to herself. "Not even my brother. Never my son."

"A game of chess?" Anna asked as Baku jumped back in her lap. "Some Mozart and some very competitive chess."

"Yes," said Lydia.

"I'm going to get a few hours' sleep," said Elena.

Anna was not a music lover. She had devoted her life to her work and had seen no plays, no movies, no ballet, no opera. Such things bored her. Even the idea of them bored her, but lately she seemed to have developed at least a high level of tolerance for Elena's collection of CDs, particularly Mozart, Bach, and Vivaldi.

So the games began. Elena knew that her aunt would enjoy the competition. Unfortunately Lydia took a long time between moves. She couldn't play under the pressure of a timer or a clock.

Elena had gone into her aunt's bedroom, taken off her clothes, and fallen into the bed, jarred into near consciousness from time to time by Lydia's shouts of triumph and defeat.

And now the weary Elena sat behind her desk looking up at Iosef standing in her doorway like Alain Delon, the French actor with the deadly smile. Sasha rose, having decided there was nothing more to say, only work to do. His head felt no better.

"I'll start making the calls to the stations," he said.

"Be tactful," Elena said. "We are asking for a second disruption."

"I will be tactful," said Sasha. "I will also evoke the specter of the displeasure of the Yak should they balk. Who knows? Perhaps we can turn a profit, sell the photographs back cheaply to each policeman when we no longer need them, split the profit three ways, and have lunch at the Metropole."

"I don't think so," said Elena.

"Why does that not surprise me?" Sasha said, moving past Iosef, who patted Sasha on the shoulder.

Elena wanted to tell Sasha Tkach to call his mother, but it was really not her place to do so. She watched him return to his cubbyhole.

Elena and Iosef could hear when Sasha began his calls. Iosef sat down in the chair across the desk from Elena and said quietly, "If you do not marry me, I will go as mad as the father Karamazov."

"I do not plan to stop being a deputy inspector," Elena said.

"Ah," said Iosef, leaning over. "A thin, white band of glowing hope. A condition. The door is open. I say, 'Fine, marry me and keep working.' "

"I don't know," she said, brushing back her hair and looking at the desk for an answer.

"That's better than no."

"It's not yes."

They could hear Sasha in the adjoining cubicle evoking the respected name of Director Yakovlev with some officer in one of the districts. Sasha sounded decidedly weary and impatient, and he had not yet really begun.

"Come to my apartment for dinner tonight." Iosef said. "I can't afford to take you out more than once every few weeks on my salary."

"We could share the bill," Elena said, "and eat cheaply. I know some places."

"You can't afford it on your salary," said Iosef with a grin.

"You come to my aunt's apartment for dinner tomorrow tonight," she said. "I have to work tonight."

"Anna Timofeyeva's apartment. I've known her since I was a small boy," Iosef said with a sigh. "I remember an enormous almost bare office. Behind the desk sat a massive, stern woman who greeted me as if I were an adult being examined carefully for evidence of a crime. She frightened me."

"And now?"

"I am not so easily frightened. What time?"

"Eight," said Elena. "I warn you. Neither my aunt nor I are good cooks. I'm a bit better, but I make no promises . . . about anything."

Iosef nodded in understanding.

"One more thing," Elena said. "Sasha's mother lives in our building. She tends to drop in without invitation at rather regular intervals."

"Lydia Tkach," Iosef said, topping his last sigh with a deeper one, the exaggerated sigh of an actor who wants you to know he is exaggerating. "Sounds as if it will be a night to remember."

TEN

LEONID SHARVOTZ FELT THE BLOW TO HIS HEAD AND another almost immediately to his kidney. He turned and slumped in confusion and pain against the wall of Georgi Radzo's small room. Leonid's face had hit the wall.

Leonid was sure his nose was bleeding. This was confirmed when he looked up from where he was kneeling to see the streak of blood down the dirty white wall.

He curled up, expecting more blows. A powerful hand grabbed Leonid's shoulder and pulled him up. The hand turned him around, and a very light-headed Leonid Sharvotz looked into the face of Georgi Radzo. Georgi's was an angry, determined, slightly stupid face with a taped broken nose.

The only positive thing about what was happening was that the smell and taste of blood blocked the almost putrid odor of sweat, unemptied trash, and bedding that hadn't been changed in months.

"*Shto ehdtah znahchyeet? Yah nyee pahnyeemahyoo.* What does this mean? I don't understand," Leonid moaned, trying to stop the bleeding with the back of his hand.

"Lean your head back. I'll hold it. Pinch your nose here and breathe through your mouth," said Georgi. "Your nose isn't broken. You want to see a really broken nose, I'll take my tape off and show you one."

Georgi's voice was strange, as if he were far away on a bad telephone connection. Part of the reason was the padding in both of Georgi's nostrils, an attempt, coupled with the tape, to give the big man's nose some semblance of shape when it healed. Another part of the reason was that Leonid's ears were now being covered by Georgi, who was massaging Leonid's neck gently with his thumbs.

"Pinch the nose," Georgi reminded him.

Leonid pinched his nose and felt blood on his fingers.

"It's stopping," said Georgi. "It was nothing."

Leonid lifted his head. The bleeding had stopped. He tasted the blood that had dripped into his mouth and felt nauseous.

"Why?" Leonid repeated. "Why did you hit me?"

Georgi had turned Leonid so they were facing each other again.

"I am not as smart as you or Yevgeny," the big man said, "but I am not a fool. If anyone is a fool, it is you."

"What . . . ?"

"Yevgeny didn't have to kill Igor," Georgi said. "There was no reason. Igor wouldn't have betrayed us. He was weak, but he wouldn't have done it because he's afraid of me and Yevgeny. I am right, Leonid Sharvotz."

"Why would he murder Igor?" asked Leonid, wanting to sit down, needing to sit.

He staggered to a straight-backed wooden chair, feeling the pain in his kidney with each step. Georgi didn't try to stop him but went on talking.

"He plans to kill me. He plans to kill you. He may even plan to kill Igor's family. He has the letter. He will destroy it and be the only one who knows where the wolf is hidden. Or maybe he'll use us to help him get it and then murder us."

"No," said Leonid, tilting his head back over the top of the chair to keep the blood from coming again. "I've known Yevgeny since we were children."

"Yevgeny wants it for himself. Yevgeny likes to kill. Yevgeny may be a bit crazy, and he is smarter than you and me."

"I don't believe it," Leonid said, pinching his nose again. "I've known Yevgeny since we were children."

"You said that," said Georgi, who had not moved. "So think back on the violent things he did in the past."

Leonid could remember only one thing specifically, but he had the definite feeling that if he spent more time thinking about it, he would find that Georgi was right. Leonid was suddenly both in pain and afraid.

"Once he pushed a girl down the stairs," Leonid said. "In school. The girl was about nine. Yevgeny had called her a name, made fun of her freckles. She had answered his insult in front of a gathering of about fifteen students in the hall by saying everyone knew he had a Jew nose. She turned. He followed her and pushed her down the stairs. I remember he was smiling when she fell. The girl broke her leg and a finger. Yevgeny said she had fallen and I said she had fallen. I don't remember her name."

"You remember Yevgeny's smile," said Georgi.

With his head still back, Leonid confirmed this with a nod.

"I propose we kill Yevgeny before he kills us," said Georgi.

Leonid sat up suddenly, still pinching his nose. He looked at Georgi and knew that the big man meant it.

"I'll do it," said Georgi. "You don't have to see or hear or be there."

"No," said Leonid.

"You know I'm right," said Georgi.

And Leonid did.

"But how do I know you won't kill me, too?" asked Leonid.

"Because you are alive," said Georgi with what might have been a smile. "I could have thrown you out the window. No one knows you are visiting me. You could have come out of any window."

"Yevgeny would know," said Leonid.

"And be pleased that he had one less partner to deal with," said Georgi.

"He would know it was you," said Leonid.

"Probably," Georgi agreed. "In which case I would have to find him quickly and kill him before he discovered what had happened to you. But I don't want to kill you. There will be more than enough money to make us both very rich. You have never acted as if you looked down on me. I like you and I need a partner with some brains to get us out of the country, to get the wolf out of Russia, to find someone to buy it."

"You suddenly seem smart enough," said Leonid, looking down at the blood on his shirt. He only had four decent shirts and this was one of them.

Georgi shook his head no.

"I've thought this through no further than I've told you. My mother said I was shrewd when I did poorly in school. She said my shrewdness would see me through life. I've exhausted whatever reserve of shrewdness I have for this project. I don't know how to go beyond killing Yevgeny before he kills us."

"You had to beat me to tell me this?" asked Leonid.

"I think so," said Georgi. "I had to get your attention. I am sorry. I could think of no other way. All I know is my own strength. I am often wrong, but I am not wrong about Yevgeny."

"I think you are not wrong," Leonid agreed, glancing away.

"I feel you are usually telling the truth when we talk," said Georgi. "I never have the feeling Yevgeny is telling the truth. You understand?"

Leonid understood. It had been his own feeling for many years, but he had not listened to it. Leonid may have been reasonably smart, but he was a follower, content to be told, first by his father and then by Yevgeny, exactly what to do. He suddenly felt a fear of his boyhood friend, a fear far greater than any in his life, a fear that was miles above his fear of Georgi.

"When will you do it?" he asked.

"I don't know. Soon. I was going to wait, but it should

probably be today, before he sees you. He'll know something is wrong. You do not lie well, Leonid. The blood from your nose we can take care of. I think the bleeding has stopped, and we can clean you up and throw away the shirt. I can give you one of mine. It will be too large. Throw it away when you get back to your apartment. Soon we will be wearing silk shirts and ties in Paris or Prague or maybe even London or New York."

The thought of wearing one of Georgi's shirts brought Leonid's nausea back.

"But," Georgi went on, "I'm not sure you will be able to walk straight. He will ask you what happened. As I said, you are a poor liar. That's another reason I think I can trust you. But Yevgeny will know you are lying, and I think you are not strong enough to stand up to him. No, I'll have to do it today with my hands or a knife. Tell me how to do it, Leonid."

Leonid sat still, finding himself thinking seriously about the best place to have Georgi murder his closest friend. Leonid found that there was a certain satisfaction in planning. He had never really done it before. He thought for a long time and came up with a plan that he shared with Georgi. Along with this new satisfaction came the realization that he would have to kill Georgi, not necessarily because he feared that Georgi would not follow through with the partnership but because Georgi was not smart. Georgi got drunk. It was one thing to get drunk among his working friends and blame the Jews for Russia's problems, but he might get too drunk one night when he was rich and say something that would put them both in danger of being prosecuted, losing their wealth, and possibly even facing a firing squad. And what was to stop Georgi from killing Leonid once they were out of Russia? Leonid had never murdered anyone. Yevgeny had murdered the Jews. But somehow, sometime, he would have to kill Georgi.

* * *

Lieutenant Valentin Spaskov of Trotsky Station had many options for dealing with his problem. All of them were bad. Some were worse than others.

He had a direct order from the ministry for himself and the major to be present in one hour to have their photographs taken for the case being investigated by the Office of Special Investigation. It seemed they were not satisfied with their last visit in which almost every police officer in the district was assembled in a demeaning lineup. The police had enough to do without such nonsense. Now they wanted to come back and take photographs of everyone who was not present at that assemblage. The major was far from happy about this order from the Yak. The Yak had connections and friends, and he was smart. They would all have to comply.

Spaskov considered getting a friend who was not a police officer to pretend he was Spaskov for the photo. This might work because the major had said the pictures would be taken in Spaskov's office. However, there was too little time to find someone, and Spaskov did not think he had a friend to whom he could tell a lie sufficient to gain his assistance. Besides, if the pictures were ever returned, the major or even Sergeant Koffeyanovich might look at them and realize that the man in the photograph was not Spaskov.

Spaskov considered a disguise of sorts, a pair of glasses from the drawer in the catch-all office on the first floor. Again, that might be awkward if anyone, including the colonel, ever saw the photograph, for Spaskov's eyesight was perfect.

Should he slouch? Make a face? Quickly shave his mustache? Shaving his mustache would be too suspicious. There would certainly be a question or two about why he chose to shave on that day.

Should he smile with confidence? Look stern with self-assurance?

Damn. Although he had not been at the lineup, he

knew they had been examined by two policemen and a tall, serious, dark, and pretty woman. Several of the officers claimed they had seen her on Moscow Television News. Others said they were just imagining it. But Spaskov knew that the ones who had claimed to see her were particularly reliable witnesses. She was the last one he had attacked. She was the one whose stubbornness had driven him to rage.

The uniform. He could get out of his uniform and put on his civilian clothes, but this was an observant woman, confident that she could identify her attacker if she saw him.

There were two real choices and a hope. The hope was that she simply might not identify him from the photograph. The night had been dark, the attack quick, her glance at him fleeting at best. The choices were to simply claim the woman was wrong if she identified Valentin. She had mistaken him for someone else. He could not possibly have done such a thing. Valentin Spaskov had risen from the ranks not through favoritism, bribes, or party connections but by his own rare honesty and bravery. He was bright. He had a wife and child and was never known to abuse either of them or consort with the women a police officer frequently encounters in his work. Many an officer actually bragged that he let some women have the choice of sex in the backseat or an arrest. Almost all chose the backseat, often with a partner joining in.

Not Lieutenant Valentin Spaskov. There was not a mark on his record. None. And he knew that if he somehow escaped this horror, he would continue to uphold the law and, when necessary, risk his life to do so, with one exception, which he was doomed to repeat over and over again. He would have to kill the woman tonight.

It would not be easy. The attacks he had made he had no control over. They had simply grown inside him till he had to rape or he would burst with a kind of madness. He attacked in a frenzy to satisfy the creature within.

After each attack, it would rest for a while only to awaken and growl anew.

Valentin Spaskov remembered the assaults: following each woman, finding the right place, occasionally abandoning one possible prey for another if the situation wasn't right. When they were over, he had only a vague recollection of the attacks, the sexual part. He had no recollection of any of the beatings.

For a long time, years, he had wondered why he was doing this. He had read files on other rapists, had even read books. He didn't think he fit the possible profiles. Somewhere buried in his past was an event, a trauma, a series of incidents, a person these women were supposed to represent, even an idea or symbol for which they stood. Maybe in the line of duty he had suffered some damage to the brain that altered his behavior. He even considered that something may have been missing or distorted in his DNA, that he had been born with an animal lust that he had successfully controlled till he was an adult. But lust was only part of it. He knew that. If it was lust that drove him, his wife was accommodating, albeit less than interested. She readily admitted that the infrequent times when he was her lover, Valentin was gentle, thoughtful, and could be very satisfying.

It had been years now since Valentin Spaskov had first tried to understand why he did what he did. He used to hope that someday it would pass just as it had come. But now he feared that it was growing. He was increasingly convinced that he would remain a sadistic rapist.

The knock on the door was firm. Valentin looked up. His was not much of an office—dirty white walls, old chairs, and a scarred desk, a battered gray metal two-drawer filing cabinet, no window, his certificate the only thing on the wall. His wife had been so proud when he had been promoted and given this office. He had immediately put a framed photograph of his family where he could see it each day. At first he had looked at it frequently with satisfaction. But for the past several years he had been looking at it with guilt. He had reached a higher level of success than anyone in either his or his wife's family.

Valentin picked up a file from the corner of his very neat desk, opened it, and said "Come in" as he turned his eyes to the papers before him. He had no idea what he was looking at.

The door opened. Lieutenant Valentin Spaskov did not look up.

Sasha Tkach entered the office wearing his heavy jacket, hair brushed back, cap in his pocket, and camera in his hand. Sasha remembered the man behind the desk from his first visit. Lieutenant Spaskov was older than Sasha. His uniform was neat and clean and he had a strong, handsome face.

"You do not have to explain," Spaskov said. "The major said you were coming."

"I'll make this fast," said Tkach. "Everything is preset. All I do is stand five feet away and click. The light flashes, the film advances, and I go on to more surly faces."

"Wouldn't you be surly?" asked Spaskov.

"Without doubt," said Sasha, brushing back his hair and moving forward to aim the camera at Spaskov, who simply looked serious. Sasha clicked. It was over.

"What kind of film are you using?" asked Spaskov.

Sasha looked at the camera as if it might help him answer.

"I don't know."

"It's a good thing to have a camera if you have a family," said Spaskov.

"I have a family," said Sasha.

"You have a picture of them?" asked Spaskov.

Sasha took out his wallet and opened it to a picture Porfiry Petrovich had taken when Illya was born. Maya was seated with the baby in her lap on their rapidly fraying couch. Pulcharia sat on her father's lap, and

Lydia sat next to her son, looking at him instead of the camera in spite of what Rostnikov had told her.

Spaskov retaliated with the picture on his desk of his own family: him, his wife, and their child in the park. It was an old picture. His golden-haired daughter had been no more than two at the time.

There really was nothing more to say as Sasha put his wallet away. One father and husband would trudge around wearily for the rest of the day taking pictures, and the other would go about his business upholding the law while planning a murder.

Karpo and Paulinin were met at the American embassy by Craig Hamilton, the black FBI agent whose specialty was organized crime. Karpo had worked with the man before, and they had a distinct respect for each other as professionals. Hamilton had gone far beyond his duty in helping Karpo track down the murderers of Mathilde Verson.

They were a strange contrast. The tall, pale white man was dressed entirely in black, and the well-groomed, handsome black man wore a light gray suit and stylish blue tie, not quite FBI uniform but nevertheless impressive.

The Russians entered the embassy identifying themselves to the American marines on duty. Karpo and Hamilton shook hands. The American had been waiting for them at the front door.

Hamilton smiled and ushered them up a stairway without speaking. He had seen Paulinin once, had a complete profile on the man, and was convinced he was both a genius and a vain, lonely borderline psychotic. Paulinin however—hatless, impatient, holding an old briefcase in his hand—troubled Hamilton far less at the moment than the gaunt figure at his side. Karpo had lost his religion, Communism, as well as the woman who had seen beneath the surface coldness to something human underneath. Now Karpo fit the profile of a suicidal personality.

He had nothing to lose. Hamilton recognized Karpo's skills and knew that the Russian would never panic, but he wondered why Rostnikov, who surely held the same opinion of the man, had chosen him to join in this, the bomber's most dangerous game. As they walked upstairs, their footsteps echoed in the evacuated building.

They stopped in front of a solid oak door.

"The package is on the desk," Hamilton said in perfect Russian. "About the size of a pen-and-pencil set, as you said. A bomb that size with the right explosive could do considerable damage."

"We are well aware of that," Paulinin said, holding his battered briefcase tightly.

"You are also aware that we have no one on our staff with sufficient expertise to deal with this bomb, if it is a bomb," said Hamilton.

"It is a bomb," said Karpo. "I heard the man who sent it. Inspector Rostnikov believes he is telling the truth."

"And you?" asked Hamilton.

"It doesn't matter," said Karpo. "We will treat it like a bomb."

"All right," said Hamilton. "We have also informed the bomb squad of the Russian National Police. Your new director, Citizen Yakovlev, insisted that since it was your case, your office would deal with it."

"The bomb squad is a waste of time," said Paulinin in disgust. "Can we begin?"

Hamilton opened the door very slowly, and the two Russians stepped in.

"I've been advised to leave the building at this point," said Hamilton.

"Then leave," said Paulinin, looking across the small room at the desk and the package, which was the only thing on it.

"I think I'll stay," said Hamilton.

Hamilton was wired. The microphone, the size of a collar button, was clipped to his tie. Whatever was said in this room was being recorded more than half a block away in a 1996 Buick Regal. The Americans simply could have planted a microphone in the room, but without someone asking questions, it was possible the two Russians might not speak.

Paulinin shrugged and moved ahead saying, "Leave the door open. If it explodes, an enclosed room could become a secondary bomb and cause more damage. The windows should be opened, but slowly, very slowly. If they offer any resistance, do not open them any further. I would like Emil Karpo to open the windows. From this point on, we move like well-fed snakes. If a time comes to move quickly, I will tell you."

Hamilton nodded as Karpo approached the windows and Paulinin placed his briefcase on the floor and opened it. Paulinin adjusted his glasses and examined the contents. From where he stood over the kneeling man, Hamilton could see a rather strange assortment of objects. The tools ranged from household pliers and wires wrapped in various colors to a roll of transparent tape, a package of brand-name oatmeal, some small zip-top plastic food bags, sharp-pointed pencils tied together with a rubber band, paper clips of all sizes, a white odd-shaped object that looked like the bone of an ape or human, a pad of paper about the size of a magazine, and other things Hamilton was at a loss to identify.

Paulinin went through the contents of his briefcase slowly, making sure that everything was in place. Then the small man rose, once again adjusting his glasses. He turned and looked up at the air vent in the wall. A near rictus crossed his thin lips. He could see the faint glint of light on glass behind the bars of the vent. He had no objection to being videotaped, no more than he objected to Hamilton's wire, which he had spotted instantly.

Paulinin had a certain level of vanity about his skills, skills he felt only a handful of people—particularly Karpo and Rostnikov—fully appreciated. He would have much preferred to be doing a complex autopsy for his audience of Americans, but from what he had seen of the work of the bomber, outwitting him would earn the admiration of the top experts in the world—if the bomb didn't go off.

He hoped there was not a timer, set to go off . . . now.

Paulinin paused for his audience and took off his coat, placing it on the floor near the door. Then he returned to the table, rolled up the unbuttoned sleeves of his faded gray shirt, and leaned over the package, holding his glasses on with one hand. He shook his head knowingly and went to his briefcase.

Karpo had opened the window and turned, arms at his sides, to watch. He knew Paulinin was doing much of this for show, which might cause him to give less than his full attention to the package on the table. That was the second real danger of this venture. The first was an explosion beyond the control of any man.

From his briefcase Paulinin pulled a long, thick rubber band that had been cut in half and looped at either end. He removed his glasses, joined the earpieces with the rubber band, and put the glasses back on. They would not slip off now.

He began to make careful, frequent trips to the briefcase to return or retrieve some object. The first was a steel dental pick. Hands steady, he probed gently at the wrapping of the package. He pried up a very small corner with the dental pick and leaned over to smell the paper.

"Standard glue. High quality to require a bit of effort to open it. That effort would probably be enough to trigger the bomb mechanism, but we must be sure."

Using the dental tool, Paulinin slowly pried open the flap of the envelope, first dabbing the flap with a cotton ball gently dipped into a clear solution in a small wide-necked purple bottle. Within a minute he had the flap open.

Then he stood up and looked down at the string that still tied the compact wooden box.

"Why the string?" Paulinin said, rubbing his chin the way he had seen someone do in a play when he was a child. He had always liked that gesture. It suggested deep thought. "It, too, could trigger the bomb. Releasing the string could cause a spring to flip up and—*boom.*"

Hamilton thought of his family. Karpo thought of nothing. They watched and listened while Paulinin suddenly began very quietly to half sing, half hum the American song "Ain't She Sweet." His English would have been unintelligible had Hamilton not known the words. The FBI agent could imagine the station chief and others smiling at this moment when they reviewed the video. He hoped he would be alive to enjoy it with them.

Paulinin carefully peeled away part of the envelope, cutting it in other places with surgical scissors, placing each piece on the table till the fragments looked like a light brown jigsaw puzzle. The string was still in place when he finished.

Then he took two broad blue elastic bands from his bag. He slowly, gently lifted one end of the box and carefully slid the band over the side that had been revealed when the paper had been removed. He repeated the procedure on the other side of the box. He then took a small white tube of a gluelike material, which he had developed himself, and squeezed some into the thin lid along the line where the box would normally be opened.

"Tzee hair walken don da street," he sang softly, waiting for the glue to harden.

It took no more than twenty seconds. Then Paulinin simply cut the string and removed it from the top of the box, making no attempt to pull it out from underneath.

"Like chess, eh, Emil?" Paulinin said, greatly enjoying his moment before microphone and camera.

"I am not skilled at analogy," Karpo said soberly.

"The bomber makes a move. I make a move," Paulinin explained, taking another bottle of liquid from his briefcase, wetting a cotton ball with it, and dabbing the liquid over the dried glue.

The next item Paulinin came up with and held high for the hidden camera was nothing more than a hinged wooden clothespin, the handles of which had been finely shaved so that they tapered up to little more than the thickness of a fine sheet of newspaper.

Paulinin now had a small flashlight in his left hand and the clothespin in his right. He leaned over and hummed as he gently inserted the paper-thin double end of the clothespin under the lip of the box. Cautiously he released the clothespin so that the spring began to open the lid. The two bands he had glued to the box kept it from popping open.

With only a sliver of the box open, Paulinin shined his flashlight into the slit, squinted, and looked back and forth slowly, opening the box only a bit more, sliding the clothespin forward gradually so that the opening became just a bit wider.

"Now I esk you wary confidential . . . hm, hm, hm," he sang as he removed the clothespin, returned to his briefcase, and brought out a thick white cardboard box. He opened the box and pulled out a small yellow object that looked a bit like a Sony Walkman with a pair of lightweight headphones attached. A thin green insulated wire dangled from the device, and a small screen lit up faintly when Paulinin pushed a button on the strange apparatus.

"Fiber optics," Paulinin explained. "Built it myself. If I moved to the West, I could patent it, make millions, live like Einstein, get an appointment to a moss league school."

"Ivy League," Hamilton corrected.

Paulinin put on his headset and began gently probing with the green wire into the space that he had reopened with his clothespin. He stopped singing, listened on the headphones, and watched the small screen on the yellow device as he very slowly moved the fiber-optic probe inside the small box containing the bomb. His movements were so subtle that if his audience did not watch carefully, they might not perceive any activity.

"Strange," said Paulinin, a slightly puzzled look on his

face that worried Hamilton, who looked at Karpo. Karpo registered nothing.

"There is a trigger spring," said Paulinin. "There is a mechanism I don't recognize and what appears to be a rectangle of soft, claylike material that may be the explosive. I don't have enough information to determine what kind of material it is. I do not have access to or funding for the most sophisticated tools. I must make do with what I can create myself while idiots stare at Japanese technology, American technology, Dutch, German technology and don't know how to use it. I am put upon, but I shall triumph. It is my move."

The headphones still on, the probe still inside, Paulinin put down the flashlight without bothering to turn it off and groped around in his briefcase till he came up with a thin metal device that looked like a delicate pliers with a small circular scissor at the end. Cautiously opening the clothespin just a bit more as he watched the small screen on the yellow box, Paulinin inserted the new instrument.

"Contact could break a circuit, create a small spark," he said more to himself than to either of the men in the room or whomever else might be listening and watching. "How clever is this man I'm playing against?"

Paulinin paused, left hand holding the tool, right hand holding the clothespin. Then he quickly squeezed the tool, and both Hamilton and Karpo could hear the small sound of metal wire being cut.

They stood waiting to die, but death didn't come, only the resumption of song from Paulinin: "Ain' she nize. Luck hair over hm, hm, hm."

Paulinin removed the cutting device from the box, pulled out the clothespin gently, and slipped off the elastic bands, holding each so it would not suddenly snap across and against the table and box.

Paulinin removed the headphones, turned off the yellow device, and put both back in his briefcase.

"Oh me oh my," Paulinin sang softly, reaching over and lifting the lid of the box. "Ain dot perfection."

He stopped singing suddenly and laid the hinged lid open.

"What's this? What's this?" he said. "His move. A bold knight, a reckless queen?"

Paulinin stood looking at the contents of the box, not singing or humming anymore.

"You two should leave now," he said.

"Why?" asked Hamilton.

"Because," Paulinin said softly, "I don't know what my next move will be. The trigger spring is attached to nothing. I recognize none of these mechanisms. If the box had been opened, it would not have exploded. The question is, why? If someone is fool enough to open the box, which does not explode, they see this. Do they stare at it, as we are, while a timer silently moves to explosion? Does the person who opens it call in others so that the bomber gets more victims? I suggest you leave."

Neither Karpo nor Hamilton moved, though the American was sorely tempted and would not be breaking any laws or rules by doing so. In fact, by remaining he may very well have been violating some FBI regulation.

"Your move," Hamilton said.

Paulinin grinned, removed his glasses, put them back on, and said, "Uncomfortable."

Then he leaned forward toward the box, inches from its inner workings. First he listened and then he smelled each part, pausing at the claylike material. Finally he delicately placed the tip of his finger on the material and put it to his tongue. The puzzled look returned and he stood thinking for an instant. An idea came. He smelled the box itself and found a scalpel in his briefcase. He carefully scraped away a small piece of the box and examined it through his thick lenses.

Paulinin looked at the open box again, put the piece of box on the table, put his tools away, closed his briefcase, and placed it on the desk. Then he reached into the open box with his right hand and pulled out the claylike material.

"Clay," he said in disgust. "Simple clay mixed with potassium. It's not explosive. The box isn't made of anything that can explode. This isn't a bomb. It's a fake bomb. A last gesture. Like the American movie I saw when I was a child, *The Phantom of the Opera*. When the angry crowd surrounds him, the phantom holds up his hand as if it contains a bomb. The crowd steps back in fear. Then the phantom opens his hand, revealing that it's empty. He laughs as the crowd closes in on him to end the movie. I've never forgotten that. The bomber has won."

"I'd call it a stalemate," said Hamilton.

Paulinin picked up his briefcase and shook his head.

"Perhaps," he said. "But he is sitting in a cell right now laughing at me."

"I doubt that," said Hamilton.

"He is laughing, smiling, gloating," said Paulinin, snapping his fully reloaded briefcase shut.

"Can we take this?" asked Karpo, looking down at the harmless box on the desk.

"I don't know," said Hamilton. "I'll see and get back to you."

Karpo nodded. Paulinin was already headed for the door, disgruntled, his moment gone. Monochov was a tormenting demon who had made a fool of him. Paulinin was quickly developing a determination never to put himself in a position like this again.

Paulinin retrieved his coat and put it on, buttoning it quickly.

Hamilton ushered the two men out of the room. As they headed back down the stairs, the FBI agent thanked them. Karpo nodded in response. Paulinin didn't even do that. He imagined that videotape. The FBI would watch it, laugh at him as he sang the foolish American song, as he played the bomber's game with surgical precision, as he stood looking down at the near jack-in-the-box of a surprise.

Instead of leading them to the front door of the

embassy, Hamilton made a turn and motioned for the two
Russians to follow him. Paulinin hesitated but moved to
Karpo's side, gripping his briefcase. Hamilton opened a
door to a small concrete-reinforced room filled with
video screens. Tapes were running. The room hummed
electronically.

"All automatic," said Hamilton. "Every once in a
while there's a glitch, a failure to record. The videotape
just made of us was automatic, not monitored. I've
turned off my microphone."

Hamilton reached over to one of the machines. On the
second screen on top was the room with the desk and the
fake bomb. Hamilton pressed a button. The second
screen went blank. A tape popped up. He removed it and
replaced it with a fresh tape from a cabinet against the
wall. He handed the tape he had removed from the
machine to Paulinin.

"The machine malfunctioned," Hamilton said seriously. "It never turned on. I'll have it repaired."

Paulinin took the tape, opened his briefcase enough to
drop it in, and closed the case. Hamilton left the room,
looking both ways down the hall, and motioned for the
two men to follow him.

The FBI agent led them back to the front door and past
the marines.

"I turned off the microphone when you opened the
box," said Hamilton softly as the three men stood out in
the cold. A sharp wind was blowing. "Electronic mal-
function is getting too common around here. A few
agents think it's some kind of jamming from your government. The microphone and recorder were a backup
for the video in case this room was destroyed, very similar to the black boxes on airplanes."

"You knew it was a fake bomb when I opened the
box?" asked Paulinin incredulously. "Before I knew?"

"No," said Hamilton. "I didn't know. I suspected only
when you opened it. I told you I know a little about
bombs. Something about it seemed off, wrong, too intri-

cate. Most bombs, even those sent by madmen, are simple. The simpler they are, the more effective they tend to be."

This, too, was a humiliation for Paulinin, but not as bad as it would have been if the FBI had wound up with the videotape that was now in his briefcase or if Hamilton had not turned off his microphone.

The FBI agent held out his hand. Karpo shook it. Paulinin hesitated, but then he shook it, too. He knew he should thank the American, but he didn't know how.

"We'd appreciate being kept informed about the bomber and his trial if it comes to one," said Hamilton, smiling. "Thank you for your assistance."

With that the agent went back into the building.

Karpo and Paulinin walked slowly away.

"Humiliation," Paulinin muttered. "I will remain in my laboratory from now on."

"Embarrassment," said Karpo. "Not humiliation. Shall we walk back?"

"It's far," said Paulinin.

"Yes," said Karpo. "And it's cold."

"Let's walk," said Paulinin.

"Good," said Emil Karpo. "That will give me ample time to tell you of one of the major embarrassments of my career, one that has remained with me for years. A woman outwitted me and almost killed me with a bomb."

They passed a parked American Buick. Three men were inside. They pretended not to look at the strange pair of Russians who passed them.

"And, if we have time, I will tell you other embarrassments and failures I have experienced," said Karpo.

"Perhaps we can stop for some tea or coffee and a sweet," said Paulinin. He held his hat in his hand, and the cold wind blew his wild hair in a winter dance.

"I see no reason not to," said Karpo, moving far more slowly than his usual pace so the smaller man could keep up with him.

ELEVEN

SARAH ROSTNIKOV SAT IN A MODEST DARK MAROON armchair in the apartment of her cousin Leon, the doctor. He sat across from her in an identical chair. Leon had not asked her but had made and poured coffee. He knew she liked hers with only a touch of sugar. He drank his black.

He was taller and leaner than most of Sarah's family and was given to wearing suits and ties even when he was not working. He did not like wearing clinical whites, though he did wear blue gowns and caps and a mask when he performed or assisted at surgery.

Sarah had come from the clinic her cousin used. Leon kept himself and his patients away from Moscow hospitals whenever possible. Unlike most doctors in Russia, and in the Soviet Union before, Leon prospered. He was younger than Sarah, no more than forty-five. He had managed to get into a Soviet medical school in spite of being Jewish, though it had taken a substantial bribe. After medical school he had supplemented the outdated medical education he had received by apprenticing under Cuban doctors, then had opened his own practice.

Leon was aware that he was known as the Jew doctor on Herzen Street. People with money came to him— government officials, businessmen, criminals—and, because of his connection to Porfiry Petrovich, an increasing number of ranking officers from the various law enforcement agencies. Leon treated them all, charged them according to their ability to pay, and, in turn, worked for nothing at the clinic to which he had sent Sarah. His patients at the clinic, in contrast to his private patients, tended to be abominably poor.

"You have the clinic report?" Sarah asked as calmly as she could.

Leon thought, as he had since he was a boy, that his cousin was a beautiful woman of great dignity. At first Leon, like the others in the family, wondered why she had married the Gentile policeman who walked with a limp and looked like a file cabinet. But Leon and the others were gradually won over. They had come to accept Porfiry Petrovich and, of course, Sarah and Porfiry Petrovich's son.

"They called about ten minutes before you got here," he said, not touching his own cup of coffee. "The X rays are being delivered here now."

"It's back," Sarah said.

"The tumor? I don't think so," he said. "I don't know, but I don't think so. That is not my specialty, but I will look and I will consult with the woman who operated on you. I think, at this point, something was touched, cut, perhaps even severed during the initial surgery. Or perhaps the tumor itself caused some minor damage before it was removed. None of this is uncommon."

Sarah knew her cousin as if he were her brother. They had grown up together. Their families had lived in the same apartment building, a building that was about half Jewish. Leon was not lying. He would not lie to her.

"And so?" she said.

"And so," he repeated, "if I am right, this is something that we may be able to treat with medication, perhaps antiseizure pills. If we can't find a good way to treat it, we may simply have to tell you to live with it unless it gets worse."

"And if you are wrong, Leon Moiseyevitch?"

"Perhaps surgery again to see if we can find and take care of the problem, but I don't think that will be necessary."

The room was warm and comfortable. Leon had made the two-bedroom apartment so. It was not filled with expensive furniture or antiques or anything that would suggest to the visitor that he was well-off. But there was an Oriental rug on the floor, a warm maroon-and-purple motif in the furniture, and contemporary Russian art on his walls. The art was all representational and non-political. There were separate entrances to the apartment and to his office and examining room next door. Leon could go to work or back home in seconds.

"Finish your coffee and we'll go take another look at you," he said. "Someone should be delivering the laboratory reports and X rays from the clinic any moment."

"You will let me know if I am going to die, Leon," she said. "I would have a great deal to do to prepare."

"You are not going to die," he said. "Not till you're as old as Grandma Rebecca. Ninety-one years. That's a promise. I will not permit another woman I love to be taken before her time."

Leon's wife had died almost seven years earlier of stomach cancer. They had one child, Itzhak, whom they called Ivan. Ivan was now nine. The woman who took care of him, Masha, a Hungarian, would pick the boy up at school and bring him home. The boy bore an uncanny resemblance to his mother, a resemblance, Sarah knew, that constantly reminded her cousin of his loss and caused him to have a protectiveness of the boy that Sarah understood, though she often thought it would not serve Leon or the child well as the boy grew.

"Shall we go?" Leon asked with a smile as he stood.

Sarah put down her cup and took his offered hand. On the way to the door to the office and through the examination room, Sarah asked about Itzhak, and Leon talked with pride about his son's accomplishments.

Sarah did not have nor did she want anyone to look after the two girls who would be waiting for her. They were old enough to make their own way home from school and find something to eat. She had left a note telling them to do their homework and then to read the books they had begun. After an early dinner she would let them watch some television.

As she lay talking and thinking, a deep part of her prayed that she would never have a seizure in front of the girls or Iosef or Porfiry Petrovich, though she knew she would soon have to tell her husband what was happening.

Rostnikov sat across the table from Yevgeny Tutsolov. Zelach stood behind the young man, who sat erect and was remarkably calm. Rostnikov had not told the young man why they had come to talk to him at the hotel where he worked in the laundry. When they had found him pulling sheets from a large dryer with the help of the hotel services supervisor, Tutsolov had seemed surprised but not at all nervous.

The supervisor was a bull of a woman in a white uniform who said they could use the small room off the laundry where the employees ate their lunch. She added that the sooner Tutsolov got back to work, the better, unless they planned to arrest him for something.

Rostnikov thanked her, smiled, and told the woman that she reminded him of Tolstoy's description of Anna Karenina. The woman's scowl had turned to a smile of pleasure.

"I've been told that before," she said over the sound of the washing and drying machines and the rolling of carts by curious employees. "Of course, that was before I put on a little weight."

"It shows through," said Rostnikov as the woman led her employee and the two policemen to the small lunchroom. "Beauty shows through."

She closed the door behind her when she left, and the three men were enclosed by windowless walls and the smell of thousands of previous lunches.

Rostnikov moved to one side of the table and sat on the bench. He had motioned Tutsolov to the other side of the bench. Zelach needed no order to know where he was to place himself—behind the suspect, close and intimidating.

"You have a slight limp," Rostnikov said.

"You noticed? One of the workers pushed a laundry cart into me about a month ago. It's getting better every day. I don't think anyone even noticed the limp except you. You, too, have a limp."

"I have an artificial leg," said Rostnikov. "Have you ever seen one?"

"No," said Tutsolov.

"The good ones they make now are marvels of technology," said Rostnikov. "My son, who used to be a poet and playwright after he was a soldier, envisions the day when as each internal organ and external limb is diseased or mutilated, it will immediately be replaced by an artificial one that works even better than the original. Everything but the brain."

"Interesting," said Tutsolov.

"Yes," said Rostnikov. "But I think it is only the poet in him. Would you like to know why we are here?"

"Very much," said the young man, folding his hands on the table and leaning forward attentively, curiosity crossing his innocent-looking face.

"You knew a young man named Igor Mesanovich," said Rostnikov.

"Yes. He was my friend. We knew each other from the time we were children," said Yevgeny Tutsolov, his eyes growing moist. "But I haven't seen him for months."

"You know he is dead," said Rostnikov, trying to find a comfortable angle for his bionic leg.

"Yes. I heard," said Tutsolov. "Someone beat him with a rock near the river a few nights ago."

"He was shot," said Rostnikov. "Not beaten. He and three others, Jews."

Tutsolov nodded. "The last time we talked, months ago, Igor said he had grown interested in Judaism. I tried to talk him out of it."

"You don't like Jews?" asked Rostnikov.

"Not particularly," said Tutsolov, "but I don't feel strongly about it, and I seldom give it even a fleeting thought."

"Perhaps you were right to try to talk him out of it," said Rostnikov with a sigh of understanding. "My wife is Jewish. My son is half Jewish, but I'm told that according to the Jews if the mother is Jewish, the child is Jewish. Here, if either parent is Jewish, then the child is Jewish. Being Jewish is hard in our country."

"Exactly," said Tutsolov. "That's what I tried to tell Igor, but he was determined. I wished him well and told him he was acting like a fool."

"Three nights ago, just before midnight," said Rostnikov, "where were you?"

"Three nights ago?" the young man repeated, shaking his head. "I don't . . . that was a Wednesday, no, a Tuesday. It doesn't matter, though. I go to sleep early. I have to get up early to get here by six. I was in bed sleeping."

"Alone?" asked Rostnikov.

The young man smiled and said, "My roommate was across the room in his bed. He has trouble sleeping and usually reads late by the light of a small lamp next to his bed. The light doesn't bother me. It's better than if he goes to sleep. Leonid often snores."

"Leonid Sharvotz," said Rostnikov.

"Yes," said Yevgeny.

"Also a friend of Igor Mesanovich?"

"Yes," said Yevgeny.

"Where can we find Leonid?" asked Rostnikov.

"He should be at the apartment," said Tutsolov. "He works afternoons and evenings. He's a perfume salesman at one of the new GUM stores. I've never been there. He gave me the name once or twice, but I don't remember."

"No one was at the apartment," said Rostnikov. "We just came from there."

There was a long silence while the washtub of a detective drummed his fingers on the table. He looked into Yevgeny's eyes till the young man turned away.

"Aren't you going to ask me if I knew any of his other friends? Anyone who might want him dead?" asked Yevgeny.

"All right," said Rostnikov. "Do you know anyone who might be able to help us, anyone who might have wanted your old friend dead?"

"No," said Yevgeny.

"Most helpful," said Rostnikov.

"You don't think Leonid and I had anything to do with killing Igor, do you?"

"No," said Rostnikov. "Of course not. We're simply obliged to follow any leads, talk to the friends of victims of violent crimes. See if they can give us any help."

"Igor was shot with three Jews?" Tutsolov asked incredulously.

Rostnikov nodded.

"I told you, as far as I know, he had no enemies," said the young man. "But you say he was with three Jews. Maybe it was just his terrible luck to be with them. Maybe . . . but I'm not a policeman. I hope you find who did this and shoot him the way they shot Igor."

"It is my experience that it seldom comes down to having to shoot criminals," said Rostnikov. "I prefer execution by the state—far more grievous, drawn-out punishment than a quick and simple bullet."

Tutsolov nodded, taking it in, appearing to absorb the wisdom of the older man.

"Yes," he said.

"That is all for now," said Rostnikov. "If you think of anything, I want you to call me."

Rostnikov awkwardly fished a crumpled card from his wallet. It was a card for an assistant manager at a plumbing supply store. Rostnikov had written his own name and office phone number on the back. The young man took the card, examined it, and carefully put it in his own wallet.

"You may go," said Rostnikov.

Yevgeny rose and nodded to Rostnikov and to Zelach, who still stood impassively behind Tutsolov's chair.

"One final question," said Rostnikov as the young man reached the door. "What is your favorite color?"

"My favorite . . . ?"

Yevgeny Tutsolov looked at the emotionless big man and the seated detective.

"I . . . when I was a boy it was green," he said. "Now, I don't know. Why?"

Rostnikov didn't answer. Yevgeny left, quickly closing the door behind him.

When the door was closed, Zelach said, "He's lying, Porfiry Petrovich."

"I know," said Rostnikov. "And he is not very good at it. He thinks he is good, but he's not. However, being a liar in Russia is not evidence of guilt. If it were, the entire population would be in prison getting tattooed and the streets would be empty. What would you suggest we do now?"

"Me?" asked Zelach. He thought for about ten seconds. "We have the rabbi, Belinsky, see if he can identify Tutsolov as one of the men who attacked him."

"A possibility," said Rostnikov. "At this point it certainly would provide the strong suggestion of a connection to the murders if he were identified. However, Belinsky saw very little of the faces of two of the men who attacked him. The one he can identify with certainty is the one whose nose he broke. So . . . ?"

"We talk to Tutsolov's roommate?" Zelach tried.

"Yes," said Rostnikov. "Leonid Sharvotz."

Zelach smiled.

Tutsolov was loading a machine with crumpled white sheets when the policemen wended their way through the laundry. The strong clean smells of bleach and detergent contrasted with the faint smell of food in the tight little lunchroom behind them where they had spoken to the nervous young man. Tutsolov smiled and waved. Zelach did nothing. Rostnikov nodded.

Rostnikov paused to thank the overweight Anna Karenina and then, with Zelach right behind him, escaped the noise of the laundry.

When they had gone, the supervisor, Ludmilla, walked over to Tutsolov and asked him what was going on. She was not sure what she thought about the young man. She, too, knew that he was a liar. He missed too much work, and his excuses were too varied and a bit difficult to keep swallowing dry.

"A friend of mine was murdered," said the young man sadly, continuing to load the machine. "Almost a brother. They wanted to know if I knew anyone who might want him dead. No one would want Igor dead. He was the gentlest person I've ever known besides my mother."

"Would you like to take the rest of the day off?" Ludmilla heard herself saying.

"Yes, please," Yevgeny said, wiping his eyes with his sleeve. "I'll stay late tomorrow."

Ludmilla touched his shoulder and said nothing. She felt him trembling. From fear, grief?

Yevgeny Tutsolov, under the scrutiny of his curious fellow workers, took off his white smock and headed for the small room near the door where the coats and boots were kept.

There was no doubt in his mind now. Leonid would have to die. He had planned that from the beginning, but he was hoping to wait till they were safely out of the country or about to leave. But if this policeman found Leonid, Leonid might well break. Georgi, up to this moment, had posed the greater problem and had been first on Yevgeny's death list, but things were changing, and quickly. It would have to be done tonight, risks or no risks. They would have to find it tonight. And he would have to kill both his remaining partners tonight. He could consider nothing else.

He put on his coat and hat and went down the echoing

corridor to the employee exit. As he left, he wondered where Leonid had gone that morning, why he had not been home when the police had come. Whatever the reason, Yevgeny was grateful that Leonid had gone out.

Two hours later Georgi arrived at the hotel where Yevgeny worked. He hid by the loading dock behind a huge metal garbage container, moving when anyone came out into the cold to dump garbage or leave. His plan was simple: come out slowly behind Yevgeny when the shift in the laundry was over, and follow him till he was alone and the other workers were scattered. He would do it quickly, in a doorway or behind a wall or truck or leafless clump of trees or bushes. If Yevgeny spotted him, he would simply have to risk killing the younger man under less than ideal circumstances. There was no point in making up a lie. Yevgeny was too smart.

Georgi moved from foot to foot, rubbed his gloved hands together, kept retying his scarf around his face, and waited till the shift ended. The workers began coming out. There were more than Georgi anticipated, but he was sure he would see Yevgeny.

The only problem was that Yevgeny did not come out. He waited almost twenty minutes more, but Yevgeny never emerged. Had Leonid warned him? Was he still inside? He had no idea that the partner he had come to murder had left before Georgi had arrived.

Not only had he left two hours before Georgi showed up—Yevgeny had headed directly for Georgi's apartment after he was certain he was not being followed. He expected Georgi to be at work. His plan had been to write a simple note saying "tonight," slip it under the door, and go to the apartment to be sure the police had not found the Kalishnikov automatic. He doubted they had. They would have arrested him, or at least said something. There was something unsettlingly odd about the crippled policeman who asked questions about colors and seemed to be thinking about other things besides the man across the table.

Yevgeny didn't even bother to knock. As he leaned over to push the note under the door, he thought he heard a sound on the other side. He pressed his ear to the door and thought he could hear what sounded like sobbing or whimpering. Georgi did not sob or whimper. Yevgeny could do both on demand, but not Georgi. Georgi didn't have the skill, intelligence, or imagination.

Who was inside the apartment?

Yevgeny hesitated and then slipped the note under the door. Almost immediately, he heard a gasp in the small apartment. Yevgeny quickly left the building and crossed the street so he could be seen by anyone looking out of Georgi's window. He went around the block, making his way among strolling pedestrians carrying colorful and not-so-colorful plastic shopping bags covered with ads for Dockers and Mitsubishi cars, people wandering, most with nowhere to go. He completely circled the block and crossed to the same side of the street as Georgi's apartment, being careful this time to stay out of view of Georgi's window. He spotted a darkened doorway across the street from where he could see Georgi's window. He went back to the corner and crossed along with a group of bundled people, half of whom walked down the sidewalk across from Georgi's building. When he got to the darkened doorway, Yevgeny stepped into the shadows, acting as if he were reaching into his pocket for keys.

His back to the corner, Yevgeny gazed up at Georgi's window. He was cold. After five minutes, Leonid appeared in the window, looking out nervously. He appeared for only an instant. In the next twenty minutes, he repeated the move to the window five times, looking as if he were trying to decide something, staying back in what he hoped were the shadows of the room.

Finally Georgi came walking down the street and entered his apartment building. Georgi should have been at work. Yevgeny watched for twenty minutes more.

When Leonid failed to come out of the building, Yevgeny carefully joined a passing group of pedestrians and moved slowly, averting his head from Georgi's window, striking up a conversation with an old man about the elections.

Not long after, Yevgeny was in his and Leonid's apartment. He took off his coat and boots and lay down on his bed after assuring himself as best he could that the room had not been searched. Later he would check on the Kalishnikov. He put his hands behind his head and began to plan, to figure out the puzzle.

It was not a difficult puzzle to figure out. The question was what would he do about it and when.

Yevgeny could not put aside the visit of the one-legged policeman who had convinced him that the move had to be that night. There was something about him, something that made Yevgeny feel that the older man might be able to see through his act. But that, Yevgeny decided as he lay in bed, was almost certainly a wrong interpretation. The policeman was like all the others he had deceived, probably not as bright as some he had dealt with.

Yevgeny closed his eyes now, trying to convince himself that he was confident, that his intelligence and willingness to kill would see him through, that he could handle Leonid, Georgi, and the police. What he needed now was a little luck, not much, just a little for the job that had to be done tonight. He had enough information from Igor's letter. He would use Leonid and Georgi to help him find the prize, and then, before they could move on him, he would kill both of his friends, kill them where they stood, and have the rest of the night and part of the morning to make his way to Belarus, pay a few bribes, and continue to Poland and then Germany, where he would become rich enough to call himself a prince and live like one.

* * *

Alexi Monochov, in his saggy and faded blue prison uniform, sat at the table in the small room. Across from him sat the same three men who had thwarted him at Petrovka only a day earlier. The one in the middle, the one with the artificial leg, pursed his lips and tapped on a large envelope he held before him. The man to the right was the erect pale vampire in black whose face showed nothing. To the left sat the large-headed nervous man with glasses, the one who had figured out that Alexi's first detonator was a decoy. It was of this man that he was most wary. There was a look on the third man's face that Alexi could not read.

"Alexi Monochov," Rostnikov said, "you are a clever man, a prankster, a man with a true Russian sense of irony."

Alexi allowed himself only a small smile of satisfaction.

"Your fake bomb at the American embassy fooled us all," Rostnikov said, returning Monochov's smile. "In addition to your sense of humor, you are a man who professes to care greatly about lives and little or nothing about individual life."

Alexi wondered if a few of the hairs on his balding head might be out of place. He refrained from patting them. He had dignity to maintain.

"To save the lives of many," he said, "it is sometimes necessary to take the lives of a few, a guilty few."

"But," said Rostnikov, "according to you there are many who are guilty, many you thought deserved to die."

"Few and many are relative terms," said Alexi.

Rostnikov nodded as if in understanding.

"Your goal was to make a point about the dangers of nuclear research, weapons, power plants. You thought you might help make the public aware of the danger."

"Yes," said Alexi. "As the Unabomber did in the United States. These people are careless, stupid, and greedy. They can destroy most of mankind. We need more bombers, more protests."

"Nuclear research caused the death of your father," Rostnikov said, looking at Alexi with sympathy.

"Yes," said Alexi.

"But not before he blackmailed some very important people who have taken care of your mother, your sister, and you," said Rostnikov.

"We've been over this," said Alexi.

"And you do not intend to give us the names of these people and the crimes they committed because you want your mother and sister to continue to receive this tainted money from men you think should be dead."

"Yes," said Alexi.

"That is a contradiction," said the gaunt man unexpectedly. "You are doing the same thing that you want stopped. You are profiting from the criminal acts of others involved in the very enterprise you wish to end. You are a hypocrite, Alexi Monochov."

"I have arranged for the sixteen names to be given to the police and the press when my mother dies," said Alexi. "She is an old woman. With my mother's help, we have put away enough for my sister, who has a good job."

"And you?" asked Karpo.

"I will soon be dead," said Alexi, head up, looking at each man across from him. "If not from my malignancy, then by execution."

"Your malignancy," said Rostnikov. "The same thing that killed your father. Isn't it odd that you chose a career in the field you hated?"

"I could be aware of what was going on and where," said Alexi, "of who was responsible and how I might be instrumental in stopping it."

"Can it be stopped, Alexi?"

The pause was long and then the prisoner said, "No, but it can be made more safe. The public can demand so, and the politicians will listen if there is enough protest."

"Maybe," said Rostnikov. "I have known politicians.

They are a patient and determined breed where money and power are concerned."

There was a sound from the scientist with the thick glasses. Alexi turned toward him, but the man was silent, watching, listening.

"I talked to your doctor, obtained all of your medical records," said Rostnikov, tapping the envelope before him. "Scientific technician Paulinin, whose medical knowledge is considerable, has examined the information and consulted with others this very day. We have confirmed without a doubt that you are not dying."

Rostnikov slid the envelope to Paulinin, who opened it and spread the contents before him, including X rays and graphs.

"The neurologist who you have been seeing," said Paulinin, "is little more than an incompetent quack. You have no malignancy. You have no cancer. What you have is a small blood clot that has grown slowly since you were misdiagnosed. Your pain increased in frequency and severity because your infection has not been properly treated. Your therapy was of no use. A simple operation to remove the clot could have been done when you were first seen. It can still be done, but it will require a competent surgeon. I know such a surgeon."

Alexi looked at the X rays and graphs. He knew a bit about reading such things but did not consider himself an expert.

"These are fakes," he finally said, handing the envelope back to Rostnikov. "I am dying. You simply want me to give you the names, the evidence. These are old X rays, old graphs. I can read the code dates in the corner."

"These are your father's medical records, Alexi Monochov," said Rostnikov, sliding another file, an old one across, to the bomber. "Your father didn't die of exposure to nuclear material any more than you are dying from it. Open the file, Alexi. Your father committed suicide. He left a note. Read the note."

Monochov opened the old file. On top of a small pile

of reports and papers was a note. It was definitely in his father's hand.

I have been exposed to high doses of radiation. The pain is unbearable. I would rather take my own life than let my family watch me suffer a long and painful death. You will be taken care of. I promise you.

He moved to the next sheet, a report, signed by his mother.

"She knew he committed suicide?" Alexi asked in confusion. "She knew all the time?"

"It would appear so," said Rostnikov.

"And you're telling me he did not die of massive doses of radiation?" he asked.

"Read the record," said Rostnikov. "It is not an external contamination from which you and your father both suffered. Put simply, Alexi, it is madness."

Alexi couldn't take in the information. It was a trick, like the bomb he sent to the American embassy. They wanted the names. Somehow they thought this would make him give them the names of those his father had blackmailed.

"This is a trick," said Alexi. "A lie."

"No," said Rostnikov.

"I don't believe you," said Alexi.

"But you do believe me," said Rostnikov, gazing into the eyes of the man across the desk.

"I will die anyway for what I have done," Alexi said, doing his best to regain a sense of dignity.

"Perhaps, perhaps not," said Rostnikov. "The director of my office is a very influential man. I have asked him if he could assure you life in prison or perhaps in a hospital for the mentally ill in exchange for the names. I grant that our mental hospitals leave a great deal to be desired, but your mother and sister would prefer that you not die."

"I don't know," said Alexi. "I have to think. My mother knew? All this time? She knew he had killed himself?"

"'You will be given the opportunity later today to ask her," said Rostnikov. "We are telling you the truth, Alexi Monochov. You have told yourself lies. You are not wrong about the nuclear dangers, but you and your family have not been singled out by them."

Monochov looked at each man. He read nothing in the face of the gaunt man. He read something like pride and vindication in the face of the man called Paulinin.

"I'll think about it," said Alexi.

All three men across from the one who had been the bomber knew that those words meant that he would cooperate, would provide the names, would live the rest of what promised to be a long life in a Russian prison or mental hospital, which many considered to be far worse than a quick death.

Rostnikov knew that Monochov wanted time to think of another option. The only other one Porfiry Petrovich knew would be for Monochov to contact some of the more influential people his family was blackmailing and threaten them with exposure if they didn't find a way to get him out of execution or prison. Corruption was almost always possible, but, Rostnikov concluded, in this case the evidence was too overwhelming. A confession had been made, and the media would be outraged. They would seek out the people who had perpetrated such an injustice, and they would be aided by leaks from the Office of Special Investigation. Monochov might try this approach, but it was doomed to failure.

"Yes, think about it," said Rostnikov. "But since this is a very important crime, you will appear before a judge within two days and the state will be ready to take you to trial within a week. Think about it, Alexi Monochov, but think quickly and let the guards know when you want to talk to me again."

Paulinin gathered the material from Alexi's files and put it back in the envelope as Rostnikov and the man who had made a fool of Paulinin continued to talk.

Who must decide now? Paulinin thought. *Which button*

do you push? Which wire do you cut? Who do you believe? A mistake, Alexi Monochov, could mean your death. Now you know how it feels. Now we are even, more than even. You have tricked yourself.

Though he said nothing, Paulinin believed that the balding man across from him would probably choose neither of the logical options open to him. Paulinin believed the bomber would try to kill himself in the next few days before having to appear before a judge, kill himself as his father had before him. That was if the bomber really had the courage to do so. He might not. In any case, should he kill himself, Paulinin wanted to conduct the autopsy. Normally he would have to wait until some incompetent pathologist butchered the body and either found nothing or drew the wrong conclusions. Only then, usually by official request from someone in Petrovka, would Paulinin get the corpse. Paulinin wanted this one first, wanted to examine the brain in detail. Rostnikov owed him that.

Rostnikov rose awkwardly, using the desk to brace himself. The two men on either side of Monochov rose also and so, finally, did Alexi. The tall, gaunt man who had disarmed him in Rostnikov's office left the room to find the guard who stood nearby.

The guard returned and Alexi followed him through the door.

When Alexi was gone, Rostnikov said, "He will give us the names. He will consider his choices and choose life."

"How do you know?" asked Paulinin.

"There was hope in his eyes yesterday when we told him he wasn't dying," said Rostnikov. "That hope was there again. And now he wants to distance himself from his father's madness. He will grow angry. He will curse his father and mother, but he will not want us to think him mad. He wants to live, even if that life is in a prison or a madhouse."

Paulinin nodded. He still thought Alexi Monochov would kill himself before the week was over.

Leonid entered the apartment about an hour after Yevgeny, who was lying in bed, hands behind his head, working out his plan for murdering Georgi and his roommate.

Yevgeny looked up.

"What happened to you?" he said.

Leonid touched his nose, turned away, and hung up his coat.

"I was robbed and beaten," Leonid said in mock rage. "A bunch of kids. They had knives, bricks, one even had a gun. I tried to fight, but they hit me, beat me, took my wallet and money, my watch and ring."

Leonid showed his empty wrist to Yevgeny, who looked up and said, "I'm sorry, Leonid. Let's take care of your wounds."

"I'll be fine," said Leonid, moving to sit on his bed.

Georgi had worked out this story with a few embellishments from Leonid, who had left his wallet, ring, and watch with Georgi. After Yevgeny was dead, Georgi would return them.

"You didn't go to the police?" asked Yevgeny calmly.

"No," said Leonid, his shoulders slouched forward. "What would be the point? They'd never find what was stolen. They wouldn't even look. And I don't think we want to go near the police. Not now."

"Anything broken?"

"I don't think so."

"Good," said Yevgeny. "We do it tonight."

"Tonight?" asked Leonid. "That wasn't our plan. I'm in no condition to . . ."

Yevgeny was aware that his frightened roommate knew full well from the note that had been passed under Georgi's door that Yevgeny had decided to move tonight.

"Our plan has changed. I have reasons. The police

came to the hotel and questioned me about Igor. They plan to question you. The policeman who questioned me suspected something. I want to do it and get out of Moscow before they find you. If they ask you questions, they might trick you. You understand?"

"I understand," said Leonid. "Tonight."

"I've already told Georgi," Yevgeny said. "I left him a note."

"Tonight," Leonid said, lying back on his bed. The move caused a punch of pain in his stomach where Georgi had hit him. Well, at least he would not have to go to work that night.

Minutes later Leonid was asleep and gently snoring.

Yevgeny looked at his friend and considered killing him right then. It would be easy. A pillow over his face. His arms pinned down. But Leonid would be useful in the night's work, and it would have been difficult to get rid of the body anyway.

Yevgeny went back to his musing after checking his watch. Eight more hours and with a little luck he would be a very wealthy man.

Elena and Iosef quickly finished their calls to the stations and began to do the paperwork that had piled up on both their desks. Forms, reports, tedium. Sasha had volunteered to go out and take all the photographs. Iosef thought Sasha had done so to leave them alone, out of either goodwill or a desire to get away from their courtship ritual. Elena, who knew Sasha better, thought he had volunteered because of his personal problems. Thanklessly running from station house to station house to take pictures of surly, uncooperative police officers would both keep him busy and let him feel sorry for himself. In any case, he was gone.

"Have you made a decision?" Iosef called from his cubicle.

"The answer is no. I will not marry you," she said.

"Is that a no for now because you want more time, or a

forever no because you don't love me and you never want to marry?"

"A no for now," Elena said, trying to read the new form on her desk.

"Then dinner at your aunt's is still firm?" he asked.

"Yes," said Elena, wondering when she would shop and cook, what she could make that was quick and easy.

Elena forced attention back to the form that lay flat in front of her. She had gotten to the fourth question: "Is the suspected perpetrator of the crime able to understand the difference between right and wrong?"

Elena had no idea. Even if she were to question the perpetrator when he was caught she would have no idea. She could ask the suspect questions about whether certain things were right or wrong, but she had learned that answers could seldom be trusted. It was how you felt about the suspect sitting before you that formed your opinion.

The question before her had no answer now and would have none later. She left it blank and went on. Of the twenty-seven questions, she left more than half blank. She was sure when she finished that the form had been created by someone who had never done any criminal investigation work. The form wanted answers where there were no answers. The form wanted certainty where there was usually uncertainty, even if there was some conviction on the part of the officer. She put the form aside and reached for another, going through the pile for something more familiar.

Perhaps there would be *sahsseeskee*, sausage, at the market. Perhaps it wouldn't cost too much, though she knew it would. Although it was against her principles, she would move to the front of the line at the market, showing her police identification. The people would boo and hiss and tell her she should be ashamed of herself. She had never done anything like that before. The people behind her would be right. She knew that many police still moved ahead, though they could no longer do so with the indifference or resignation of the people behind them as they had in the Soviet Union.

Am I capable of knowing the difference between right and wrong in such a case? Elena thought. She decided quickly that she was capable, that what she considered doing, annoying as it might be, would cause little harm. It was wrong, but it was expedient and, she felt, necessary if she was to prepare dinner tonight, a task she would never leave to her aunt with a guest coming. But she also knew that she wouldn't do it. She would wait her turn, read a book, pay more than she could afford for inferior food, and not complain.

It is not whether the person knows right from wrong but whether they believe what they have done, no matter how terrible it might be, was done because it was necessary and expedient. Right and wrong, Elena thought, were lost concepts in the new Russia. She believed in obsolete ideas.

Sasha was on his last roll of film in his last station. He took two group photographs and three individual ones. A few policemen protested mildly. Most simply looked bored.

From this final station, he called home. Maya answered. The baby was doing well.

Nonetheless, a quiver in her voice told him there was something else happening, that the baby was doing well but Maya was not.

"Lydia is here," Maya said. "She has given me many suggestions on how to take care of the baby. Would you like to talk to her?"

Sasha definitely did not want to talk to his mother, but Maya had given him no choice.

"Yes," he said, wearily playing with the most recently shot roll of film, a roll marked in black with the number of the police station.

Seconds later his mother screamed into the phone.

Across the room an officer taking another call looked up at the sound.

"Mother," Sasha said as calmly as he could. "The baby is fine now. You can go home."

"My grandchild needs me. Your wife needs me. Where are you in this crisis?"

"Working, Mother, and there is no crisis."

"I'll judge for myself when there is a crisis," she said, her voice only a meaningless decibel or two lower.

"The doctor told us the baby would be fine," he said.

"No he didn't," Lydia said.

"Ask Maya," he said.

"I did. She said the same thing. I don't believe it."

"You think Maya and I are lying."

"I didn't say that," his mother countered. "You believe the doctor said that. I don't believe the doctor said that. We respect each other's beliefs."

Sasha was momentarily confused.

"I should respect that you think my wife and I are liars?" he said.

"You believe what you want to believe. I believe what I want to believe. This is a democracy now. I can believe what I want."

Sasha took a deep breath and, as calmly as he could, said, "Mother, you must leave now. Maya needs rest. She'll get no rest with you there."

"She'll get more rest," said Lydia. "I'll take care of the children. She can go rest."

"I don't think so," said Sasha, surprising himself. "I believe she'll get more rest if you leave. You believe she will get more rest if you stay. This is a democracy. You believe what you want to believe. I believe what I want to believe. Go home now."

"But Maya wants me to stay. Ask her," Lydia shouted.

Sasha knew that Maya would never bring herself to tell her husband's mother to leave. The rift in the relationship of the two women would be too wide to bridge.

"No," said Sasha. "I'll call you later. We'll have you over for dinner in a day or two."

"If that's the way you feel, that's the way you feel," she said, resigned and obviously feeling sorry for herself. "I'll go."

"And, Mother," he said, now that he had the nerve, "I think you should call before you come to the apartment. Don't just drop in. Anyone who simply drops in can be coming at a bad time."

"You want to get rid of me?" she said angrily.

"No," he said.

The man on the other phone was looking at him.

"I don't want to get rid of you," Sasha continued. "You're my mother. I love you. I need your warmth, your wisdom, your caring."

She had ample reason not to believe any of this, but this time she chose to.

"I'm going back to my little apartment now," she said. "I will take comfort in the always welcoming company of Anna Timofeyeva. I will call you when you are more calm and we can talk about this sanely."

"Fine," Sasha said, putting the roll of film back in his pocket.

"You can come to my apartment and we'll talk calmly," she said. "Tomorrow."

"Tomorrow won't be good for me," said Sasha. "I'll call you. We'll make arrangements."

"We'll see," said Lydia skeptically.

Before Sasha could say more, his mother hung up.

"I'll be late again," Valentin Spaskov said into the phone.

"Very late?" asked his wife.

"I don't think so," he said.

Spaskov's wife had begun to think there was another woman. Once she had called the station to give him a message when he was supposed to be on duty and had been told that he was not working that night. More and more often he'd been coming home late, almost too depressed to play with his daughter if the girl was still awake. On those nights, Valentin had clung to her in bed.

Did he feel guilty? Did he want to confess? What about the blood he had hidden? She bore it silently, hoping it would end.

"I'll have food ready for you," she said as she always did.

"Good. I'll probably be very hungry," Spaskov said. "Good-bye."

"Good-bye," she said, and hung up the phone.

So did Spaskov, who stood looking down at it for a minute or two, his hands flat on the desk.

If everything went as planned, Spaskov was certain he would have no appetite this night.

TWELVE

PORFIRY PETROVICH GRUNTED MIGHTILY, HIS HAIR and brow damp with sweat, his purple-and-white Northwestern University sweatshirt with the tiny hole in the sleeve turned nearly gray from his perspiration. If he did two more bench presses, just two more, it would be a new record for him.

To the voice of Dinah Washington singing "Down with Love" Porfiry Petrovich, in the corner of his living room in his apartment on Karasikov Street, willed his arms and chest to move. Two things other than his own determination were helping him toward the new record. First, using extrastrength green plastic piping, he had designed and built a simple stand onto which he could place the weight as he lay back on the narrow bench. Placing the weight on the stand made it easier to get the weight in the air by not having to awkwardly lift it from the floor. He had no one to spot him on either side, so he had to be sure of the safe extent of both his weights and repetitions. He should have considered such a device years ago. He had seen them, used them in many weight rooms, even one in a small navy weather station in Siberia, but building one had only recently occurred to him. The second thing that made it easier to do the bench presses was the new leg. With his crippled leg he had balanced awkwardly on his right leg while doing the presses. It had taken a major effort just to get the weight to his chest and then down again when he finished.

The new leg served as a brace, like the strong leg of a table.

The two girls, as always, sat watching Rostnikov. They sat quietly, listening to the music and to his grunting. Grunting and blowing air were not only part of the ritual, they actually helped him get through each exercise.

They had finished dinner, chicken tabak, Rostnikov's favorite. He did not ask Sarah where she got the chicken, but he had not eaten with his usual hum of satisfaction. Sarah had something to discuss. He could see it in her face, her movements, in the fact that she had served him his favorite meal. They would talk later, either in bed or seated on the sofa with the lights low.

He, too, had something to tell his wife, but he was somehow sure that what she had to say was more important. It was her look, the look of a witness who had decided after hours or days or years of agony to come forth with what she knew and could no longer keep to herself.

Dinah Washington and Porfiry Petrovich finished together. He placed the weight back on the stand, and the singer concluded with a plaintive low note that nearly brought tears to the detective's eyes.

He sat up, reached for his towel, and wiped himself as he looked at the girls, who seemed to find even his wiping of sweat fascinating.

"You are the strongest person in the world," said the older girl.

Rostnikov looked over at Sarah, who sat in her chair across the room reading a book.

Although neither of the two girls had spoken much since their grandmother was taken from them and sent to prison, they had done reasonably well in school from the day the Rostnikovs had taken them in. And now the girls were gradually beginning to speak more and more.

"Sometime I will take you to watch the Olympic hopefuls working out," he said. "If we're lucky, we'll see one of the former champions, a few of whom are now coaches, demonstrate. Then you will see some of the strongest men in the world. And the strongest ever was . . ."

"Alexiev," finished the younger child.

Rostnikov smiled. Normally at this point he would turn off the record player, which he now did, put away the bench and weights in the space he had made behind the doors of the bookcase against the wall, which he now did, and change his clothes and shower, which he did not do.

Rostnikov had many loves, beginning with his wife and son and, more recently, the two little girls who were looking up at him from where they were seated. Following his family on his list, a list of which he was never overtly conscious, were his work and his coworkers, weight lifting, American mysteries, particularly those about the police by Ed McBain, and plumbing.

On his days off Rostnikov would often spend hours searching the outdoor stalls around the city for mystery novels in English. An Ed McBain was always a treasure, as was anything in English translation by Georges Simenon, but close behind were Lawrence Block, Donald Westlake, and many others.

When the weights and bench were compactly stored and the bookcase door closed, Rostnikov wiped his brow, neck, and head once more and said to the girls, "Shall we go to work?"

Both children nodded yes and smiled. Rostnikov glanced at Sarah, who looked up and smiled at the trio across the room, but there was something plaintive in her expression.

Rostnikov went into the bedroom and came back with his big plastic toolbox in one hand and five four-foot-long plastic tubes under the other arm. Bulianika and his wife on the fourth floor had come by earlier and left a message with Sarah that their sink was backed up. Sarah had said that if nothing came up at Petrovka, she was sure Porfiry Petrovich would take care of it later.

He told the older girl to get his plastic bucket from the storage box in the kitchen area. She moved quickly.

Rostnikov loved plumbing. He owned books on plumbing and pored over the diagrams even when the books were in German or any other language he could not read. From time to time Rostnikov would drop in on the Detlev Warehouse, a great indoor expanse that had once been a lightbulb factory. Now it was piled with neatly organized building parts, including piping, fittings, and tools for plumbers.

In exchange for the not inconsiderable right to evoke Rostnikov's name and rank when trouble arose, Detlev and his son, who looked like nearly identical well-built Italian construction workers, complete with dark mustaches and faded overalls, supplied the detective with parts and tools free or at a laughably low price. The Detlevs firmly believed that they were getting the better of the deal by saving the money they would normally have to pay to the police and one of the new mafias. At night an armed guard, an off-duty police officer, protected the warehouse, but the Washtub's reputation was far more effective.

"We should not be long," Rostnikov said as the older girl opened the front door with one hand, carrying the bucket in the other.

Sarah nodded.

On the way to the Bulianikas' apartment, the two girls took turns opening doors for Rostnikov, who moved slowly on his new leg, walking before him with a serious demeanor suitable to the serious business at hand.

For Rostnikov, this building, with its ancient and ill-built pipes, was his challenge. Eventually, if he lived long enough and the building continued to stand, he would probably replace every pipe, joint, toilet, and sink. Behind the walls was a network of metal and plastic that worked like a system of the human body. Water came in supposedly clean and left, usually dirty.

The Bulianikas, an old Hungarian couple whose son

had moved back to Budapest years ago, welcomed the
repair trio, offering tea and cookies. The girls each took
one cookie, as they had been instructed, and Rostnikov
said they would all have a quick tea when the job was
finished.

The job turned out to be an easy one. The sink, old and
cracked, was backed up with foul-smelling water and
almost full to overflowing.

"First rule in a case like this," said Rostnikov to the
two attentive girls, "is not to immediately use a plunger
or drain auger, that long spring. The cause may be in the
fixture drain, right here, or in the main drain, which col-
lects waste from the fixture drains. Or the problem could
be in the sewer drain that carries liquid and solid waste
out of the house and to the sewer. We've had no other
complaints, so we can tentatively conclude that the scene
of the crime is in the fixture. So we start by clearing the
drain opening."

One of the first things he had done when taking on the
circulatory system of the ill-constructed building was to
collect a few kopecks from each tenant to buy strainers
for each sink. It would not solve any problems, but it
would go a long way toward cutting down on clogged
drains.

Rostnikov, sweating even more through his white
sweat suit, removed the stopper and, using a flashlight,
looked down the drain to the first bend a few feet away.
He could see nothing.

Then, using his plunger, he created suction and pulled,
his neck muscles bulging red, the girls standing back in
awe. Nothing.

Next Rostnikov forced the long, flexible metal coil of
his auger down the drain. He cranked the handle, which
rotated a stiff spring when he hit what he thought might
be a slight blockage. This accomplished nothing.

"Next," said Rostnikov like a seasoned surgeon ad-
dressing a group of interns rather than two fascinated
little girls, "we can do one of two things. We can use a

chemical cleaner, which would probably not work because the drain is completely clogged. If it didn't work, we would then have to contend with caustic water. So we must dismantle the trap and use the auger on the drainpipe that goes into the floor."

The girls nodded in understanding as Rostnikov dismantled the trap, found it a bit dirty but clear, and inserted the auger into the floor drain. Again no result. He reassembled the trap and, awkwardly holding on to the sink, pulled himself up.

"The clues lead us elsewhere," Rostnikov said, picking up his piping and toolbox.

After reassuring the Bulianikas that he was on the trail of the problem, Rostnikov took his equipment and, with the girls ahead of him opening the stairway doors, went to the apartment below, where Vitali Sharakov lived alone. His wife had left him two years earlier. She had stayed with him for years only because he had been a member of the Communist Party, the ranking member in the apartment building, who earned a good living as a district sanitation supervisor, though he knew nothing about sanitation. But Sharakov was now a sullen stoop-shouldered man whose bush of dark hair always looked as if it needed cutting and who frequently looked as if he had forgotten to shave.

He let Rostnikov and the girls in with the air of a man who was accustomed to being intruded upon and had resigned himself to a lack of privacy.

"Plumbing problem upstairs," Rostnikov said.

Sharakov was wearing socks, a pair of wrinkled pants, and a white T-shirt with short sleeves from which his thin arms dangled like winter birch twigs.

Sharakov nodded. The room was dark except for the light from the television set placed directly in front of an old armchair. As far as Rostnikov could see, the room was neat and clean.

From the television came the voices of a couple of

actors arguing about a woman who was married to one of the characters.

"No trouble with your sink or toilet?" asked Rostnikov.

Sharakov shrugged and said, "No more, no less than normal."

He went back to his chair and his television show and let Rostnikov and the girls find their way to the sink. Rostnikov put down his toolbox and piping and turned on the water. The flow was weak. Then the work began. Rostnikov got on his back and moved awkwardly to open the little door that revealed the drain that was connected to the apartment above. Rostnikov stopped and asked Sharakov if he could have more light.

"Yes," said the man in the armchair, but he didn't move.

The older girl found the switch, and a hundred-watt bulb came on. Rostnikov took out his flashlight and a few tools and began to remove the metal plate under the sink. The screws were rusted. Rostnikov would replace them with new ones from his toolbox. For now he needed a careful but firm grip to turn each screw, not wanting to crack the grooves. Once he got each screw out slightly, he put a few drops of oil from a small aluminum can into the space behind the screw head. After giving the oil a few seconds to soak through, he removed the plate and searched the space behind it with his flashlight.

The coupling of the two sections of drainpipe was directly in front of him, a piece of luck since many of the joints in the building were difficult to reach. He had both the right wrench and the strength, after using more oil, to turn the coupling. It took about four minutes to loosen the ring and free the pipe. Each twist brought forth an ear-punishing squeak of rusted metal nearly locked by time and decades of polluted wastewater.

Rostnikov placed the coupling carefully on the floor, pushed the freed lower pipe gently out of the way, and called for the bucket and the flexible auger. The older girl handed him the bucket. The younger girl handed him the rolled-up metal coil.

Rostnikov, lying on his back, pushed the coil upward slowly. Gradually the coil almost disappeared, and then he paused, feeling some resistance. He reached for the bucket and held it in one hand while he twisted the handle of the auger. He paused, pushed it a second time, and then quickly pulled it out of the pipe as a trickle of dark liquid dribbled down, falling deep inside the wall of the building. Rostnikov got the bucket under the pipe just in time. The trickle suddenly turned into a torrent as the combination of hair, pieces of metal, paper, and items of unknown origin came thundering out.

He turned his head away and held the bucket tightly. The muck was almost to the top of the bucket when the flow suddenly stopped.

Rostnikov carefully removed the bucket, which gave off a foul odor that got even Sharakov's attention.

"What is that?" he called.

"I think it best not to know," said Rostnikov.

He wanted to replace the two sections of pipe with two of the new plastic sections he had brought, but he checked his watch. He did not have the time. He did, however, replace the rusted connecter with a new plastic one. Then he put the plate that covered the piping back in place and replaced the old screws with new plastic ones.

Sweat-drenched and dirty, Rostnikov gently eased his way out from under the sink, grabbed the countertop, and pulled himself up. The girls were looking in the bucket.

"I think I see a bug, a big bug," the younger child said.

"It would not surprise me," said Rostnikov, washing his hands in the sink and drying them on his sweatshirt. He would wash off thoroughly in the shower when he got back to his apartment.

"I'll be back when I can to put in new piping," Rostnikov said as he and the girls moved past Sharakov, who grunted and continued to watch his melodrama.

Rostnikov had to carry the bucket. It was very heavy now and dangerously near to overflowing. He let each of the girls carry two sections of the relatively lightweight plastic pipe. They managed with difficulty and dignity.

"Go tell the Hungarians that their drain is fixed," he said to the girls, who nodded like solemn, dutiful soldiers. "Then bring the pipes back to our apartment. You have done good work."

Both girls smiled and hurried away.

By the time he got back to the apartment after going downstairs and outside to dump the putrid mess directly into the sewer, the girls were already in their nightclothes, men's extralarge black T-shirts with the words THE TRUTH IS OUT THERE printed in English across the front.

Sarah finished getting the girls ready for bed while Rostnikov removed his left leg, placed it nearby, and showered using the heavy-duty grainy Chinese soap that went through even the dirtiest grease. He shampooed with just the right amount of American liquid Prell and was dry, leg back on and fully dressed, in ten minutes. He said good night to each girl and thanked them for their help.

"I'm going to dream about that bug," said the older girl.

"It wasn't a bug," Rostnikov lied. "It was a piece of black rubber."

The child sighed with relief, and Rostnikov went into the living room, closing the door behind him. Sarah sat at the table, a cup of tea for her husband in front of the empty chair across from her.

Rostnikov sat, sipped some tea, and said that he had to go back to work. He didn't know for how long. Maybe an hour or two, maybe most of the night. He told her he still had almost two hours before he had to leave. Then he waited for her to tell him what was troubling her.

Sarah spoke softly, calmly, telling him what she felt and thought and what her cousin had said.

"I've been having seizures," she explained. "I have medication from Leon that should stop them, but I may have more. I go blank. I think I shake. I wet myself. I don't want the girls to see this happen. I don't want you to see it happen, but you should be prepared. I should tell the girls and Iosef."

"Yes," said Rostnikov, reaching across the table to touch his wife's hand. "I was wondering why I got chicken tabak tonight."

"I will survive," Sarah said, a confident smile on her full lips and pale face.

"And we will endure," said Rostnikov. "Surviving and enduring are what Russians do best. We have almost made an art of it."

"If the medication doesn't work," Sarah said calmly, "we will try another medication. If that, too, fails, the woman who operated on me, removed the tumor, will conduct a procedure to relieve the pressure in my brain. It is not an operation in the same sense as the one I had. This is a simple procedure that is almost certain to work and poses no threat to my life."

Rostnikov said nothing.

"Porfiry Petrovich," Sarah said softly, "Leon would not lie to me."

While Rostnikov had been lying on his back under the pipe holding the plastic bucket, Valentin Spaskov was sitting in the unmarked car across from the Moscow Television News office. The engine was off. Spaskov did not want to draw any attention. He had signed the vehicle out for surveillance of a suspected illegal arms dealer.

He watched each person exiting the building, waiting for Magda Stern. He knew she was inside. He had called from a public phone five minutes before he parked across from the building and asked if she was there. The woman who answered said she was, but she was in a meeting. Spaskov said he was Inspector Tkach and asked to leave Magda Stern a message that the new photographs would be ready for her to look at the next morning.

Valentin hardly noticed the cold. He was wearing civilian clothes and a lightweight jacket so he could move quickly when the time came. In the holster under the jacket was a fully-loaded Colt Delta 10mm Gold Cup that he had taken from the Trotsky Station evidence room. After he killed Magda Stern, he would clean the weapon and return it to the evidence room on a shelf containing dozens of weapons.

He had decided to use it because the killing might then be linked to a shooting in front of Moscow Television News almost a year ago. A popular newscaster and commentator had been shot as he exited the office. The man had, on the air, been critical of both the government and the rise of extremists. Valentin had no idea what Magda Stern's political position might be. He simply planned to kill the woman nearby in the hope that it would be blamed on the same people who had committed the earlier murder and had never been caught.

If this were his district, he would have carefully supported such a suggestion. But this wasn't his district, and he wasn't at all certain whose district it was, considering the recent drawing of districts by the Ministry of the Interior. On more than one occasion, Valentin had been called upon to step in to negotiate jurisdiction over a crime because both Trotsky Station and another station claimed the territory.

The detectives from the Office of Special Investigation would, he was sure, not accept such a motive. The death of Magda Stern the night before she was to look at new photographs in the hope that she could identify her attacker would be too much of a coincidence. The detectives would conclude that her attacker and murderer was in one of the photographs. But which one? They would check, to the best of their ability, where each man photographed this day was at the time of each rape and beating. They might even eventually grow suspicious of Lieutenant Valentin Spaskov.

He would remain calm, cooperative. That wasn't the problem. The problem was that he would now, this night, have to murder an innocent woman. The problem was that he did not know if he was capable of stopping his attacks. And now he considered that once he had murdered Magda Stern he might well murder his next victim.

She came out of the building walking quickly, pulling the collar of her coat around her neck to temper a winter wind that came out of the darkness carrying drifts of snow from the street and sidewalk. A few people came out with her. If she went somewhere with them, he would follow and have to kill her elsewhere, but the group went to the right and she moved alone to the left. The group was moving toward the nearby metro station. She was walking into a darkness that was barely relieved by streetlights blurred by blowing snow. She was cooperating fully in her own murder.

Valentin got out of the car quietly, normally, looking like a man who had someplace to go in the area. He crossed the street and slowly followed the woman. He remembered her cool, pale, pretty made-up face. He remembered her tall body and erect posture.

"God," he said to himself, "I'm going to do it again, do it before I kill her." It was the wrong thing to do. It would definitely point to the serial rapist and not to the political fanatics who had murdered the newsman, but Valentin knew that he could not control himself.

He quickened his pace, closing the distance between himself and Magda. She did not look back. There were no footsteps to be heard in the thin layer of snow on the sidewalk. He waited, following. There were hardly any people on the street. It was cold. It was late. A few cars were parked nearby, their hubcaps and windshield wipers removed for the night by their owners to keep them from being stolen. It was reasonably safe for him. Besides, he had little choice. The obsession had taken him. It had overridden his conviction that he had to murder the woman in front of him. Murder her he would, but first . . .

Valentin closed the distance between them to no more than six feet and then he knew. He felt it before he saw them. It was confirmed by the look of revenge on the hard, lovely face of Magda Stern, who turned suddenly to face him. Valentin stopped.

"Halt," came a voice behind him. The voice was familiar. "Hands behind your head."

Valentin did not think about what he did next. He closed the distance between himself and Magda Stern in three long, quick steps, moved behind her, and with one swift instinctive motion, put his left arm over her neck, pulled out the pistol, and put it to her head.

In front of him, over her shoulder, Valentin could now see Sasha Tkach and Elena Timofeyeva no more than a dozen yards away with pistols aimed at him.

"What is the point of this, Spaskov?" Elena asked him. "If you pull the trigger, we will kill you."

"You know who I am now," said Spaskov, the concern of the honest policeman coming to the fore. "I will not be taken in to face this woman's charges, to stand in front of other women, to be humiliated, to have my family humiliated. It would be better to die in the street. I have nothing to lose by killing her."

Magda Stern stood tall, making no sound, determined to give no satisfaction to the man who had attacked her and now threatened to kill her.

Both Elena and Sasha knew that Valentin Spaskov would probably not shoot Magda Stern first. His first shot would be at Sasha and then, whether Elena hesitated or fired knowing she might hit Magda, Spaskov would shoot Elena. Magda would be last.

The only one of the four people in the stalemate on the silent street wearing gloves was Magda Stern. The three police officers had no gloves so that they could more easily handle their weapons. Their hands were cold but steady.

"I need time to think," said Valentin, pushing the woman slowly forward. "Move into the street. Give us room to pass. Don't try to get behind me. Move now."

"You have a wife, a beautiful child," said Sasha. "Remember, I saw their pictures."

"And you have a wife and two children," said Valentin as Sasha and Elena moved into the street. "What would they do? What would they think if they found you were like me? I don't want to kill you, but I will if you don't give me time."

Sasha was silent.

"You see?" said Valentin. "You have a great deal to lose."

"You could get help," said Elena. "We could get you psychological help. You haven't killed anyone yet."

"No," said Valentin, turning Magda to face the two armed officers as he moved back toward the Moscow Television News office. "I'll go to prison. My wife and child won't be able to face me. Can't you see I need time to think? How many times must I say it? Do you want to push me into doing something without having the chance to think?"

"Take your time, then," said Elena. "Stop. Take your time. We won't do anything as long as you don't hurt her."

Valentin continued to move, keeping Magda between himself and the two in the street with guns. As they approached the corner, Valentin moved himself and his captive into the street.

"I'm going to my car," he said. "Stay back. Stay careful. I would guess that I am a better shot than either of you. I don't want to shoot police officers. None of us wants a massacre. I just want time to decide what to do."

"We can't let you drive off," said Sasha. "You know that."

"You may have to," said Valentin as he backed his way across the street, his arm tight around Magda's neck. She was not cooperating, so he had to half drag her, causing his arm to tighten around her neck. Even with the increased pain and the difficulty breathing she refused to cooperate. Valentin admired her, and in spite of what was now happening, he wanted to have her. It was at this moment he knew he was surely mad.

Sasha and Elena followed, guns leveled as he moved to the car. He had left the door unlocked so he could get away quickly. Now he opened it and said, his voice shaking, not with fear but with emotion, "I am going to put her in the passenger seat. I will have to let her go, but I'll keep the gun against her head. We are at the moment when you will have to shoot me and risk her life or let us get in."

Valentin pushed Magda into the car. Sasha and Elena did not fire as he got in after his hostage and closed the door. But they did stand directly in front of the car, weapons at the ready, hands numb from the cold.

Spaskov did not try to start the car. He kept his weapon against Magda Stern's head. Both Elena and Sasha realized at the same time what he was doing. The inside of the car was definitely not warm, but it was much warmer there than the outside. Soon Elena's and Sasha's hands would begin to lose feeling. Already the prickling sensation had begun.

Valentin looked at them through the frost-covered window. He could see their shapes in the street before him, and they could see the faint outline of Spaskov with the gun to Magda's head.

The standoff was definitely in Spaskov's favor. All he had to do was wait till the hands of the two who stood in front of the car were too cold to shoot.

The car was a Mercedes. Many police cars, marked and unmarked, were Mercedes, which were far more reliable than Russian-made cars. Even cold it would start quickly. He could run right into them and over them before they could react. Neither Elena nor Sasha could tell if the front window was bulletproof. It probably wasn't, but they couldn't be sure with the frost and shadows covering it.

Elena felt as if she were in a dream. Less than two hours ago, when Sasha called her to say he was picking her up and that Magda Stern would be leaving the Moscow Television News office at ten, she had been sitting in her aunt's living room. The meal was over. Elena was confident that she had done a good job, not because Iosef had said so but because she knew she had. The conversation had been fine, and Anna had retired to her room to leave them alone.

Elena and Iosef had cleaned the dishes together, talking softly about work, family, his ideas and ambitions, her ideas and ambitions. The conversation had ranged from politics to books and movies, and they had discovered even more remarkable coincidences in their views, though Elena was a bit more pessimistic about the future of Russia and the world than Iosef. He attributed the difference to his experiences in the army. Almost naively, he assumed that things could probably not get much worse than that.

He had kissed her when the last pot was cleaned and the last dish put away. He had kissed her deeply and she had responded eagerly and when he had again asked her to marry him, she had been about to say "yes, yes, yes" when the phone rang and Sasha told her to come quickly.

She had expected the call, but not quite this early.

Iosef understood. He, too, was a police officer. It was another thing they had in common, that made him understand this sudden action in a way that might well be impossible for a husband or lover who was not a police officer. Iosef said he would go with her, but she had stopped him. It wasn't his case. It was hers and Sasha's, and if she showed up with Iosef, Sasha would surely feel offended by not having been consulted. Elena knew that she would feel the same in his place. Iosef had kissed her again, less passionately, but a long, moist kiss nonetheless. And then he had left, telling her to thank her aunt again for having him to dinner. He didn't tell Elena to be careful. He knew she would be as careful as the situation allowed.

Now she stood next to Sasha, absolutely unsure of what the situation allowed, and her hands were definitely stiff with the cold. She could hold the gun in one hand

and try to warm the other in her pocket, but she was right-handed and a weak shot with her left hand. If either she or Sasha tried to put a hand in a pocket, Valentin Spaskov might well take that moment to act. Besides, the pocket by now was not much warmer than the air. And if the windshield was bulletproof?

Sasha's evening had not been as dramatic or romantic as Elena's, but it had not been at all bad. Maya was clearly pleased with him and far more affectionate than she had been in a long time because of the stand he had taken with Lydia. The baby, Illya, was definitely getting better. Pulcharia, before she had gone to bed, had sat warm and close in Sasha's lap listening to him read "The Snow Maiden."

Now he was here, hands freezing to his gun, facing a car that could suddenly come to life and kill him. Or the policeman with a gun in a warmer hand inside the car, who could probably shoot better than Sasha could even with warm hands, might decide to come out shooting.

There was no knowing how long the standoff would have lasted or what the result would have been had Magda Stern not made the next and decisive move. Valentin was looking ahead, thinking about what would become of his wife and child regardless of what happened and gradually coming to the horrible conclusion that he would have to kill not only the woman at his side but the two police officers as well.

Valentin felt his hand pushed forward and a terrible pain as Magda bit him, bit him hard and deep enough to draw blood. Valentin fired, but the bullet thudded into the passenger-side door. Magda opened the door and jumped out, kicking it closed behind her and rolling away into the street.

Elena and Sasha moved instantly out of the direct path of the car and fired almost at the same time. And at the same time they realized that it was difficult to shoot straight with frozen fingers and that the car window in front of them was, indeed, bulletproof. They kept firing, knowing that even a bulletproof window was, in truth, only bullet resistant. The question was, how resistant was this window?

The window cracked, forming a beautiful spider web design. Magda Stern was on her feet now, running toward the doorway of the Moscow Television News offices.

The firing stopped. Elena and Sasha were almost out of bullets, and they had not penetrated the window. But what they had accomplished was to make it impossible to see out of the window. Suddenly the driver's-side door opened.

Elena and Sasha went to the ground on their stomachs, aiming toward the open door. Lieutenant Valentin Spaskov put out his left hand and Sasha shouted, "Come out slowly. Hands high. You know what to do."

Valentin obeyed. In his bloody right hand he still held a gun. He stepped out onto the sidewalk.

"Now," said Elena, "drop the gun."

Blood was dripping in the snow. Spaskov hesitated, fathered the whisper of a sigh, and said, "Tell my wife I am sorry. Tell her I love her. Tell her I couldn't help myself. Tell her I would like her to try to understand and to raise our child without telling her what her father did."

"Drop the gun," Elena repeated.

It seemed for an instant that he was about to drop his weapon. Instead he quickly put the barrel of the weapon to his ear and fired. Sasha closed his eyes. Elena watched in horror.

The body of Valentin Spaskov crumpled to the sidewalk.

Sasha and Elena got up, brushing snow from their coats, and approached the body. There was no doubt that he was dead. The blood and lack of motion told them that. But beyond what they saw, they could feel death before them.

Even so, Sasha kept his gun pointed at the body of Valentin Spaskov while Elena tucked her gun into the holster in her pocket and reached down to feel for a pulse she knew would not be there.

Yevgeny had insisted on sitting in the backseat of Georgi's heap of a car with his automatic rifle across his lap. There wasn't much room for him back there because the springs came through on one side of the seat, leaving little space for a passenger. Usually Leonid sat in the back, but Yevgeny had insisted, making Georgi and Leonid decidedly uncomfortable.

"It's dark," Georgi said, looking across at the old church that the Jews had converted to a temple. "There's no one there."

"Five more minutes," said Yevgeny. "Eleven o'clock. I want to get started as badly as you do. We said eleven. We wait till eleven."

"We wait till eleven," Georgi said with a shrug.

"You have all the tools?" asked Yevgeny.

"You asked me that," said Georgi.

"I'm asking again," said Yevgeny.

"All the tools. In the trunk," said Georgi.

He knows, Leonid thought. *He knows. He's never wanted to sit back there before. He wants to keep his eyes on us. Maybe when it's over, he'll shoot us. Maybe I should try to get behind him when we're inside. Hit him with one of Georgi's tools. Kill them both. Take my chances.*

"It's eleven," said Georgi. "Let's go."

"Yes," said Leonid, trying not to sound nervous and failing. "Let's go."

In answer, Yevgeny got out of the car, holding his gun low in one hand, pointed toward the ground. The door squeaked as he pushed it shut and waited for Georgi and Leonid to get out.

Yevgeny stood, as the wind blew and the snow danced, facing his two partners while Georgi opened the trunk as quietly as he could and handed Leonid some tools. Georgi himself hoisted a tarnished black crowbar over his shoulder and closed the trunk.

"In back. No talking till we're inside," Yevgeny whispered.

Georgi led the way with Leonid almost at his side and Yevgeny several steps back. The street was, as they had all expected, quiet. It wasn't a residential neighborhood, mostly a row of old brick three- and four-story buildings housing offices and businesses.

The snow was thick behind the building. No one had been there for weeks. Yevgeny had anticipated this and worn his boots. Georgi always wore boots. Only Leonid was in shoes and found his socks and the cuffs of his pants growing moist and cold.

There was only a dim light from a street lamp nearly a half block away, but they could see well enough to make it to the rear window. Georgi propped his crowbar against the wall and reached for the window. He tried to simply push it open, but it didn't budge. He reached for the crowbar and wedged it under the bottom of the window. The wood was old but frozen. He had to move the bar back and forth four or five times to get it in. When it was firmly in place, Georgi began to pull the bar down slowly. The window creaked, resisted, and then began to move upward as Georgi pulled down. Ice in the corners of the window crackled, and the lock snapped much louder than any of them had expected.

They stopped for a moment and looked around. Nothing.

The window was open. Georgi placed the crowbar so that it would keep the window from falling closed as they climbed in. Georgi went first, then Leonid and finally Yevgeny, entering the most awkwardly of all because he kept his finger on the trigger of his weapon and his thigh still hurt from where the rabbi had kicked him.

Yevgeny's shoes touched something only about two feet inside below the window. He had heard a metallic sound when the other two had climbed in, and now he caused the same noise.

Georgi reached toward Yevgeny in the almost non-existent light. Yevgeny stumbled to his left out of the bigger man's reach and tumbled onto his back. He rolled quickly and leveled his weapon at Georgi, who removed the crowbar from the window with one hand and brought the window down slowly and quietly with the other.

Yevgeny pulled his small flashlight from his pocket and shined it on the faces of his two partners. If there had been any doubt before, now there was none. This was a partnership that would end in hell. Yevgeny lowered his weapon.

Both Georgi and Leonid turned on their flashlights, bending low. There was a small platform with a podium. Behind the podium was a cabinet. On either side of the cabinet were framed documents written, Yevgeny was sure, in Hebrew. In front of the podium was the expanse of the floor. Folding chairs were piled in one corner of the room.

"They made it easy for us," Georgi whispered, continuing to move his beam around the room. The entrance to the temple was to his right. He knew there was a small alcove there with a tiny office big enough for a table and chair.

All three men could now see the aluminum tubing that they had stepped on. The tubing ran around the room, connecting to four stoves with pipes that went out through the ceiling. The stoves were cold and so, too, was the room.

Yevgeny cradled his weapon and moved to the center of the room, shining his light across the floor, getting his bearings.

"We start in each corner and take five steps toward the center of the room," Yevgeny said.

This was the first the other two had heard of such a plan. Either Yevgeny had a plan that they could not fathom or he had information that he had not shared with them. In fact, Yevgeny had taken Igor's letter and discovered that Igor had not told them the precise location inside the old church, but that didn't matter now.

"We move quietly. We work as quietly as we can. The boards should come up easily, and it should be buried no more than a foot deep. The ground will be frozen. We have no time to waste."

The plan meant that one corner was not covered, but the odds were three to one in their favor, and if they were wrong, all three could work from the last corner. They had time if they worked quickly and hard.

Yevgeny had no hope of putting the dirt and floorboards back before they fled. Instead he planned to push over the cabinet and podium and, if they could do so quietly enough, pull at least one of the stoves from the wall and tip it over. The goal was to make this look like a desecration tied in to the killings. He had even had the foresight to bring a small can of black spray paint so he could leave a few crude swastikas on the walls. The can bulged in his jacket pocket.

Yevgeny took a long iron bar from Leonid, who backed away from him. Then they all retreated to separate corners and began to pace off toward the center of the room. They placed their small flashlights on the floor, the beams crossing one another. Yevgeny put his weapon on the floor at his side, where he could reach it quickly. The men were now separated by about ten feet.

Yevgeny reached down to find a space between the boards at his feet into which he could insert the steel bar. His fingers touched the wood beneath him and he pulled at it hard. The board came up easily, suddenly hitting him across the cheek.

He dropped the board and went to one knee for his weapon. In the light that shone up from the floor, the faces of Leonid and Georgi looked ghostly pale, sunken holes for eyes, dark, upward shadows in skeleton grins.

Each of them had found the same thing. The boards beneath them had simply come up with a slight pull. It was Georgi who picked up his flashlight first and shined it at the ground under the board he had placed at his side.

"Someone's been here," Georgi said. "Someone's been digging here."

"And here," said Leonid.

Yevgeny turned his light downward and said nothing. The other two were right.

"How did you know where to start digging, five paces from the corner?" asked Georgi, hoisting his crowbar like a baseball bat.

"Igor had a letter," said Yevgeny, trying to think.

"One of us came here and got it," said Georgi.

"Yes," said Yevgeny as Georgi stepped forward and Leonid stepped back.

"No," came a new voice.

The three men threw the beams of their lights across the walls and into the corners and then toward the alcove as overhead ceiling lights came on and two men stepped into view. One was the rabbi who had beaten them in the street. The other was the policeman, the Washtub, Rostnikov, holding something in his arms. Whatever it was, was covered by a white cloth.

"This is what you are looking for," said Rostnikov, pulling the cloth away to reveal a tarnished stone-encrusted figure of a dog or wolf. Even after a century under the earth, the creature was magnificent. "When it is expertly cleaned and restored, it will go to either the Hermitage, from which it was stolen, or to the Kremlin Museum. You have murdered for nothing. You do not even have the excuse of murdering for hatred, simply greed."

"Put it down and back away," said Yevgeny, aiming his weapon at the two men.

Rostnikov didn't move.

"How many are outside waiting?" Yevgeny asked.

"None," said Rostnikov.

"Leonid," said Yevgeny.

Leonid went to the window and looked out cautiously,

half expecting a bullet through his forehead. He rushed across the room and did the same on the street side.

"I don't see anyone," Leonid said.

"You can't be that stupid," said Yevgeny.

"Thank you," said Rostnikov, still holding the golden wolf.

"Georgi," Yevgeny said, "when I shoot, you take the wolf. Leave the tools here. We go through the front door. Leonid, you turn off the lights and close the door."

There was nothing more to say. Yevgeny pulled the trigger. Nothing happened. He pulled again. Nothing.

"We found the gun while you were at work this morning," said Rostnikov. "Behind a panel in the ceiling of the bathroom down the hall from your room. We disarmed it."

"You knew before you came to the laundry," said Yevgeny.

Rostnikov shrugged.

"You wanted to catch us here," Yevgeny went on.

Belinsky could take no more. He strode across the floor, pushed Yevgeny's gun to the side, and slapped the young man with the back of his right hand. Yevgeny's head spun to the side. A tooth spat from his open mouth. The young man staggered back, dropping his gun, stunned, mouth bloody. The rabbi slapped him five more times and said, "One for each of the men you murdered."

"I don't think we'll need guns, will we?" asked Rostnikov.

Georgi took another step forward past the rabbi, hoisting his crowbar high. Once past the smaller man he advanced on Rostnikov, who still held the wolf and blocked the doorway.

"Give it to me or I'll break your head," Georgi threatened.

"That will be a problem," said Rostnikov. "I don't think you can hold it in one arm. It is quite heavy and if you use both arms, you will have to put the crowbar down. It is a dilemma."

Yevgeny was on the floor, using his sleeve in an effort to stop the blood from his nose and mouth. Leonid had backed against the wall and sagged to a sitting position on the aluminum tunnel.

"Now," demanded Georgi. "Leonid, come."

Leonid paid no attention.

When Georgi, crowbar upraised, stood directly before Rostnikov, the inspector dropped the wolf. It landed on Georgi's right foot. Every man in the room heard the bones cracking followed by a shriek of pain and the crowbar clanking across the room in a wild spin into the aluminum tubing, which clanged loudly. Even this did not rouse Leonid.

Georgi's eyes rolled back and he slumped to the floor and onto his back, unconscious with the shock of sudden, horrible agony. For an instant, Rostnikov wondered if the big man on the floor would lose his foot.

With the help of Rabbi Belinsky, Rostnikov handcuffed Yevgeny and Leonid together and got them out to their car, where Zelach sat behind the wheel. Rostnikov then went back into Congregation Israel for the wolf, which he put in the trunk of the car. Finally he returned to carry the limp, semi-conscious Georgi Radzo, who, Belinsky estimated, weighed well over 220 pounds. Rostnikov had lifted him with no great effort in spite of having to do so with only one good leg.

Outside, after turning off the lights and locking the door, the rabbi took a handful of snow and gently put it to the mouth of Yevgeny Tutsolov, who sat in the backseat of the police car handcuffed to the zombielike Leonid, who did not even react to the weight of Georgi unconsciously slumped against him.

"That should stop the bleeding," said Belinsky, examining Yevgeny's face.

Yevgeny didn't answer. His hand was cuffed to the dead weight of Leonid, and he was at the mercy of the mad Jew.

A little more than an hour later, when the three murderers were behind bars and Belinsky had gone home, Rostnikov entered Petrovka and went up to see the director of the Office of Special Investigation. The lights were on and the door open. Rostnikov entered, holding the wolf in one arm, and then walked in front of Pankov's desk to the inner door. It came open before he had to shift the burden again.

Director Yakovlev stood back to let him in and pointed to the conference table, where a thick towel lay. Rostnikov placed the wolf on the towel. The Yak said nothing. He shook Rostnikov's hand and stood at the door ushering his deputy director out. He closed the door behind him.

Twenty minutes later Rostnikov took off his left leg and crawled into bed under the thick blanket next to Sarah.

"You're all right?" she asked dreamily.

"I'm all right," he answered.

And then they slept.

THIRTEEN

IT WAS A NARROW STREET IN THE OLD PART OF MOS-cow, a street that had been fashionable a century ago and now withstood the crumbling of its stores and brick houses, which had been turned into apartments.

Karpo knew the street well.

It was where, for several years, he had come to meet Mathilde Verson, where they had gone to a small room, a neatly decorated and quite comfortably bright room where they initially had sex and eventually did something very close to making love. Mathilde was smart, a flaming red-head with good teeth and extremely fair skin. She was a little over forty. During the day she filled in as a telephone operator. For the last six months of their relationship, Mathilde had refused to take money from him, though the thought of anything but a business arrangement made Karpo uneasy. Yet resistance to the life force that was Mathilde, the good-natured fun she made of his serious-ness and his lack of a sense of humor, was impossible.

When Mathilde was caught in the crossfire between two gangs and torn to pieces by bullets from automatic weapons as she sat in a small café drinking tea, Karpo had, with Rostnikov's support, joined with Craig Hamil-ton, the American FBI adviser on organized crime, to find, confront, and destroy those who had taken her life.

This retribution had given Karpo little satisfaction, and he had stepped back into total dedication to his work. He had also, Porfiry Petrovich had told him, begun behaving like a man who was now courting death. If that was true, Karpo was not consciously aware of it.

Now it was a Thursday again, and he was on the same street where he had first begun meeting Mathilde. It was also almost the same time of day.

Emil Karpo had only broken one law in his life. He had believed fervently in Communism from the time he was a boy and his father took him to his first party meeting. He had believed in its laws and promise. There were weak and corrupt government officials and police, but Karpo, erect, dressed in black, pale-faced and determined, walked like death in Ingmar Bergman's *The Seventh Seal*, a film he had never seen, through the streets of Moscow.

The law he had broken was that of frequenting a prostitute. He wanted no wife and was not sure of the kind of woman who would have him even had he so chosen. He was aware, not just from the teachings of Lenin and Marx and Chairman Mao, that men were potentially superior animals, but that did not stop them from being animals.

Emil Karpo had decided that to fulfill his function as a citizen of the Soviet state he had to acknowledge his existence as a sexual animal or he would lose at least some of his ability as a police inspector. It had been a difficult position to arrive at for Karpo, especially in a Soviet Union that proclaimed prostitution did not exist.

Now Karpo walked. The sun was out, but the snow was not melting. People, carrying their plastic bags and bundled up, avoided him on the street, and only an occasional young man would look directly at him.

The shop was small, the walls cracking. An icon of the Madonna and the baby Jesus hung where only a few years ago Lenin had looked off into the future. The owner of the small coffee and tea shop, much smaller than the one in which Mathilde had been killed, was not a Communist or a Christian. He was a survivor, a Turk by birth, with a round body and mustache and a look of constant consternation on his face.

The prostitutes had paid him a token fee for taking up table space in his shop. He didn't mind having the place look a little busy. But those were the old days. Now prostitutes plied their bodies openly near the big hotels that made special arrangements for visiting businessmen. The newly rich, proudly unscrupulous capitalistic entrepreneurs and the mafias had their own contacts for obtaining prostitutes and seldom accepted the offers of the women who were reduced to walking the streets.

The shop was nearly empty. There were only five tables, in any case, with a counter against the far wall that was only a dozen paces from the door. One table held a couple, a man and woman about the same age. Maybe they were married or lovers, or maybe this was one of the last vestiges of the old days and they were talking money for favors.

At another table sitting alone, looking out of the frosted window, was a dark-haired young woman, thinner than Mathilde and wearing more makeup than Mathilde had ever used. She was wearing a reasonably modest green dress, and she was seated far enough back from the small table to reveal a black belt around the middle of the dress. Draped over her chair was an expensive-looking black jacket.

Karpo approached the young woman. Before her was a demitasse of dark coffee and a smoldering cigarette in a clear glass ashtray.

"Amelia?" he asked, standing over her.

The woman turned to look up at him. She was definitely pretty. She was also older than she had looked in profile, which, he decided, was probably why she had been looking out of the window instead of at the door when he entered. She was somewhere in her thirties. Beyond that, he couldn't be sure.

She smiled, a very small but sincere smile, and held

out her hand. It was slender and her nails were cut relatively short and painted bright red.

"Please sit," she said, putting out the cigarette. "Would you like a coffee? Tea?"

"Nothing," he said, sitting, not unbuttoning his coat.

"You are going to make this difficult for me, aren't you, Inspector?" she said with a sigh.

"That is not my intention."

"We have met, you know?" she said.

"Almost two years ago," he said. "On the street. Mathilde said hello to you. You were with two other women."

"Quite a memory," she said, looking impressed.

"I am a policeman," he said.

"I thought it might have been me who impressed you," she said.

There was a teasing in her voice and manner that reminded him of Mathilde. Was she imitating Mathilde? Was it part of her act? Was he seeing the real woman?

"You asked to see me," he said. "You said it was important."

"Down to business," she said, slapping both hands on the small table. "All right. Mathilde and I were friends. We talked. I knew about you. I knew something close existed between the two of you toward the end. But you want to get to business. Fine. If you are interested, I will take Mathilde's place. Not in a personal relationship but a business one. My rates are low and my time flexible. I would like to be able to do it for Mathilde."

Karpo, who had mastered the skill of not blinking, looked directly at her and decided, at least for the moment, that she was telling the truth.

"Why aren't you working a hotel or . . . ?" he began.

She laughed. Not Mathilde's ringing laugh, but a low, deep laugh and said, "I'm too old. The girls in demand are near amateurs, teens or in their early twenties. I hold on to my regulars and pick up extra money doing . . . well, things. I refuse to walk the streets in front of second-rate restaurants and hotels. Are you considering? It's difficult to tell looking at you."

"I'm considering," he said.

Consideration of such a thing was not something Emil Karpo could do quickly.

"You have a last name, Amelia?" he asked.

"The real one or the easy one?" she asked.

"Both."

"The real one is Boroskovich, Amelia Boroskovich. The professional one is Boros. I thought it sounded exotic when I began my profession. Now I am stuck with it."

Karpo rose and looked down at the young woman. He spoke deliberately with no trace of emotion.

"I will consider," he said. "If I decide to engage in the relationship, it will be for one time initially. We can decide what, if anything, happens after that. I want only the business relationship."

"Your gallantry is flattering," she said with a smile on her very red lips. It was an ironic comment worthy of Mathilde.

"If I decide affirmatively, will this time and place a week from now be acceptable?" he asked.

She shrugged and said, "Now would be acceptable, but, I know, you want to consider."

"Yes," he said. "I may decide negatively. It would have nothing to do with your appearance or personality, which are quite acceptable."

"A real compliment," she said, showing more teeth, which were white and remarkably even. "I'll be here a week from this moment, Emil Karpo. If you come, I will smile. If you don't, I will drink a cup of strong coffee, have a cigarette, and whisper to the memory of Mathilde that I tried."

Karpo nodded and left the shop. He walked the way he had come without looking back. He told himself he would consider, that he would check on Amelia's background, but unless he found something truly damning, he knew he would be back at the shop in exactly one week at the same time.

The Yak stood looking out the window of his office. His hands were clasped behind his back when Rostnikov entered and closed the door.

"It would be nice to have some fresh snow," said Director Yakovlev, still turned away from his deputy.

There really was nothing intelligent to say about the comment, so Rostnikov stood silently. Written reports on the bomber, the rapist, and the men who had murdered the Jews were in his hand.

Yakovlev turned around, approached Rostnikov. He took the reports and placed them on his desk without looking at them.

"Last night our bomber, Alexi Monochov, was transported by plane to a mental hospital in Irkutsk, Siberia. An evaluation by a psychiatrist and a decree from a judge were obtained."

Rostnikov said nothing.

"Monochov turned over the names of the eight profiteers and criminals his father had been blackmailing," said the Yak, "along with the evidence against them."

Again Rostnikov said nothing, though he knew from his last conversation with Monochov that there had been sixteen people of substance being blackmailed. He had more than a good idea of where the evidence against the final eight, probably the most influential people on Monochov's list, might now be.

There was a pause while Director Yakovlev waited to see if Rostnikov would react. Rostnikov did not.

"You've made me look like a genius in my first week," said the Yak with a touch of what may have been relief. "Three major crimes brought to resolution. My decision to put you in charge of all ongoing investigations has brought me reluctant praise from several sources."

"I'm pleased to hear it," said Rostnikov.

"Would you like to sit?" asked the Yak, moving behind his desk.

"Not if we will be brief," said Rostnikov.

"We will be very brief," said the Yak, touching the tips of his fingers together. "I have only one more piece of information. Regrettably the statue of the wolf you brought in yesterday proved to be nothing but a cheap replica of the original. Sometime in the past century someone must have made off with the original and buried the imitation in its place."

Rostnikov said nothing. There was nothing for him to say. He knew that the statue he had brought in was authentic. He had been a police officer long enough to know when he was touching real gold, emeralds, diamonds, rubies. He had touched them the night before. He had placed a real treasure on the desk where the report files now stood. In addition, Rostnikov was certain that the Yak didn't think he was deceiving his deputy.

"A certain member of the government, one who is high in rank and shows promise of being president one day, came here last night," said the Yak. "I do not know how he knew the statue had been delivered to me. He looked at it, examined it, and proclaimed it a fraud. Then he took it with him."

The Yak, Rostnikov knew, did not have to tell him about the unidentified member of the government. It was clear that the Yak wanted Rostnikov's respect. Yakovlev was not after the wealth to be derived from a rare treasure any more than he would use a list of nuclear criminals to gain wealth. Yakovlev sought only that which would yield influence and favors. Conclusion: the director had the eight missing files, and an influential government official had the wolf.

"It will be a disappointment to the staff of the Hermitage," said Rostnikov.

"I have already spoken to Colonel Snitkonoy and explained the matter," said Yakovlev.

"And each of the three thieves has explained in lengthy

statements how the other two were responsible for the murders of the Jews," said Rostnikov.

"They are all guilty," said Yakovlev. "Their trials will be swift, and the zeal with which we have pursued and caught these killers will be made very public."

"There turns out to be one irony," said Rostnikov, now wishing that he had taken the director's offer to sit. "The four men thought they had some right to the wolf because their ancestors had originally stolen it."

"Twisted logic, but not ironic, Porfiry Petrovich," said the Yak.

"Two of them, plus the one they murdered, Igor Mesanovich, were descendants of the original band of anticzarist thieves," said Rostnikov, "but the fourth, Yevgeny Tutsolov, was not related to any of the original thieves. His family were all laborers and factory workers in Moscow from long before the original theft. He lied to the others."

"Interesting," said Yakovlev.

Rostnikov stood silently and met the other man's eyes.

"Perhaps the wolf will be found one day," said Rostnikov.

"Perhaps, who knows," said the Yak. "Meanwhile, what we have said here this morning must remain confidential."

And what we have not said, thought Rostnikov.

"I'll tell no one," he said.

"In which case, I would like to do you a favor, both for your outstanding work and your discretion. Thanks to what I have told you, the extent of my influence has expanded significantly."

Rostnikov thought for only a few seconds and then told his superior what he wanted. Two favors.

"Name them," said Yakovlev.

"First, Lieutenant Spaskov's death will be listed as having occurred in the line of duty. He will not be officially listed as the serial rapist. He has a wife and a daughter."

"Your people can so report," said Yakovlev. "You have another request?"

Rostnikov told him.

"I think that can be arranged," said the Yak.

"May I ask when?" asked Rostnikov.

"Perhaps as early as this afternoon," said the Yak, rising and holding out his hand.

Rostnikov moved closer to the desk and reached over, supporting part of his weight on his left hand. They shook and Yakovlev said, "We have a new set of cases." He reached into his desk drawer and pulled out three files: two thin, and one very thick. He handed them to Rostnikov. "Keep me informed."

The meeting was over.

"No Lydia?" asked Elena when she entered her aunt's apartment early that evening.

Elena had the late afternoon and evening off after working all night and most of the morning, not to mention almost being killed.

Anna Timofeyeva was sitting at the window, looking over her glasses at her niece. The apartment was a bit on the cold side, which Anna rather liked and Elena didn't mind. Anna wore a thick beige turtleneck sweater. On her lap was a book she had been reading. In the chair opposite her was Baku. The cat was curled up sleeping.

"Lydia was invited out to someone's apartment for dinner," said Anna. "She didn't expect to be home early, but she promised that if the hour was not too late, she would stop for a moment."

"May we be so lucky," said Elena, hanging her coat in the corner cabinet as the phone began to ring.

Anna didn't move, though the phone was within reach.

"It's him," she said. "He's called four times. Out of respect for my health and his father, I have displayed a politeness my closest relatives and colleagues in the procurator's office would never recognize."

The phone kept ringing.

"Hello," said Elena, picking up after the fifth ring.

She stood, supporting her elbow in her hand, the phone to her ear and her legs spread.

"I would have told you, but you were out of the office all day," Elena said, turning her back on her aunt in the hope of a semblance of privacy. "I want to take more time to consider. I do not want presents. I do not want flowers. I do not want poems. I want time. It is not that I don't . . ." She looked at her aunt.

"Say it," said Anna Timofeyeva, looking down at her book through her glasses. "I've heard it before. It does not make me ill."

"It's not that I don't love you, Iosef," she said, "but I have to imagine my future beyond the immediate romance—a year, two years, two decades. Don't you understand? . . . Thank you. . . . Yes, Saturday night would be fine. An American movie will be fine. And yes you can make the dinner. . . . Yes, Sasha and I did have to tell Valentin Spaskov's widow and child that he was dead. . . . We lied. Porfiry Petrovich approved the lie. Lieutenant Spaskov died in the line of duty on his way home saving the life of a man who was being attacked by a gang on the street. . . . Yes. . . . Saturday. Good-bye."

She hung up and turned to her aunt, who looked up and said, "Sometimes I think I look like one of those old women in the movies and on television, the ones who wear shawls over their shoulders and sit in rocking chairs knitting sweaters no one wants and blankets no one needs."

"I'm waiting," said Elena. She picked up Baku, sat down across from her aunt, and put the cat on her lap. The cat continued to sleep.

"I never thought this would be my future," Elena's aunt said, taking off her glasses and looking around the room. "I thought I would die at my desk. Overwork. A massive heart attack. A well-attended funeral where I would be laid out in my uniform. And the surprise is, Elena, what has happened to me, what is so different from what I expected and even wanted, is not so bad. In fact, I am growing to like my existence. I like occasional visitors, like Porfiry Petrovich, who ask my advice and help from time to time, but I am learning to savor my repose, my view from the window, and my reading. You've read this?"

She held up a copy of *Crime and Punishment*.

"Yes," Elena answered, looking out the window and petting the sleeping cat in her lap.

"I was not a reader of literature as a young woman, or even as a middle-aged woman for that matter," said Anna. "I read dictums, laws, revisions to the law, orders, cases being made and presented. I had no life outside of my work. No marriage. I never came close to considering marriage. I am very close to celibate, and those few experiences took place a long time ago and far from Moscow. Unlike your mother, I have never had very much in the way of a sex drive. Therefore, I do not regret my decisions, and I do not brood over my present state, though it has taken me some time to come to it."

"That's your advice?" asked Elena.

Anna shrugged.

"I don't give advice anymore except to recommend reading and to be decisive about what I want to eat," said Anna. "I like Iosef. I see his father and mother in him. It is a good combination. I also see something behind his good looks and his eyes. He has a sense of humor. He is creative. Whether you wish to keep your independence for a while or for the rest of your life is your decision. I can't tell you what it's like to share one's life with a man. As you see, I am not much good at this kind of advice."

Elena did not answer. If Iosef would give her the time, she would take it and probably in the long run she would truly accept him. If he grew impatient and wanted an answer soon, she would probably reject him as nicely as possible. Iosef was a man of both intellect and intuition. She doubted that he would continue to press her for an answer. He might, however, go on with his life if she took too long to decide.

"What have we to eat?" Elena asked.

"Cheese, lots of cheese, bread supplied generously by Lydia Tkach, one onion, one half of a sausage left over from last night, one suspicious-looking tomato, four imitations of American cola in cans with those pop-up things, and a half-empty package of chocolate cookies, which are forbidden to me but I am unable to resist."

"Sounds fine," said Elena, getting up and putting Baku back on the chair. "I'll get it ready. I plan to go to bed very early."

The surprise had been perfect. Rostnikov had taken the girls out for an ice cream. Russians eat ice cream in spite of the weather. It is a love, a need, an obsession that poets, psychiatrists, philosophers, and writers of novels have been at a loss to explain. Old men have been known to get into fights in near zero weather while waiting in line for an ice-cream cone. Children save almost meaningless kopecks for weeks to buy one small packaged ice-cream sandwich.

The girls had eaten their ice creams slowly, savoring them. Rostnikov had tried to do the same, but the habits of a lifetime die hard. He was done in five chilling but satisfying bites.

When they got back to the apartment, the girls were looking forward to reading and maybe a little television if there was something on that Sarah Rostnikov would let them watch. Porfiry Petrovich had done his workout before dinner, and no one was in need of a plumber. He might, however, read to them. Sarah wouldn't let him read them American or French detective novels, though he said they could learn a great deal from Georges Simenon and Ed McBain. Sarah said they were too young. She had a neat pile of storybooks, with chapters, for them to read or have read to them.

They opened the door and looked across the room at

the table where three women were sitting: Sarah Rostnikov, Lydia Tkach, and their grandmother, Galina Panishkoya. The girls stood for a moment with the door open, glanced at Rostnikov, who was smiling, and ran into the waiting arms of their grandmother.

Rostnikov took off his coat, hung it up, and looked at the table now surrounded by happy weeping women and children. The only one not crying was Lydia Tkach, not because she didn't want to, but because she had an image to maintain, an image she had spent a lifetime perfecting.

"Do you have to go back to jail?" the older girl asked.

"No," said her grandmother.

"Your grandmother will live here with us for a while," said Sarah. "It will be a little crowded, but we'll manage."

"Apparently," said Rostnikov, "your grandmother was confused. She didn't do the thing we thought she did. It was someone else who has yet to be found. Your grandmother got caught in the middle of an unfortunate event. My superior reviewed the record of the trial and came to the conclusion that she should be released immediately. He exerted some influence to see that justice was done."

"And I have a job," said Galina, still holding her granddaughters, who had not yet taken off their coats. "I'm going to be working in the bakery of Lydia Tkach. I am going to sit on a stool, take orders, and learn how to use a cash register."

"Older women are better workers than girls," said Lydia.

Neither Sarah nor Porfiry Petrovich was sure of such an all-encompassing statement, but neither was going to engage Lydia Tkach in argument on this point.

They didn't get to bed till nearly eleven, much too late for the girls, but this was a special night. Lydia insisted that Rostnikov not walk her down the steps and to the metro station when she left.

"No one is going to attack me from here to the metro station," she said. "And, besides, I would have to walk slowly so you could keep up with me. It is cold outside and I want to move quickly."

Sarah set up the bedroom for the girls and Galina. When they had gone in, Rostnikov and Sarah could hear them whispering for about ten minutes.

Setting up the living room to sleep in was a little awkward. Rostnikov knew how Sasha and Maya had done it when Lydia lived with them. A one-legged man getting onto a mattress on the floor was a sight best reserved for himself and his wife.

Sarah turned the lights out and got in under the blankets next to her husband after she had changed into her pullover nightshirt. Since the girls had come into their lives, he had taken to sleeping in boxer shorts and a variety of extra-large T-shirts of various colors and carrying various messages on front, back, or both. The orange one he wore tonight bore the words PLANT A TREE in black letters. Rostnikov found the shirt reasonably comfortable, though he planned to plant no trees. Before the girls had come, he had slept with nothing on, and so, usually, had Sarah.

"How did you do it?" Sarah asked in the darkness.

"Do what?"

"Porfiry Petrovich," she said with mock exasperation, "Galina Panishkoya. How did you get her out of jail? She killed a man."

"It was a mistake," he said. "You heard me tell the girls."

Rostnikov rolled over to kiss his wife and then rolled back, his arm touching the prosthetic leg next to the bed.

She touched his hand and he spoke very quietly. "Do you think a beautiful woman might consider making love to a one-legged policeman tonight?"

She answered by rolling on top of him as she pulled the nightshirt over her head.

Somewhere during that night in Moscow, two drunks passed out in doorways and died, frozen. A husband and wife who lived with another couple in a single room had a fight over his snoring. He threw her out of the fourth-floor window. There were two murders, five beatings, dozens of breaking-and-enterings, and countless drug deals and illegal transactions between midnight and dawn.

Sometime during the night, the snow began to fall again. It was falling when the members of the Office of Special Investigation awoke and looked out their windows. There was Pankov the anxious clerk; Zelach the slouch; Elena Timofeyeva, who had not slept that night; Iosef Rostnikov, who had been up most of the night writing some very bad poetry that he threw away; Sasha Tkach, who had fallen asleep with his wife in his arms in the darkness thinking of how close he had come the night before to being killed; Yakovlev the ambitious director; Emil Karpo, who had worked at his desk till midnight and immediately fallen asleep when he got into his narrow bed; and Porfiry Petrovich Rostnikov. They all looked forward to a day in which Moscow would be covered in clean, soft, pure, cold whiteness.

DEATH OF A DISSIDENT
Inspector Rostnikov almost wishes the investigation of
a dissident's murder won't turn out to be too easy.
Before the case is over, he will remember that wish and
regret it.

BLACK KNIGHT IN RED SQUARE
A shocking string of murders pits Rostnikov against the
deadly accuracy of international terrorists.

RED CHAMELEON
The violent and inexplicable murder of an old man in
his bathtub sends Rostnikov on a hunt into the past.
But the trail leads to a most unexpected and dangerous
place.

A FINE RED RAIN
Someone is killing the stars of the New Moscow Circus,
and a stalker threatens the city's prostitutes. Rostnikov
takes the case as multiple murders sweep Moscow.

A COLD RED SUNRISE
At an icebound naval weather station in remote Siberia,
two grisly murders are committed. Inspector Rostnikov is
ordered to solve one of the murders, but not the other. . . .

THE MAN WHO WALKED LIKE A BEAR

A string of coincidental crimes turns into connections, and Rostnikov finds himself enmeshed in a catastrophic conspiracy.

ROSTNIKOV'S VACATION

Under orders from his superior, Inspector Rostnikov leaves Moscow for some time off—only to become involved in the mysterious murder of a vacationing fellow officer.

DEATH OF A RUSSIAN PRIEST

The cryptic last words of a murdered priest make Rostnikov wonder if the death was a political assassination or a murder with a motive closer to home.

HARD CURRENCY

When a former Russian advisor is accused of murdering a Cuban woman, Rostnikov is dispatched to Cuba on a criminal investigation-cum-diplomatic mission.

BLOOD AND RUBLES

Crime in post-communist Russia has only gotten worse: Rostnikov and his police team find themselves up against the Mafia, murderous thieves, and a theft of Czarist treasures.

The Inspector Rostnikov Mysteries
by STUART M. KAMINSKY

Published by Ivy Books.
Available at your local bookstore.

784·0246

MURDER ON THE INTERNET

Ballantine mysteries are on the Web!

Read about your favorite Ballantine authors and upcoming books in our monthly electronic newsletter MURDER ON THE INTERNET, at **www.randomhouse.com/BB/MOTI**.

Including:
- What's new in the stores
- Previews of upcoming books for the next three months
- In-depth interviews with mystery authors and publishers
- Calendars of signings and readings for Ballantine mystery authors
- Bibliographies of mystery authors
- Excerpts from new mysteries

To subscribe to MURDER ON THE INTERNET, send an E-mail to **srandol@randomhouse.com** asking to be added to the subscription list. You will receive the next issue as soon as it's available.

Find out more about whodunit! For sample chapters from current and upcoming Ballantine mysteries, visit us at **www.randomhouse.com/BB/mystery**.